*lton, believe me,*
*...w how I feel,"*

whispered, throwing all pride to the wind.
since last summer I've dreamed about you,
for you."

He took her face between his hands. "Ah,
Cassie..." His hands dropped. "You're just a—"

"Kid," she finished, mortified. "That's what you
think, right?"

"You're more than a child," he said slowly, his gaze
moving meaningfully to her breasts. "But you're
playing with fire, Cass."

"You don't love me," she said. Wrenching her hand
from his, she fought the urge to cry. She'd bared
her soul to him, and he'd as much as laughed in her
face. She started running along the sandy strip of
shoreline to the woods.

"Cassie, wait! I'll take you home."

"I'll walk!"

"No way!" Colton caught her and circled her waist
with his strong arms.

His eyes searched hers, and the protest on her lips
died a quick death. She knew he intended to kiss her.
As he lowered his head, she tilted hers up eagerly.

"Stop me," he whispered hoarsely.

But she couldn't...

Dear Reader,

Welcome to the Silhouette **Special Edition** experience! With your search for consistently satisfying reading in mind, every month the authors and editors of Silhouette **Special Edition** aim to offer you a stimulating blend of deep emotions and high romance.

The name Silhouette **Special Edition** and the distinctive arch on the cover represent a commitment—a commitment to bring you six sensitive, substantial novels each month. In the pages of a Silhouette **Special Edition**, compelling true-to-life characters face riveting emotional issues—and come out winners. Both celebrated authors and newcomers to the series strive for depth and dimension, vividness and warmth, in writing these stories of living and loving in today's world.

The result, we hope, is romance you can believe in. Deeply emotional, richly romantic, infinitely rewarding—that's the Silhouette **Special Edition** experience. Come share it with us—six times a month!

From all the authors and editors of Silhouette **Special Edition**,

Best wishes,

Leslie Kazanjian
Senior Editor

# LISA JACKSON
# Tender Trap

*Silhouette Special Edition*

Published by Silhouette Books New York

**America's Publisher of Contemporary Romance**

SILHOUETTE BOOKS
300 East 42nd St., New York, N.Y. 10017

ISBN: 0-373-09569-4

First Silhouette Books printing December 1989

Printed in the U.S.A.

**Books by Lisa Jackson**

# LISA JACKSON

was raised in Molalla, Oregon, and now lives with her husband and two sons in a suburb of Portland, Oregon. Lisa and her sister, Natalie Bishop, who is also a Silhouette author, live within earshot of each other and do their writing in Natalie's basement.

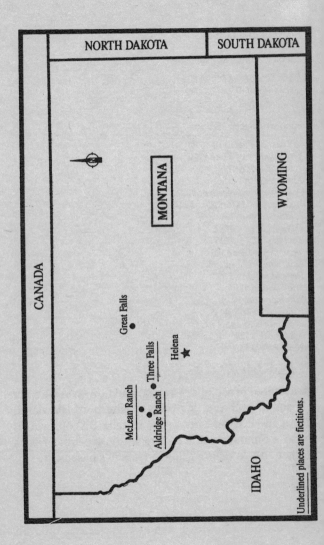

## Chapter One

Damn it all to hell!" Colton McLean growled, kicking at the straw and slamming the stall gate so hard the timbers of the old stable rumbled. Several horses snorted nervously. "Where's Black Magic?" Colton whirled to face Curtis Kramer, the ranch foreman.

"Gone."

"I can see that."

Curtis rubbed his silver-stubbled chin. "I already checked the paddocks and the south pasture."

"What about the other barns? Maybe someone put him in the wrong place."

Squinting at the younger man, Curtis slowly shook his head. "Nope. Len searched all the buildings and the paddocks. Black Magic's nowhere in the yard."

"He couldn't disappear without a trace!" Colton strode out of the stallion barn, ignoring the restless grunts of the other horses. Black Magic was the single most valuable asset of the McLean Ranch. And he'd vanished into thin air.

"I knew I should never have agreed to stay here," he muttered, thinking unkind thoughts of his older brother, Denver, who, with his wife, Tessa, had left Montana three weeks before in order to "tie up some loose ends" of the engineering firm he was moving from L.A. to the nearby town of Three Falls. This ranch was Denver's business as well; Colton didn't want any part of it.

Outside, the night was as dark as Colton's black mood. Rain from the vast Montana sky fell relentlessly, bending the grass in the surrounding fields and turning the ground to muck.

Curtis had to run to keep up with Colton's long strides. "If ya ask me," he said, catching his breath, "this is all the doin' of Ivan Aldridge."

Jolted at the mention of a sworn enemy, Colton turned on the older man. "Aldridge? What's he got to do with this?"

"He's stolen Black Magic, sure as I'm standin' here!"

"Bah!"

Curtis lifted his chin. "As sure as he stole that horse last spring, he's taken him again."

"Last spring? What the devil are you talking about?"

"Didn't anyone tell you?"

Colton's patience snapped. He was cold and wet, and the last thing he wanted to do was stand in the driving rain and discuss Ivan Aldridge. "No one knew where I was last year," he reminded the older man.

"Well, while you were getting shot up in Northern Ireland, Black Magic disappeared for nearly two weeks."

Colton didn't want to think about the bar in Northern Ireland where, six months before, someone—Colton didn't know who—had witnessed him snapping pictures, taken offense and turned his gun on him. Colton was lucky to have gotten away with his life. "The horse escaped last spring?"

"I think he had help. No one could prove it, of course, but the way I figure it, Ivan Aldridge stole the horse, used him to service some of his mares, then let him go before anyone was the wiser.''

''That's crazy.''

''Yeah, that's what everyone told me last year. And then when the horse showed up, everyone got busy again and conveniently forgot that he'd been gone. No one dug very deep. The insurance company and the rest of us were relieved.''

''So what's this got to do with Aldridge?''

''Old Ivan always swore to get even.''

Colton scowled. He knew better than anyone just how deep Ivan Aldridge's hatred ran.

''No way. The horse hasn't been stolen! And as for the feud—let's not bring it all out in the open again, okay?'' Colton suggested, irritated. Just the mention of Ivan brought back memories of Cassie—memories he'd sworn to destroy.

''Suit yourself.'' Curtis delved into his shirt pocket for his cigarettes. ''But it's not my neck on the line. When Denver finds out the most valuable stud in the state of Montana is missing, there'll be hell to pay.''

''Maybe he never should have left me in charge.''

''Maybe you never should have agreed.''

''Don't remind me,'' Colton bit out. He needed a drink—a hot drink. Irish coffee.

Curtis cupped his hands around a cigarette and lit up. ''You're the boss,'' he said, plucking a piece of tobacco from his tongue. ''But if I were you I wouldn't let my feelings for Ivan's daughter get in the way.''

Colton took a menacing step toward the older man. ''I don't have any feelings for Cassie Aldridge.''

Curtis shrugged. ''Eight years ago—''

''Eight years is a long time,'' Colton cut in, closing the subject.

Curtis knew when to quit. ''Okay, okay. Forget about Cassie.''

"I have," Colton lied.

"So what should we do about Black Magic?"

"Find him!" Colton rubbed the back of his neck. It was wet. "We'll split up, go over every field. Len and Daniel can check the western fields, you check south and I'll take the north."

"Fair enough. Just be sure to check the property butting up to Aldridge's place."

"I will," Colton promised as he climbed into his Jeep and headed north. He'd check every inch of fence line, every square foot of the northern corner of the property, if for no other reason than to prove Curtis wrong. He and Curtis had a tenuous relationship at best. For years Colton had thought Curtis responsible for the fire that had cost his parents their lives. However, he'd been wrong, and in the past few months he had discovered just how much Curtis knew about ranching. The old man, once he'd given up the bottle, was loyal, true-blue and Denver's father-in-law.

Now, with Denver in California, they had to work together—at least for a few more weeks. Then, once Colton's shoulder healed from the wound he'd received while on assignment in Northern Ireland, he'd take off. Colton couldn't wait to leave Three Falls, Montana. As soon as his doctor gave the word, Colton McLean was history in big sky country.

Two hours later Colton hadn't found any trace of the horse. His shoulder throbbed and his muscles were cramped from the cold. Angry with Black Magic and the world in general, he squinted past the rain-spattered windshield.

"That's what you get for letting your brother talk you into sticking around and looking after things," he jeered, glancing at his reflection in the rearview mirror. Two gray eyes glowered back at him. He turned his attention to the acres of Montana ranch land stretching past the beams of the headlights. "Damn horse."

Colton yanked on the steering wheel, guiding his Jeep along the fence line. Maybe he'd get lucky and find Black Magic. But maybe not. The chronic pain in his shoulder reminded him that his luck had run out some six months before.

The wipers slapped the rain off the glass as he studied the sagging wire. Easing up on the throttle, he slowed near a thicket of oaks in the northeast corner of the property. The Sage River cut through Aldridge property on the far side of the fence.

Colton was about to give up, but a gaping hole between two fence posts caught his eye.

Jaw clenched, Colton yanked on the emergency brake, let the Jeep idle, then hopped out. His boots sank into an inch of mud. His eyes never left the fence—or what was left of it.

Sure enough, the fence wire had been cut, all four strands neatly snipped. The rusted wires sagged, leaving more than enough room for a horse—or an entire herd—to slip through to the stretch of land between the fence and the river.

Fingering a clipped end, Colton noticed a clump of ebony hair—probably from Black Magic's tail—clinging to a barb. Beneath his beard, Colton's jaw grew rigid. Rain and wind lashed at his face. "Son of a—"

Thunder cracked over the hills.

Colton swung the beam of his flashlight over the ground. Hoofprints and bootprints were clearly imprinted in the soft earth. A cigarette butt had been tossed on the wet stones flanking the river. Thick, heavy-treaded tire tracks followed the jagged course of the Sage. Swollen by spring rains, the river rushed by, shining silver, roaring so loudly he barely heard the next clap of thunder.

Colton glared at the swift current. The Sage was a natural dividing line between the McLean Ranch and the Aldridge spread—as deep and wide as the feud that had existed between the two families for nearly a generation.

So Curtis had been right. Black Magic hadn't just disappeared, he'd been stolen! Again. This time from under Colton's very nose. Transported to heaven-knew-where by a truck that had been waiting on Aldridge land.

With all the proof he needed, he strode swiftly back to the pickup. He ignored the rain pouring down the collar of his jacket and the sharp jab of pain in his shoulder as he yanked open the door and crawled into the battered old rig.

Ramming his Jeep into gear, he stared through the windshield toward a scraggly thicket of oak and pine, beyond which stood the Aldridge ranch house. The house where Cassie still lived.

Colton's fingers curled over the gearshift. Cassie's image swam before his eyes. Impatiently he shoved the vision aside. Eight years had passed since he'd last seen her. If he had his way, he would never lay eyes on her again, never stare into her luminous face nor touch the lustrous sheen of her blue-black hair.

Stomping on the throttle, he turned the pickup toward the road leading to the Aldridge ranch. He hoped Ivan was home. Tonight was as good a time as any to drag the truth from the old man.


Cassie twisted off the faucet and stepped out of the shower. Through the bathroom window she heard Erasmus, her father's crossbred collie, barking and growling loudly enough to wake the dead.

"I'm coming!" she called. "Hold your horses!" Muttering to herself about Erasmus's particular lack of brains, she snatched her favorite robe from a hook on the bathroom door and stuffed her arms down the sleeves.

She was so tired she wanted to drop. After spending the past twelve hours at the Lassiter ranch, trying to save some of George Lassiter's heifers from a serious case of milk fever, she was beat. Two animals had survived. Three had died. Veterinary work wasn't for the fainthearted, she decided as she cinched her belt around her waist.

She dashed down the threadbare red runner on the stairs. Outside, Erasmus was going out of his mind. Barking gruffly and snarling, the old dog paced the porch and scratched at the front door.

"What's gotten into you?" Cassie asked, flinging open the door. Fur bristling, teeth bared, Erasmus streaked past her and dashed around the corner to the kitchen. "What the devil?" Cassie whispered.

"Down!" a male voice commanded from inside the house.

Cassie froze.

Erasmus quit whining.

"Miserable beast," the voice muttered again.

Cassie's heart slammed against her rib cage. Who was in the kitchen? Her throat cotton-dry, she silently crossed the worn living room carpet, opened her father's gun closet and cringed at the soft click of the lock. Quickly she withdrew her old .22. It was unloaded, of course, but the intruder, whoever he was, wouldn't know that.

Did Erasmus know the man? she wondered wildly, disturbed that the dog had obeyed the rough command. She clenched her fingers tightly around the stock and barrel and padded noiselessly to the kitchen. Lifting the rifle to her shoulder, she stepped into the light.

"What's going on here?" she demanded, then stopped dead in her tracks. She nearly dropped the .22.

There, in the middle of the room, was Colton McLean—the one man in the world she detested. Big as life, his wet Stetson low over his eyes, he straddled one of the chipped maple chairs and scratched Erasmus's ears. The traitorous dog whined in pleasure.

His gaze, as cold as silver, clashed with hers. "Cassie," he drawled. "It's been a long time."

## Chapter Two

Cassie's heart nearly dropped through the floor. "What're you doing here?"

Tipping his Stetson back, Colton surveyed her through slitted silvery eyes. "Waiting."

"For?"

"Your father."

"He's not here."

Colton merely shrugged. His gaze narrowed on her, his expression murderous. His face was rugged, craggier than she remembered it. A full beard covered his jaw, and his features were lean and jaded with the added years. His denim jacket, stretched taut across his shoulders, was wet from the rain. His attention drifted to the rifle. Its barrel gleamed blue in the dim light from a single low-watt bulb mounted high on the ceiling.

"What're you going to do, Cassie? Shoot me?"

"I haven't decided yet." She lowered the rifle.

"I've been used for target practice before." His teeth flashed beneath his beard, and her stomach knotted as she remembered the rumors she'd heard about the shooting in Northern Ireland—how he was lucky he hadn't been killed.

"How'd you get in?"

"The door wasn't locked."

"So you just waltzed in and made yourself comfortable?"

His lips twisted. "Believe me, Cass, I'm not comfortable."

"But you had no right—"

"Probably not." His cold gaze slid slowly up her body before resting on her face. She felt stripped bare.

Several heart-stopping seconds ticked by before she found her voice. Her hands were clammy; her voice threatened to shake. Colton McLean was the last person she'd expected to find in her kitchen. Though he'd been back in Montana for nearly six months, he'd been reclusive and, according to the rumors circulating in town, hadn't been seen much. Cassie hadn't run into him once. "Don't you believe in knocking?" she asked.

He glanced at the open door and the unlatched screen. "Don't you believe in locking your doors?"

"Dad lost his key—oh, never mind!"

"I knocked. Twice. No one answered."

"I was in the—"

"I can see where you were. I heard the shower running."

Suddenly aware of her damp hair, her towel-buffed skin and her naked body protected only by a ragged terry robe, she clenched the rifle more tightly. She wasn't afraid of Colton McLean, not really, but the sight of him brought back too many memories—dangerous memories—of a love affair she'd rather forget.

"You knew I was upstairs taking a shower? And you came in anyway?"

"I knew the water was running. That's all."

"Nervy of you."

He sighed and rubbed his jaw. "When's Ivan coming back?"

"I don't know, but you can't wait here for him."

"Why not?"

"Take a wild guess," she invited, her temper flaring.

"I couldn't begin to," he drawled.

"Try." At first she'd been surprised that he'd landed, dripping and ready for battle, in the middle of her kitchen, but as she slowly recovered, her shock gave way to anger. It had been over eight years since she'd seen him, eight years since he'd walked out the door of this very house! And now he had the nerve to straddle one of her kitchen chairs as if he owned the place!

"Why don't you just tell me?" he drawled.

"Because I don't want you here! I've had a long day and all I want to do is curl up in bed with a good book!"

"Don't let me stop you," he taunted.

"I'm in no mood for games, Colton."

"Neither am I."

"I'll tell Dad you stopped by and he'll call you."

"Sure he will."

She clenched her teeth. "Hasn't anyone told you it's dangerous to bait a woman holding a rifle?"

He laughed, a short derisive sound that conjured up half-forgotten images of a warm summer filled with young love. "I remember how good a shot you were, Cassie. You couldn't hit the broad side of a barn."

"I've improved."

He cocked one dark brow, and his eyes glinted. "Have you, now?" he asked, his voice low, almost seductive.

"Get out, Colton!"

"You haven't even heard why I'm here."

"I'm not interested."

"No? Not even if I told you Black Magic was missing?"

"Black Magic?" she repeated.

"You've heard of him?"

"Of course I have—the whole county has," she said, remembering the fiery charcoal stallion with the jagged white blaze running the length of his nose. "I treated him once last year."

"Oh, that's right, you're a veterinarian now," he jeered, his lips twisting.

"And you're a famous photojournalist, right?" she threw back at him, agitated. He had no reason to mock her career, no right to barge into her house and badger her! He'd left her life in shambles, and she'd managed to pull herself back together. Alone. "So what are you doing hanging around here?"

"Marking time," he replied, never taking his eyes off her.

She set the rifle against the wall and forced a thin, impatient smile.

Colton watched her. "I just want to ask Ivan a few questions."

"About Black Magic?"

"Yes."

Cassie frowned. "You think Dad might know where your horse is?"

"Denver's horse," he shot back.

"That's right. You're not into ranching, are you?"

"Never have been."

"Neither was Denver. He changed," she flung out, hoping to wound him a little, though any hope she had that Colton had mellowed over the years died when she noticed the hard angle of his jaw.

"I won't." His eyes were steely gray as he scrutinized her. She saw the room as he did—peeling paint and scratched counters, worn, overwaxed flooring, blackened kettles hanging from dusty ceiling beams. His eyes were restless, and there was a wariness about him, a hard edge she didn't remember.

"Why're you here? Why not your brother?" she finally asked.

"Denver and his wife are in Los Angeles."

She remembered now. In her work as a veterinarian, she'd overheard snatches of conversation at the surrounding ranches. Denver and Tessa would be away for another few weeks. "And you're stuck with the ranch," she taunted, unable to resist goading Colton. "So how did you manage to lose the most valuable horse on the spread?"

"I didn't lose anything. He was stolen."

Finally she understood why he was sitting in the middle of the Aldridge kitchen, his expression hard with unnamed accusations, his bearded chin jutted in fury.

Her voice, when she found it, was barely a whisper. "You're not here to suggest that Dad had something to do with Black Magic's disappearance, are you? Because if you are, you can just haul your self-righteous backside out of here right now!"

He didn't move.

Cassie advanced on him. "Dad would never—"

"He's made threats."

Her lips twisted. "That was a long time ago, Colton."

"Feuds have a way of smoldering—then flaring when you least expect them."

"Not this one!" She poked a finger at his chest. Her skin collided with rock-hard denim-clad muscles. "You'd better leave. Now! Just get in your truck or Jeep or car or whatever it is you've got parked outside and take off, before *I* decide to start the feud all over again by strangling you!"

"Strong words, Cass," he chided.

"Strong accusations, Colt."

He eyed her speculatively. "You've changed."

"Thank God."

His gaze lowered to the hollow of her breasts displayed all too vividly by her gaping robe. "But in some respects, you're still the same—"

"Get out, Colton."

"Not until I talk to Ivan," he said with infuriating calm.

"He may not be back tonight."

"I'll take my chances."

"You can't."

Colton didn't budge.

Emotions, old and new, roiled deep within Cassie. She hated him—hated the very sight of him. Or at least that's what she'd been telling herself for eight years. "Dad doesn't want you here—don't you remember?"

His eyes narrowed. "How could I forget?"

"Then take a hike and do it fast! Or I'll call the sheriff's office."

"Go ahead." With a jaded half grin, he motioned toward the phone. "I know a deputy there, Mark Gowan. You've probably heard of him."

She had. Mark was one of the best the sheriff's department employed.

"Go ahead. Call him. When Gowan gets here, I'll explain about Black Magic and the fact that the fence was cut—the fence between your property and mine. Then I'll repeat every threat Ivan's made against the McLeans to the good sheriff!"

Cassie blanched.

"And if that isn't good enough, I'll tell my tale to the local press—I've got connections, you know. Friends in high places. It comes with the territory."

"You bastard!"

He winced a little.

"You wouldn't!" she whispered, grasping at straws. "You'd look like a fool!"

"And your father would look like a criminal," he growled.

He was bluffing! She knew it. He couldn't risk another scandal with the McLean name. Not after the last one—when John McLean had seduced Cassie's mother! She reached for the phone, but he caught her wrist. The receiver clattered against the wall. "This would be a whole lot easier, you know, if you let me take a look around myself."

His fingers were hot and hard against her flesh. "Dad's never stolen anything in his life!"

"So prove it."

She glared at him indignantly. Why bother explaining? The stern set of Colton's jaw told her he'd already tried and convicted her father, just as he had her, years before. "Let go of me, Colton."

He didn't.

She tried a new tack. "This happened before—right? Last year. I heard it from Milly Samms, Denver's housekeeper. The horse was missing, then just showed up. This is probably the same kind of mistake."

"This is no mistake, Cassie. Someone took Black Magic. I want to know who." His grip tightened, the warm pads of his fingers playing havoc with her pulse. She tried yanking her hand from his, but he wouldn't let go. "Come on, Cassie. Here's your chance to prove me wrong."

Her gaze burned into his. "One of your ranch hands just got careless."

He dropped her hand. "Then you won't mind if I walk through the barns and stables?"

"Are you crazy? I'm not going to let you go poking around, disturbing the animals—"

"After I see what I came to see, I'll leave."

She wavered. She wanted him to leave, and the opportunity to prove him wrong and put him in his place was tempting. "Okay—but this isn't going to take all night. We check out the stables and that's it."

He nodded.

"It'll take me a few minutes to change."

"Don't bother. I can find my way around—"

"No way!" she sputtered. "You can't march over here with ridiculous accusations and then start tearing the ranch apart board by board! Your stallion is probably just lost, and I'm not about to let you turn this place upside down just because you 'suspect' Black Magic was stolen. If that's the case, go to the sheriff! If not, just give me five minutes to change.''

He spread his palms, and an ingratiating smile stole across his bearded chin. "By all means . . ."

Goaded, she stomped out of the room and took the stairs two at a time. Her mind was spinning as she tied her hair away from her face and yanked on a pair of jeans. Cassie didn't believe Black Magic had been stolen—not for a minute. The cut wires were just an accident. Most likely someone had been repairing the ancient fence earlier in the day. As soon as she spoke with her father, the downed fence would be explained. And Colton McLean would have to eat crow!

Smiling at that thought, she pulled a wheat-colored sweater over her head and hurried back to the kitchen.

Colton was leaning against the door, one booted foot propped on the seat of a chair as he stared impatiently through a rain-spattered window. Thick brows converged over his eyes, and his face was a hard, rough-hewn mask. He'd matured in the past eight years. Living a dangerous life as a photojournalist who snapped pictures of war-ravaged political hot spots had stolen any trace of boyishness from his face. Even his coffee-colored hair had a few strands of gray at the temples, and his skin was lined near the corners of his eyes.

"You won't see anything from here," she pointed out.

He swung his gaze back to hers, and for just an instant she remembered him as he had been, handsome and warm. He'd smiled often then, his irreverent grin spreading from one side of his tanned face to the other. There had always been a dangerous side to him—his temper was infamous—but there had been a kind side, too, and she'd loved him with all of her naive young heart. There had been a few other boys she'd had crushes on while growing up, but deep in her heart, from the time she had turned fourteen, she'd harbored a love for Colton so deep it had kept her awake at night. But that was years ago, she reminded herself.

"Let's go," he said gruffly.

Without a word she swept past him. On the back porch she snatched her faded jacket and a flashlight from the cupboard, then tugged on her boots.

Outside, the wind slashed at her face. Rain peppered the ground and slid down Cassie's collar as she followed her flashlight's unsteady beam. She half ran to keep up with Colton's long strides.

"Don't upset the horses," she warned.

"Wouldn't dream of it."

"Good." She reached for the door. "Several mares are due to foal, and I don't want anything disturbing them."

He slanted her a hard glance. "I'm not interested in your mares. I just want to find Black Magic."

"Then you're going to be disappointed."

"It won't be the first time," he said, his gaze locking with hers. For an instant she hesitated, lost in his stare. Her throat felt suddenly swollen and hot.

Giving herself a mental shake, Cassie strode inside. The familiar smells of oiled leather, warm animals and horse dung mingled with the dust. She snapped on the lights.

Cobwebs clung to the rafters, and a fine layer of grime covered the windows. Horses snorted and rustled the straw scattered over the floor of their stalls. Inquisitive dark heads poked over the top rails, and a few mares nickered at the sight of Cassie.

"It's okay," she murmured, petting each velvet-soft muzzle thrust her way.

Colton's gaze swept the boxes, taking in every detail, each swollen-bodied mare and shifting, nervous stallion. One wild-eyed gray pawed anxiously in his stall, tossing his head at the unfamiliar scent of Colton. "Friendly guy," Colton observed dryly.

"Like you," she shot back.

Colton's boots echoed against the concrete floor. "Black Magic's not here," he muttered under his breath. His face was drawn, his expression clouded.

Cassie felt like smirking. "Satisfied?"

"Not yet."

"Come on, Colton," she jibed, unable to hide the sparkle in her eyes. "Admit it. You were wrong."

"Aren't there any other barns?"

"Just for the cattle—"

"Let's check them."

"No!" She reached for the door, wrenched it open and flipped off the lights in one swift motion. "I put up with this—this stupid idea of yours, just to prove that you were wrong about Dad. But I'm not about to let you rip apart every blasted building on the ranch just to prove my point!"

He moved swiftly, curling his hand around her upper arm. "I'd like to think that your old man is as honest as you claim he is," he said slowly, his eyes glittering dangerously in the darkness. "But I've got to be sure. Your family has a history of lying."

She thought her heart would break. Though she'd told herself he could never hurt her again, she'd been wrong. Struggling against the old wounds, she whispered, "I never lied to you, Colton."

"Ha!"

As she tilted her chin up defiantly, her gaze collided with the naked cynicism in his. "Believe what you want, but I swear by everything I believe in, that I never lied to you."

A muscle worked in his jaw, and for a second, indecision flashed in his eyes. His expression became gentler as he gazed down on her, and Cassie sensed he was wrestling an inner battle. "Maybe you just twisted the truth."

"And maybe *you* did," she whispered as his breath, warm and familiar, filled the air between them. Her throat went dry at the nearness of him.

If only she could forget how much she had loved him, how much she had cared....

Then, as suddenly as it had appeared, his uncertainty vanished. His jaw slid to the side, and he surveyed her through narrowed eyes. "I played the fool for you once, Cassie," he admitted, his lips thin as he tossed her arm away in disgust. "Believe me, it won't happen again."

"You arrogant bastard," she cried, stepping away from him. "You've got a lot of nerve...." Knowing she was fighting the inevitable anyway, she led him to the barn across the yard. She barely felt the rain and mud as she marched into the tall building and switched on the lights. A few white-faced Herefords lowed and shoved their heads through the manger, hoping that she would toss some more feed in the trough.

Colton followed her inside. He noticed the challenge in her eyes and the pride that stiffened her slim shoulders as she waved her arm in a wide arc. "Be my guest," she invited caustically.

"I will." He strode through the building, searching it from one end to the other and found nothing, not one bloody trace of Black Magic. Swearing under his breath, he wended his way through the bins of feed, oats and loose bales of hay to the door where Cassie leaned insolently against the dusty frame. Her arms were folded under her breasts, and her generous mouth was curved into a fair imitation of a smirk. "Find him?" she asked, pretending interest in her nails.

"No."

"You're sure?" she drawled.

"Positive."

She cocked her head to one side and glanced toward the ceiling. "Better check the hayloft," she suggested sweetly savoring her revenge. "Dad could have used the grain elevator to lift your precious horse up there."

Unexpectedly Colton grinned. He eyed the loft, a platform built some ten feet above the wooden floor. Tightly stacked bales were piled to the apex of the roof, where a small round window reflected the beam of Cassie's flashlight. "You've made your point, Miss Aldridge."

"About time." Shoving open the door, she shined her flashlight on his dented truck. "Now, if you're done accusing my family and searching this place from stem to stern, I think I'll go into the house. It's been a long day."

"It's not over yet."

"Oh, yes it is!" she said succinctly. "At least for me." Her eyes blazed. "The next time you go around accusing innocent people of crimes they didn't commit, you'd better get your facts straight."

"You're a good one to start talking about the truth, Cass."

The words cut deep, stinging like the bite of a whip. "As I said, Colton, I never lied to you. You just weren't man enough to trust me!"

"Trust you?"

"Yes. You didn't even have the guts to let me explain!"

"Explain what? That you were trying to trap me into marriage by imagining a baby that didn't exist?"

"No!"

"Don't, Cassie," he whispered, his voice low, his eyes dark.

"Get the hell off my land, McLean!" she ordered. Spinning on her heel, she took off for the house.

Colton watched her sprint across the yard. Her black hair streamed behind her; her hips moved gracefully as she hurried up the back steps and slammed the door in her wake.

Seething, his jaw clenched so hard it ached, Colton strode to his pickup and climbed inside. What was it about her? She was a liar—a woman who at seventeen had tried to trick him into marriage—and yet there was something captivating about her tantalizing smile and wide hazel eyes.

He jammed the old truck into gear and stomped on the throttle. He'd known women before and since his brief affair with Cassie, but none had been able to get under his skin the way she had.

"Never again," he told himself as the old truck whined and he shifted into second. "Never again."

## Chapter Three

You're an idiot!'' Cassie muttered, kicking off her boots as she heard Colton McLean's Jeep drive away. Angry with herself as well as the whole lot of McLeans, she marched through the kitchen and upstairs.

She had, over the years, convinced herself that she was long over Colton. But tonight, after seeing him again, she wasn't quite so sure. The hate she'd sworn to harbor was tangled up with an emotion she'd rather not examine too closely. Their love affair, long dead, seemed closer than it had in years.

"What love affair?" she taunted her reflection as she yanked a brush through her wet hair. Love had never been a part of that summer.

A familiar ache, an old feeling she'd buried along with her foolish notions of love for Colton, wrenched her heart. Sinking unsteadily onto the edge of the mattress, she clenched her fists around the edge of her quilt. Her memory tortured her with vibrant images of a young man unjaded by the years. It seemed that it was just last night when she'd been seventeen and hopelessly in love....

It was a summer to remember, a beautiful hazy time when anything was possible. Cassie sprinted playfully along the edge of the lake. The lapping water tickled her toes, and sandy soil squished under her bare feet. The summer sun had already settled behind the western hills. Vibrant slashes of magenta and orange streaked the wide Montana sky.

"Bet you can't catch me," she called, glancing over her shoulder.

"Why would I want to?" Colton asked. His back propped against the scarred trunk of a pine tree, he plucked a twig from a low-hanging branch. He lifted one side of his mouth lazily as she waded ankle-deep.

"Figure that one out for yourself," she teased.

He tossed the twig into the water, then shoved his hands deep into the pockets of his cutoff jeans, as if he didn't care what she did. But she noticed the gleam in his eyes, the involuntary flexing of his thigh muscles, the tension in his stance. Though he attempted to appear nonchalant and uninterested, Cassie knew he was only fighting her—and fighting a losing battle.

Bending forward and running her fingers through the cool water, she grinned. She'd loved him for so long, and now he was finally returning those feelings. For the past six weeks they'd been seeing each other, on the sly, of course. Her father would kill her if he thought she was dating a McLean.

Today her heart soared as high as the hawk circling distantly overhead.

Feeling Colton's gaze searing her backside, she turned. He had moved from his spot near the tree and was sauntering closer to the lake.

"Maybe we should go," he suggested restlessly. His voice had grown husky, his eyes dark.

Cassie's heart somersaulted. "We just got here." She moved deeper; the cool water lapped against the hem of her shorts.

"Isn't your father expecting you?"

"He's in town. Won't be back for hours." Tossing her hair over one shoulder, she wiped her hands on her shorts.

"Ivan wouldn't like it if he knew you were here with me."

"Ivan doesn't have to know."

He arched one of his dark brows insolently. "Don't use me to rebel against your father."

"I'm not!" she vowed, her throat swollen as she gazed at him. Colton was everything she'd ever dreamed of—and more. Against a backdrop of pine and cottonwood, he stood at the water's edge, his tanned chest bare, corded muscles visible beneath a swirling mat of black hair. His jaw was lean and sharp, less boyish than it had been the summer before, and his eyes glinted like newly forged steel.

Colton moved closer, rippling the water's surface. Cassie's heart hammered so loudly she could barely hear the gentle thrum of insects or the lapping of the lake.

"I don't like sneaking around."

"Neither do I."

"Think about it, Cass. We both know your father would skin us alive if he found out we'd been meeting behind his back."

"I have thought about it."

"Have you?" he asked distractedly. His eyes slid from hers to the halter top that covered her breasts in pink gingham. The fabric was stretched taut, and she could feel a slow trickle of sweat on her skin, the tangle of damp curls against her neck.

He swallowed hard. "What do you think my dad would say?"

Cassie's carefree mood faded.

"And then there's Uncle John. He'd kill me."

She cringed at the mention of Colton's uncle. She didn't want to think about John McLean, nor of the affair he'd had with her mother. That time, so long ago, still caused a horrid aching in her heart—an aching she didn't want to experience. Not today. She'd heard the rumors—knew that her mother had abandoned her long before because of John McLean. "Because I'm Vanessa's daughter?" she asked, thrusting out her chin.

"Because you're Ivan's."

Bravely, for she'd never dared mention the feud to him before, she said, "What happened between your uncle and my mother is in the past." A love affair that had soured. A love affair that had cost Cassie her mother and her father his pride.

"Tell that to your dad."

"I have."

His head jerked up, and his gaze, bright and seductive, drilled into hers. "And what did 'Ivan the Terrible' have to say?"

"Nothing." She hated it when Colton referred to her father as if he were a monster; and yet she understood why. Ivan had never gotten over his wife's betrayal, and he'd blamed John and anyone else cursed with the surname of McLean for ruining his life. That curse included Colton.

"You're lying. Ivan's made no bones about the fact that he blamed John and everyone related to him. Vanessa never came back, did she? She just left your dad to take care of himself and you. You really can't blame the man for being bitter!"

Cassie's throat constricted as painful memories clouded the otherwise perfect day. "I—I don't want to talk about Mom."

"Do you ever hear from her?"

"Of course," she lied, avoiding Colton's eyes.

"Sure."

"Besides, it doesn't matter. You and me—that's what's between us. What we have doesn't have anything to do with Dad or Mom."

"Cassie," he whispered. He was so close she noticed the shadows of suspicion clouding his gaze. He touched her shoulder and lifted the tiny strap that was knotted behind her neck. "It does matter."

She swallowed hard. "Dad lives in the past, Colton. There's nothing we can do or say to change that. We can't worry about it."

His lips curved sardonically. "And when he finds out?"

"He won't," she said mutinously, thrusting out her chin. "I'm seventeen and I've already graduated from high school! I can make my own decisions."

He sucked in a swift breath and let his hand fall to his side.

She wanted to kick herself for bringing up her age. For some reason, he thought her a child, though he was only four years older than she.

"Come on," he said hoarsely, "I'll take you home."

"But we've got all night." Never before had she been so forward, but she'd never been with Colton before—not alone.

He swore violently, his gaze sweeping the swell of her breasts peeking from beneath her halter, to her flat, tanned abdomen and the curve of her hips. "We do *not* have all night."

He wrapped strong fingers around her wrist as he started back for the shore, dragging her through the water quickly.

"You just think I'm a kid," she pouted as she tried to negotiate the slippery bottom.

"You are."

"Colton, I love you!"

"Oh, Cass, no!" He stopped then, and she ran into him, her legs giving way. She started to fall, but he caught her and lost his balance. They plunged into the ice-cold depths.

Water swirled over them both, and she sputtered as he hauled her to her feet. "Love?" he repeated, his chest heaving. Drops of water clung to the dark hair from his chest to the waistband of his wet cutoffs. "What do you know about love?"

"I know that I can't think straight when I'm around you, and when I'm not, I can't wait to see you again!"

"You've been *in love* with half the boys around—"

"I have not!"

"What about Dave Lassiter?"

"We had one date—and he's just my best friend's brother," she said, thinking Dave was just a boy. Colton, on the other hand, was so mature. Then she smiled to herself. Obviously Colton had been keeping track.

"And Mike Jones?"

"He asked me to the prom." She forced her eyes to his. "I've had dates, Colton, sure. I've even thought I liked a couple of the boys. But it's not the same as I feel about you."

"Oh, Cass, no. Don't—" His gaze appeared tortured.

"Why won't you believe me?"

"Because it *can't* happen. You're too young and I—I have plans for my life. I can't be stuck in this Podunk town, feeding livestock and talking about property taxes...." He clamped his mouth shut, and for a moment she thought she saw a flicker of love in his eyes. "Oh, hell, what's the point?" he growled, swearing roundly.

Cassie flushed, feeling incredibly young and naive. But the hand over her wrist never let go, and Colton's gaze lingered before dropping.

Glancing down, she saw the wet fabric of her halter top hid very little. Her raised nipples pressed intimately against the sheer scrap of gingham.

"Oh, Cassie, what are you trying to do to me?" he groaned.

"Nothing—I—"

He jerked her forward quickly, capturing her lips with his. Her breath was lost somewhere in her lungs. She couldn't breathe, could only feel the dampness of his muscled chest, his hair tickling her skin, and his lips, hard and sensual, moving anxiously against hers.

The driving beat of his heart was matched only by her own.

She leaned against him, and he stepped back, his eyes narrowing to hide the desire smoldering in his gaze. "Nothing, my eye. You know exactly what you're doing to me. I should never have agreed to meet you here!"

"But you did."

"It was a crazy idea."

"Why?" Hope swelled again. "Colton, believe me, I know how I feel!" she whispered, throwing all of her pride to the wind. "Ever since last summer I've dreamed about you, waited for you."

"You don't know what you're saying! Before the summer's over you'll change your mind."

A hard, tight ball filled her throat. "You don't love me," she accused.

He took her face between his hands. "We barely know each other." His hands dropped. "Besides, you're just a—"

"Kid," she finished, mortified. "That's what you think, right?"

"You're more than a child," he said slowly, his gaze moving meaningfully to her breasts. "But you just don't know what you're getting into. You're playing with fire, Cass."

"I love you—"

"Stop it," he commanded roughly. "You don't know the first thing—"

Wrenching her hand away from his, she fought the urge to break down and cry. She'd bared her soul to him, and he'd as much as laughed in her face. To save what little pride she could still claim, she started running out of the lake and across the sandy strip of shoreline to the woods. Intent on walking barefoot all the way back to her father's house, she struck out through the trees.

"Cassie, wait!"

"Leave me alone!"

But Colton caught her at the forest's edge and circled her waist with his strong arms. He tugged her kicking and clawing against him. "Where do you think you're going?"

"Home!"

"Like this? Barefoot?"

"Yes!"

"But it's almost dark."

"I don't really care. Let go of me, Colton. I think I've suffered enough embarrassment for one night, don't you?" she accused, trying to deny the weakness in her knees, the constriction of her lungs. She struggled to get away from his musky male scent and the coiled power of his arms.

"I'll take you home." His voice sounded rough.

"I'll walk!"

"No way." His eyes seared hers, and the protest on her lips died a quick death.

Wrapped in the strength of his arms, feeling the heat of his body, the raw sensuality of his wet skin rubbing against hers, she couldn't find her voice or the self-righteous anger that had flared so quickly only seconds before.

She knew that he intended to kiss her. As he lowered his head, she tilted hers up eagerly. His lips covered hers and stole the small whisper of breath in her lungs. Moving slowly, expertly, his mouth molded against hers. His tongue gently prodded, sliding easily between her teeth, exploring and plundering.

All thoughts of leaving him fled into the shadows of the towering pines. Cassie slid her arms around his neck, and she leaned against his muscular chest. Her body responded easily to Colton's kiss; her skin tingled when he splayed his hands against her bare back, shifting slowly, sensually, fanning the forbidden flames of desire that heretofore she'd only dreamed of.

"Stop me," he whispered hoarsely.

But she couldn't. She felt one of his hands slide around to caress the burgeoning fabric of her halter. She gasped when his palm covered her breast, and the wet gingham slid erotically against her nipple. "Don't stop," she breathed. "Colton, please, don't stop."

He groaned a deep primal moan of surrender that turned her blood to fire. Heat swirled deep inside her as he untied the thin straps and bared one soft breast to the night. He gulped as he gazed at her. "You're too young to look this way," he protested, but let one thumb graze her nipple, watching in fascination as the stiff peak responded.

"Just love me," she murmured.

"I can't—"

"Please. Colton, oh, please—"

Groaning, he lowered his head. His lips moved gently along the column of her throat, and one hand became tangled in her hair as he dragged them both to their knees. "This is dangerous," he rasped.

"No—"

"And so are you."

Instinctively she let her head loll back and arched her neck as he kissed her slowly, sliding downward until his mouth was poised over her breast.

"You're so beautiful," he murmured, his hot breath fanning her nipple before he took all of that rosy button into his mouth and suckled hungrily.

She wound her fingers in the thick strands of his hair, and the warm ache within her, a new and frightening passion, stretched and yawned deep within. She didn't protest when his weight forced her back against the sand, where her halter fell completely away.

She kissed his head and smooth shoulders as he laved her breast, teasing and tormenting with each supple stroke of his tongue. Cassie shuddered, unable to think beyond the delight of his body molding to hers.

His muscles were rigid and hard. Sweat beaded his brow. He lowered the waistband of her shorts. Her abdomen flattened expectantly.

"This is a mistake," he whispered.

"No, Colton, it's right. So right. I *love* you."

He squeezed his eyes tight for a minute, as if he was trying to get a grip on himself. For a heart-stopping second, Cassie thought he would tear himself away. But he didn't. And when his lips found hers again, they were hot and hard and hungry. All his self-control fled. His fingers worked feverishly on the snap and zipper of her shorts.

He stripped them from her so quickly she gasped. His hands ran anxiously along her thighs, smoothing her skin, parting her legs easily, stroking her panties until she began to writhe anxiously, her blood thundering wantonly, throbbing with desire.

"I want you, Cassie," he murmured against her hair. "Damn me to hell, but I want you."

Somewhere in her passion-drugged mind she knew she should stop him, that lust didn't mean love. But she didn't care. In time he'd learn to love her just as she loved him.

"Touch me," he breathed, guiding her hand.

Hesitantly she reached for the top button of his cutoffs. Her fingers flitted against his abdomen, and he drew in a swift breath, his own fingers delving, searching.

He groaned when she touched him, his muscles flexing. "Oh, Cassie." Lips, full and hungry, captured hers, and he kicked off his clothes, his body in all its young, virile glory straining over hers. "I—I don't have anything for protection—"

"I don't need anything but you," she whispered, watching him through glazed eyes.

Shuddering, he parted her legs with his own. He moved quickly then, thrusting into her, past the thin barrier of her virginity.

She gasped with the searing pain, a white-hot burst that he assuaged with his gentle, rhythmic movements. Cassie closed her eyes, and the sounds of the night faded. She could no longer hear the gentle drone of crickets, the quiet lapping of the lake, the wind soughing through the pines. She heard only the beating of her heart and the thundering cadence of Colton's, felt only the liquid heat within her building with each joyful, binding thrust.

She dug her fingers into his shoulders as his tempo increased. Moving with him, she arched upward, her spine curving, her breasts full against him.

"I can't hold back," he cried, just as the first spasm sent her rocketing into a new, wondrous world. Light splintered before her eyes, and she heard him cry out lustily, the sound echoing through the trees.

"Cassie, Cassie," he whispered, hoarse and clinging, his body fused to hers. He gazed down at her, and regret darkened his gaze. "Oh, God—"

"Shh..." She pressed a finger to his lips and smiled, but he closed his eyes and clung to her, as if blocking out an image he couldn't bear.

"I'm sorry," he said.

"For what?"

"You—you were a virgin."

"Of course I was!" She held his face between her hands. "There's no reason to be sorry."

"Oh, God, Cass, there are a thousand reasons," he whispered, levering himself on one elbow and gazing down on her.

His eyes moved over her slowly, and his expression turned pained, guilt-ridden. "This wasn't the right time," he muttered, his muscles still glistening with sweat.

"It was perfect."

"That's the trouble, Cassie. You see things the way you want to see them. I see them for what they are."

"And what was this?" she asked, almost afraid to know.

"This..." He smiled wistfully for a second before he swallowed hard. "This was—a mistake."

"No!"

"Cassie, you're not ready for any of this."

"I know what I want."

"You couldn't," he said, looking up to the darkening sky as if searching for answers.

"Colton? Talk to me."

He ran a hand through his still-wet hair, and his fingers trembled. "I-I think we'd better get dressed."

"So soon?"

"For God's sake, Cassie!" he exploded. "Think about it." Muttering under his breath, he yanked his cutoffs on.

"I'm not ashamed."

His head snapped up. "Good. You shouldn't be," he said quickly.

"Neither should you."

He pinched his lips together. "Forget it."

"Colton, it was beautiful! I love—"

"Don't!" he said, rubbing the back of his neck nervously and biting the corner of his lip. "I care about you, Cass. Hell, you know that. But you're so young.... I just think we should slow things down a little."

"What do you mean?" she asked, crushed.

"That we're moving much too fast."

Reluctantly she stepped into her panties and tried not to cry. Tears formed in the corners of her eyes, but she forced them back. Maybe Colton didn't love her now, right this minute, but he would! She knew it! Surely he couldn't have touched her so intimately, caressed her skin so fondly, if he didn't—

"What the hell do you think you're doing?" a strong, familiar voice demanded.

Cassie froze, grateful for the shadows cast by the trees.

Colton, lifting his head, scrambled to hide her from his brother's incriminating gaze.

Astride a rangy bay gelding, Denver McLean glared down at them. His face was lined with disapproval, his brows drawing into one thick black line. "Have you lost your mind?" he demanded harshly.

Colton coiled, his muscles flexed as if he was about to leap up and drag his brother from the saddle. "I think you'd better leave!"

"So you can go back to bedding Ivan Aldridge's daughter?" Denver sneered. "Not on your life."

Cassie wanted to die! She struggled into her halter and shorts.

Standing, Colton snapped the closure of his cutoffs. "It's none of your business!"

"No? And what happens if she turns up pregnant? What do you think her old man will say?"

"I swear, Denver, if you don't leave . . ." Colton warned, still using his body to shield her.

"Come on. Take your best shot." But Denver didn't slide to the ground. He glanced at Cassie and sighed. "Hell, Colt, she's only a child!"

"I'm seventeen," Cassie insisted, her clothes finally intact even if her pride was shredded to ribbons.

"Sweet Mary! Seventeen?" Denver exclaimed, his furious gaze ricocheting back to Colton. "Ivan Aldridge will personally nail your hide to the wall!"

"That's my problem," Colton retorted, standing next to Cassie, one hand curved protectively around her waist.

"That's everybody's problem," Denver pointed out. "There's still a lot of bad blood between the two families. If Ivan finds out that you and his daughter are lovers, there'll be hell to pay."

"I'm warning you," Colton ground out.

"It's none of your business," Cassie cut in, her temper flaring.

"Isn't it?" Denver's blue eyes glinted. "I hope to God that you're old enough to protect yourself," he said furiously. "I don't know how your dad would feel about becoming a grandfather to a McLean."

"Protect myself?" Cassie repeated.

"It hasn't come to that, Denver," Colton lied, his jaw tightening.

"But not far from it."

Colton bristled. "I can handle myself."

"Just use your head."

"Oh, like you do whenever you're around Tessa?"

Denver's face became a mask of iron. "Leave Tessa out of this," he warned in a low growl. "You'd better get back to the house. Dad wants to talk to you. And you, Cassie—"

"I'll take care of her," Colton bristled.

"If you haven't already." Yanking on the bay's reins, Denver swore furiously. The horse twirled on his back legs and took off in a cloud of dust.

"Come on," Colton said gently, "I'll take you home."

"I don't want to go home."

A muscle tightened in Colton's jaw, and his silvery eyes sparked. "Denver's right, you know. This'll only cause trouble." He took her hand in his and guided her to the truck.

"But all I want is you! I want to marry *you*!"

"Oh, God, Cassie. Marry me?"

"Yes."

He shook his head violently. The fading light was reflected in his eyes. "You'll change your mind a dozen times before—"

"Don't tell me I'm too young to know what I want," she said, tears flooding her eyes as he helped her into the dented Ford pickup. She hated being only seventeen—hated it!

"Okay, I won't. But I'll tell you what I want. I want to finish college. I want to travel. I want to be the best photographer in the newspaper business." He ground the old gears, and the truck lurched forward. "And I'm not interested in a wife—at least not now."

He couldn't have wounded her more if he'd taken a knife to her throat. Huddled miserably on the passenger side of the pickup, Cassie wondered how she could change his mind. He'd wanted her, and there was more to their relationship than simple lust, she thought wretchedly. There had to be. Somehow she'd prove it to him.

The next morning Cassie was working out her plan to see Colton when her father cornered her in the kitchen. "You were out yesterday," he said. Seated at the battered old table, he sipped coffee from his favorite chipped mug.

"Umm." She kissed her father on his crown. "But I wasn't late."

"Who were you with?" he asked.

"Just a friend." She reached into the cupboard and found a cup for herself.

"Boyfriend?"

"Yes," she said, naively thinking she could end the feud right then and there. "Colton McLean."

Her father's head snapped back and a steady flush crept up his neck as he glared at her. "I thought I told you the McLean boys were off limits."

"And I thought that it was time to start mending fences."

The back of her father's neck turned scarlet. "Some fences are never meant to be mended. Don't you remember what the McLeans did to us? To our family?" He shoved his plate across the table.

"That was John."

"I never want to hear that name in this house!" he warned. "And you may as well realize all the McLeans are the same—cut from the same bolt of rotten cloth. Especially Colton. He's wild and irresponsible, that one!"

"You just don't know him."

"Don't I?" Ivan's hands were shaking. He rolled his fingers into his palms, and his jaw clenched and relaxed several times before he found his voice. "Use your head, Cassie. Colton McLean doesn't care for you."

"You don't know anything about him!" she cried.

Ivan cocked both eyebrows. "I know this—you're not to see him."

"You can't stop me!"

"You're still a minor, Cassie. You're living under my roof, by my rules."

She clenched her fingers tight around the cup, her knuckles white. She swallowed hard. "I love him, Dad," she admitted, cringing a little when she saw his shoulders slump.

"You're too young to know about love."

"Mom was seventeen when she married you."

"And look what happened. She ran off with John McLean. Then, when he was through with her, she didn't bother coming back."

"And so you blame everyone with the McLean name."

"The same blood runs through their veins." He stood and jammed his hat onto his head. "You're not to see Colton McLean again, hear?"

"And what if I do?"

His old eyes saddened. "Don't be forcing the issue, Cassie. It's a mistake to choose between family and a man who doesn't want or need you."

"You're wrong about Colton!"

"Am I?" Ivan paused at the door. "Then if he wants you, he'll have to court you. I won't have you sneaking off behind my back!"

Colton didn't call. Not that day, nor the next, nor any day that week. Her father never mentioned his name again, but Cassie thought of him constantly. She rode along the fence line, hoping to catch a glimpse of him working on the ranch, and she spent hours in town with her friends, hoping to run into him. Once in a while she'd see him and he'd be staring at her, but guilt would change his expression and he'd quickly look away.

Two weeks later she was seated in a corner booth in Jerry's, a local burger hut. Cassie had purposely chosen this booth near the window facing Main Street so that she could stare outside and watch the traffic, just in case Colton or someone from the McLean spread drove into Three Falls.

She sat there for fifteen minutes, sipping cola, pining for Colton, when Beth Lassiter, her best friend, breezed through the front door.

Spying Cassie, Beth waved, dashed to Cassie's booth and slid excitedly onto the red plastic seat. "I'll have a Coke and onion rings," she said to Bonnie, the waitress, then trained worried blue eyes on her friend. "Guess what?" she whispered, her brown ponytail falling forward, her cheeks flushed.

"What?" Cassie swirled her straw in her drink, watching the ice cubes dance.

Beth bit her lower lip. "Colton McLean's dating Jessica Monroe."

Cassie gasped, her stomach turning over. Her hands began to shake, and she hid them beneath the table and tried to appear as calm as possible. "No—"

"I didn't believe it, either, but I got the word from Ellen."

Ellen was Jessica Monroe's younger sister. There were three Monroe sisters in all. All blond, blue-eyed, petite and gorgeous. Jessica was the oldest and probably the prettiest.

"That's impossible," Cassie said, finishing her Coke. She wouldn't believe that Colton had betrayed her—couldn't. Already she suspected that her lovemaking with Colton had cost her more than her virginity. Her period was late, and Cassie was certain that she was pregnant.

Beth rolled her eyes. "Look, Cassie, I know you've got a major crush on Colton, but you may as well forget it. He's

only got a term or so left in college in California and then
he's history. He won't be coming back here.''

"You don't know that—"

"Sure I do. He's as much as told everyone he's met that
he's going to be some hot-shot journalist. Face it, this town
*bores* him."

"Maybe he's changed."

"Are you kidding? Cass, what's gotten into you? He's
more like his Uncle John than the rest of his family and—
oh, jeez, I'm sorry," Beth said, grimacing. "I—I forgot
about your mom."

"It's okay." Cassie forced a smile that threatened to fall
from her face. The back of her eyes burned when she
thought of her mother and especially when she thought
about making love to Colton McLean. "But you're wrong
about Colton."

Bonnie, a heavyset woman with a once-white apron
strapped around her thick waist, deposited onion rings and
Beth's drink on the table.

Beth handed her a couple of dollars, then poured a thick
glob of catsup into her paper-lined plastic basket. "If I were
you, I'd forget about Colton," Beth advised. "There are
other fish in the sea."

"So I've heard."

Beth sighed. "Colton's just not for you."

Cassie didn't believe her. She'd seen the way he'd looked
at her, felt the electricity charging the air between them,
known the ecstasy of lying in his arms.

But another week passed and she didn't hear from Colton. Because she loved him with all of her heart and she felt
she was carrying his child, Cassie thwarted her father.
Though he'd ordered her not to chase after Colton Mc-
Lean, she couldn't stop herself. Not with a baby on the way.

Lying on her bed, listening to the sounds of the night
through her open window, Cassie waited until her father was

asleep, then sneaked down the stairs and hurried outside. Erasmus yipped at the sight of her, and Cassie jumped.

"You scared the life out of me!" she whispered. "Hush!"

Shoving her hands into the pockets of her jean jacket, she crossed the yard, letting moonlight guide her into the barn.

She couldn't chance starting the engine of the truck, so she slipped a bridle on Tavish, her favorite chestnut gelding, then led him outside. Not bothering with a saddle, she swung onto the chestnut's broad back and dug her heels into his sides.

The gelding bolted; his hooves thudded against the dry fields as he fairly flew over the hard ground. The dry summer wind streamed through Cassie's hair, and she blinked against tears collecting in her eyes.

She knew what she was doing was dangerous. The horse could trip in the darkness, throwing her. Or her father might wake up and discover her gone. But she had to talk to Colton.

Closer to the edge of the property, she pulled back on the reins and slowed Tavish to pick his way through the pines near the river. She heard the roar of the rushing Sage.

Tavish stepped from between the pines, and Cassie saw the river in the moonlight, the turbulent white water splashing over stones and slicing through the dry earth.

The horse shied near the edge of the river. Cassie talked softly to him, patting his sleek neck. "Come on, boy. We can do it. We have before."

Tavish tossed his head before stepping into the river. The dark water swirled around his legs and belly. As she twisted the reins in her fingers, the first icy touch of the Sage brushed against her bare legs. Tavish stepped deeper, then began to float.

Cassie felt his legs stretch as he swam, carrying them across the current and toward the opposite shore. "That's it," she said, encouraging, soothing, though her throat was dry, her lungs constricted. "Hold on—just a little more..."

Finally his hooves struck bottom. Scrambling over the rocks, Tavish lunged from the river. Once on land, he shook, snorting and blowing, the bridle jangling loudly.

"Good boy!" Cassie cried, climbing off his back and tying him to the sagging fence separating McLean property from Aldridge land. "Wait for me."

Her canvas shoes squished as she slipped under the barbed wires. She ran through the fields by instinct. Her heart was pounding, and though her shorts were damp from the cold water, she began to sweat. What if Colton wasn't home? What if he wouldn't see her? What if, God forbid, he was there with Jessica?

"Don't go borrowing trouble," she told herself as she approached the center of the McLean ranch. The stables, barns and outbuildings loomed ahead, glowing eerily beneath the security lamps. Beyond the buildings and across the yard, lights gleamed in the windows of the McLean house.

Cassie nearly lost her nerve as she climbed the final fence and started across the yard. She was sure someone would look out the window and see her. And then what?

She was almost to the front door when a car approached. Headlights bobbing, engine whining, the sports car sped up the hilly lane leading to the house. Cassie's heart sank, and she ducked behind a tree, silently praying she wouldn't be seen.

The car screeched to a stop not far from the tree. A car door banged open.

"I never want to see you again!" a woman screamed, and Cassie recognized the voice as belonging to Jessica Monroe.

"Don't you?" Colton drawled.

Cassie's knees gave out. She leaned against the rough bark for support. So it was true. He was seeing Jessica! After he had made love to her. Her stomach roiled, and she thought she might throw up right there on the lawn.

"You're a lying, two-timing bastard, McLean."

"I didn't call you," he reminded her.

"It's that Aldridge girl, isn't it?" Jessica charged.

"Leave her out of this," Colton warned.

"God, Colton, she's barely out of diapers! And her father would murder you if he ever got wind—"

"Stop it!" Colton cut in, his voice low.

"Don't I mean anything to you?" she wheedled, and a long silence followed.

So Colton didn't care about Jessica! Cassie, flattened against the tree, heard her heart slamming against her ribs.

"You're a fool, Colton McLean!" Jessica charged.

"Probably."

Cassie heard footsteps crossing the gravel driveway and the sound of a car door slam loudly. She peeked around the tree trunk just as the convertible roared to life again and tore down the drive. Jessica's long blond hair waved like a moon-dusted banner behind her.

Cassie turned her gaze to Colton. He was standing in the middle of the yard, but he wasn't paying the slightest attention to the disappearing car. Instead, an amused smile curved his lips. His hands on his hips, he stared straight at Cassie.

"See enough, Cass?" he taunted.

Cassie swallowed hard. She wanted to run as fast as her legs would carry her back to the fence where Tavish was waiting, but she forced herself to step forward. She felt young and stupid and incredibly naive. "I heard you were dating Jessica," she admitted, forcing her head up to meet the questions in his eyes.

"Not much of a date," he said sarcastically. "It was her idea."

Cassie managed a poor imitation of a cynical smile. "Seems like you have all sorts of women chasing you down."

"Not many. Some are girls."

She bristled. "How can you say that? After...after—"

Colton sighed, plowing his hands through his hair. He closed the gap between them and grabbed her arm, drawing her into the shadows away from the house. "You are a girl, damn it," he ground out, more exasperated than angry. "Seventeen, for crying out loud!" He dropped her arm and swore. "I don't know what to think of you, Cassie."

"We made love."

He sucked in a swift breath. "I haven't forgotten."

"Then why haven't you called or stopped by?" she asked, her heart pounding wildly with fear—fear that he would reject her, fear that he wouldn't want the baby.

"Oh, God, Cass," he whispered, his voice rough, "if you think this has been easy—"

"Don't you want to see me?"

His jaw worked. "More than I should."

"Then, why—"

"Because I don't want to make the same mistake twice."

"Mistake?" she whispered, her throat closing. "Mistake?" Unbidden, tears filled her eyes. "How can you call what we shared a mistake? I love—"

He held up one flat palm. "I don't want to hear it!"

"Why not, Colton? Because you're afraid?"

"Yes, damn it! I *am* afraid." He grabbed for her again, his hands clamping over her forearms. "I'm afraid of what's happening to me—to you—to us. What about the rest of our lives, Cassie? You have dreams, don't you? Didn't you tell me you want to become a veterinarian?"

"Yes, but—"

"And I want to finish school, get a job with the best goddamn paper in the country."

"You can—"

"With a wife?" he mocked. "Because that's what you're after, Cassie. You as much as said it before." He stared down into her eyes and groaned. "You're beautiful, Cass, and loving and smart, and you've got your whole life stretched out in front of you. You can have anything you want."

"Except you."

Colton swallowed hard, and his eyes searched hers. For a split second she thought he might kiss her. "Give it time," he pleaded, his voice rough.

"Maybe we haven't got time," she whispered.

"Of course we do...." He stared down at her, as if noticing for the first time how pale she was, how pinched the corners of her mouth had become. "What do you mean?"

"I'm pregnant," she whispered, her voice raw.

His arms dropped to his sides, and he leaned one shoulder against the house, sagging. "Pregnant?" Stunned, his face chalk-white, he asked, "You're sure?"

"Of course I am."

"You've been to the doctor?"

She shook her head, fighting against tears. "Not yet."

"Then maybe—"

"I'm positive, Colton. It's not something you guess at. I've been around a ranch for years. I know the facts of life."

"But until you've seen the doctor, you really don't know," he protested.

Cassie was firm. "I'm nearly two weeks late, and I've already started throwing up before breakfast."

"Oh, God," he muttered. Pinching the bridge of his nose between his thumb and forefinger, he squeezed his eyes shut.

With a sinking heart Cassie understood just how little he wanted the baby, how little he cared for her. She hurt all over. "Look," she finally said, her voice barely audible, "this isn't your problem. I—I can handle it." She started walking, faster and faster, away from him, before the tears burning behind her eyes began to fall.

"It's as much my fault as yours."

"It's no one's *fault*, Colton. It just happened."

He let out a long breath. "I'll marry you."

She stopped short, barely believing her ears. "You don't have to—"

He caught up with her, and every muscle in his face was hard and set. "I won't run away from my responsibilities, Cassie. You're pregnant, the child's mine, and we'll get married."

"There's no need to be noble."

He snorted. "Oh, this is far from noble."

*If only she could believe him!* "What about your career?"

His eyes searched the heavens, and a wistful smile curved his lips. "There's time. It'll wait. We'll live here until we get on our feet, then we'll find a place of our own. When we can afford it, we'll both finish school."

It sounded so clinical, so hollow. Where was the happiness? The joy? The love everlasting? The earth-shattering knowledge that this love—their love—would bind them together always? "I don't want to get in the way, Colton," she whispered, suddenly feeling as if she'd made a big mistake in telling him about the baby. "You have your plans—"

He grabbed her again, his fingers tightening over her arm. "We'll make it work, Cassie," he vowed, "but it won't be easy. You've got to understand that."

"I'm willing to work at it."

"Good. So am I." He glanced up at the moon, smiling wearily. "This isn't what I'd planned," he admitted, "but maybe it's just what I, we, need."

"Of course it is!" she cried, forcing their happiness.

He held her then, wrapping his arms around her waist and kissing her full on the mouth. Warmth spread through her, and she clasped her hands behind his neck, dragging them both to the ground. "I love you, Colton," she whispered over the pounding of her heart, "and I always will."

"Shh, Cass, I know. I know," he said, sighing.

So he hadn't said he loved her. But at least he wanted her. She saw it in his eyes, felt it in the urgency with which he cast their clothes aside. Cassie gazed up at him, filled with the wonder that this virile man would soon be her husband.

Two days later, Cassie squirmed in the hard, plastic chair.

Dr. Jordan, a man in his fifties with glossy white hair and small, even features, stared at Cassie over the tops of his glasses. He was seated behind his desk, his fingers toying with the edge of her medical chart. "The lab results are back. You're not pregnant."

Cassie froze. "Not pregnant?" she repeated, disbelieving.

"Your test was negative. This should be good news," the doctor said, though obviously from his expression he could see the disappointment on her face.

"There must be some mistake—"

"No mistake, Cassie."

"But I've been sick and my period is late!"

"You probably had the flu, and sometimes that can affect your cycle."

"No..."

The doctor smiled. "You've got plenty of time."

Did she? She felt as if all the sand in her hourglass had just slipped through her fingers.

As she walked outside, a warm summer breeze caressed her face and tugged at her hair. Overhead, leaves turned in the wind and squirrels chattered and raced nimbly through the branches. The air felt fresh and clean, but she felt cold inside. What would happen now? How could she tell Colton that she'd been wrong?

She wrapped her arms around her waist as she walked along the dusty sidewalk. She tried not to notice young mothers pushing strollers or a happy couple, obviously in love, sneaking kisses in the park.

Walking past a boutique, she eyed a lace wedding dress in the window. Would Colton still want to marry her? Two doors down she paused at the only children's store in Three

Falls. Her throat went dry. Rattles and blankets and sleepers in a rainbow of pastels were strewn around a bare wooden rocking horse with glass eyes and a hemp mane and tail.

"Maybe someday," she whispered, her fingers trailing over the glass. She strolled into the store and touched the soft clothing and adorable stuffed animals until she could stand the self-inflicted torture no longer.

"Fool," she whispered to herself as she drove home, squinting against the lowering sun. Knowing she had to tell Colton the truth, she drove straight to the lane leading to the McLean ranch, but at the last minute she changed her mind and sped past the gravel drive. What would she say? What if Denver answered the door? Or worse yet, Colton's parents or his uncle John? No, she had to wait until she got Colton alone.

She was still lost in thought, worried sick about breaking the news to Colton, when she parked the pickup near the barn.

"Where ya been?" her father asked as she raced through the back door. Seated at the kitchen table, working the crossword puzzle in the morning paper, he glanced up at her.

"In town."

"Get anything?"

*Just bad news.* "Nope—nothing caught my eye." She forced a smile she didn't feel.

Ivan turned his attention back to the open newspaper pages, and she ran upstairs and changed, feeling miserable.

She considered calling Colton, but couldn't risk it, not until her father was away from the ranch. If Ivan heard her end of the conversation, he'd go through the roof. And she couldn't chance another midnight ride; she might get caught by the McLeans or her father.

A little voice in her mind nagged at her—told her she was just putting off the inevitable, but she wouldn't listen. She had time, she assured herself. Besides, it was better to be safe than sorry.

In the next few days her father never left the ranch. And, unfortunately, he expected her to help with the hay and wheat harvest—so she was in the fields as much as he. Cassie spent nearly twenty-four hours a day with him. If Colton had called, she'd been out and missed him.

One evening while her father was doing the chores, she forced herself to take a chance. Her insides churning, she reached for the phone, dialed, and waited.

"Hello." Denver McLean's voice rang over the wires. Was it her imagination or did he already sound hostile?

"Hello?" he said again. "Hello?"

Cassie swallowed hard.

"Is anyone there?" Denver asked, his voice angrier than ever.

"Cass?" her father called.

Whirling, Cassie hung up.

"Don't let me bother you," her father said, nodding toward the telephone.

Shaking her head, Cassie mumbled. "I was finished anyway."

"Who was it?"

Cassie thought fast. "Just Beth," she lied, hating herself for the deception.

Her father chuckled. "You two would tie up the lines around here all day if you had the chance," he said, and Cassie felt worse than ever.

Her father grabbed his cap from a hook near the door, then disappeared outside again.

Cassie sagged against the wall. Somehow she had to find Colton and tell him the truth—in so doing, she would relieve him of his obligation and set him free to do what he really wanted with his life. Sooner or later they had to talk.

As the next few days passed, she felt more and more guilty. And there was a tiny part of her that kept hoping that even when he knew that there was no baby, he would smile and say, "It's all right, Cass. I love you. We'll get married anyway."

By the end of the week she'd gathered all her courage and found an excuse to go riding alone. The sun was just setting over the western hills, and Cassie knew that it was now or never. She followed the same path she'd taken the night she'd told Colton she was pregnant. Tavish streaked across the fields to the river, where, after snorting his disapproval, he eventually swam with Cassie clinging to his neck.

Her heart was pounding, her hands sweaty, as she tied Tavish's reins to the fence, ducked under the sagging barbed wire and ran through the bleached stubble of the McLean pasture.

*Please, God, let him be home,* she silently prayed. Climbing the final fence, she nearly lost her nerve. The yard was empty, but she saw Katherine McLean in the garden near the house.

Cassie combed the tangles from her hair with her fingers, squared her shoulders, and ignoring the fact that the hem of her denim skirt was damp, she forced herself down an overgrown path to the garden.

"Mrs. McLean?"

Katherine, bent over a row of bush beans, cast a glance over her shoulder. From beneath the brim of her straw hat her blue eyes widened a bit. But if she thought it strange that Ivan Aldridge's daughter was standing in the middle of McLean property, she didn't show it. "Cassie! How're you?"

"Fine," Cassie said, her fingers twisting nervously in the folds of her skirt. She could feel the flush in her cheeks, knew her heart was slamming a million times a minute. "Is—is Colton here?"

Katherine dusted her hands, and her dark brows drew into a thoughtful frown. "No, he left over an hour ago. He was going into town, and then I thought he said he was stopping by your place. He should be there by now."

Cassie swallowed hard, and the color that had invaded her face drained. "I must've missed him," she whispered, a thousand horrid scenarios flitting through her mind. What if at this very minute Colton was talking with her dad, explaining about the baby, telling Ivan he intended to marry her? She started backing up. "Well, uh, maybe I'll catch him there."

Katherine winced and rubbed the small of her back. "Are you sure? You look pale. Maybe you should come into the house for a drink. I know I could use a break. There's sun tea in the refrigerator—"

"No—no thanks," Cassie said quickly, feeling miserable. She hated turning down Colton's mother and this chance to help bury some of the bad feelings lingering between the Aldridges and McLeans, but she couldn't take a chance that Colton might be telling Ivan that he was going to sacrifice himself by marrying Cassie—all because of a baby!

She fairly flew across the arid fields, her hair streaming behind her in the wind. At the fence she ducked quickly, snagging her blouse, feeling the prick of one sharp barb on her back. She didn't care.

Her fingers fumbled with the reins. The wet leather had partially dried, tightening the knot. "Come on, come on," she whispered, finally yanking the reins free and jumping onto Tavish's broad back.

Digging her heels into the gelding's sides, she urged him into the river, not even noticing the Sage's icy water against her calves and thighs.

Tavish scrambled up the bank, and Cassie leaned forward. "Come on, boy—now!" As his hooves found flat ground, she slapped the reins against his shoulder and he bolted, streaking down the path through the trees and across the open, windswept fields. Grasshoppers flew out of Tavish's path. Jackrabbits scurried through the grass to the protection of brambles. The chestnut's strides reached full length, and tears blurred Cassie's vision.

"That's it," she whispered, riding low, her legs gripping Tavish's heaving sides.

She yanked on the reins at the stables, and the gelding slid to a stop. Not bothering to walk him, nor take the bridle from his head, she looped the reins over the top rail and scrambled over the fence only to spy Colton's truck parked in the yard.

"No..." she cried. Her throat closed, and for a minute she had to stop and lean against the rough boards of the barn to catch her breath. Maybe it wasn't too late. He couldn't have been here long, though the lavender streaks of coming dusk told her that time had passed, perhaps too much time.

With as much dignity as she could muster, she climbed up the steps to the back porch, flung open the door and stepped inside.

Ivan and Colton were in the living room, both standing, surveying each other as if they were mortal enemies. Colton's back was to the fireplace, where the old clock on the mantel ticked softly near the faded pictures of Cassie's mother.

"I—I didn't know you were coming here," she whispered, her voice barely audible. She felt Colton's gaze on her, knew he could see the tangles in her hair, the flush on her cheeks, the dampness discoloring her skirt.

"I should have called," Colton said tightly, and she knew instantly that he was furious. His face had whitened under his tan, and his mouth had thinned to a hard, cruel line.

"What in blazes is going on here?" Ivan demanded, hooking an insolent thumb at Colton. "McLean here says he wants to talk to you—alone. When I told him you'd gone riding, he said he'd wait."

Cassie's heart dropped through the floor. "It's—it's okay, Dad."

Ivan scowled. "Whatever you have to say to my daughter, you can say to me."

"I don't think so," Colton replied.

"Please, Dad—"

"You know how I feel about this."

"It won't take long," Colton told him.

Ivan hesitated, glanced at Cassie and swore under his breath. "I need a drink," he said, his eyes narrowing on Colton before turning to Cassie. "I'll be on the back porch." With one last disparaging glance at Colton, Ivan strode stiffly into the kitchen, rummaged in the cupboards until he found his favorite bottle of rye whiskey and a glass, then stomped loudly outside. The screen door slammed behind him.

"Is—is something wrong?" Cassie asked, not knowing how to break the ice.

"You tell me," he said flatly.

"As a matter of fact, there is," she admitted. "I—I was just over at your place looking for you."

"Were you?"

She could feel the loathing in Colton's gaze. His nostrils flared angrily, and disgust curled his lips. Why was he so angry? she wondered...and then it hit her. He knew. Somehow, some way, he'd found out! Frigid desperation settled in her soul. "There—there is no baby," she admitted.

"And you weren't going to tell me." His voice sounded flat, lifeless.

"Of course I was. I just wanted to wait until we were alone." She turned pleading eyes up at him, begging him to understand.

The anger in his eyes died for just an instant, and Cassie's hopes soared. "When—when did you find out?"

"Last Monday," she answered, watching in dread as his features hardened to stone.

"Last Monday! A week—nearly a week ago! And you didn't tell me? When were you planning to give me the news, Cass? *After* the wedding?" he demanded, his hushed voice growing louder, a vein throbbing in his neck.

She reached for his arm. "No, Colton, I swear—"

"Don't bother," he muttered, yanking his arm away from her in disgust.

"But I called—I was just at your house, looking for you—"

The back door flew open, and Ivan raced into the room. "What the devil's going on?" he demanded, his eyes darting anxiously from Colton's stiff spine to the tears rolling soundlessly down Cassie's cheeks.

Colton's face turned to stone. He started for the door, but Cassie ran after him, catching him just as his fingers curled over the knob.

Throat knotted, tears streaming from her eyes, she clutched Colton's sleeve. "Wait—I can explain—"

"I just bet you can!" He yanked open the door. Hot night air streamed into the room. "How do you think I felt when I told a friend of mine you and I were going to be married?" he demanded.

"But—"

"That's right, I let Warren Mason know. Warren just happens to work at LTV labs. He was congratulating me all over the place, then asked who the lucky girl was. When I mentioned your name, he got real quiet, I mean *real* quiet."

"Oh, no—"

"I asked him what was wrong, and he told me—reluctantly, mind you—that he'd seen your pregnancy tests. I was stupid enough to think he was going to congratulate me on becoming a father, but he didn't. Instead he let it slip that the test was negative.''

''Oh, God,'' Cassie whispered.

''There never was a baby, Cassie, and you knew it.''

''Then why would I have the test done?''

''To convince me,'' he growled.

''No—''

''Then why didn't you tell me *last Monday*?''

''I wanted to—''

''Did you?'' Seeing her fingers curled into the folds of his denim jacket, Colton snarled, ''Let me go, Cassie.''

''I can't—I love you.''

''It's over!''

''I didn't mean to—''

''Didn't mean to what? Lie to me? Deceive me? Trap me into marrying you?''

''I never—''

Slowly, he peeled her hands off his jacket. ''Save it, Cassie. Save it for someone who'll believe it. Maybe the next guy you seduce!''

She shrank back at his cruelty. ''I can't let go,'' she whispered pathetically.

''You don't have a choice.''

Wounded beyond words, she felt her shoulders begin to shake, her body droop heavily against the wainscoting.

''Get out, McLean!'' Ivan commanded, his voice a deadly whisper as he stalked into the entryway. His face was purple, his eyes bright, his fists clenched at his sides. ''I don't know what the hell's going on here, but I don't care. You get out and leave my daughter alone! If you ever so much as step one foot on this property again, I swear, I'll kill you!''

''Dad—no—''

Colton's gaze moved slowly from Cassie to her father and back again. ''Like father, like daughter. Always swearing something that doesn't mean a damn thing.''

"No!" she cried, colder than she'd been since that devastating night when her mother, her eyes red with tears and her coat billowing behind her, had left through the very same door. "I love you!" she cried, and saw Colton's shoulders stiffen.

"Don't, Cassie," he rasped, shaking his head as if convincing himself that he didn't care. "Just don't!" His jaw set, he strode out of Cassie's life.

"Okay, Cassie," her father whispered, his lips tight, "I think you have some explaining to do."

"What do you want to know?" she whispered.

"Everything."

"Oh, Dad—"

"Come on, now," his voice was gentle, but firm. He wrapped one arm around her shoulders. "It can't be that bad."

"You don't know."

"Whatever it is, we'll get through it," he said as they listened to Colton's Jeep racing out the driveway. "Didn't we before?"

"This is different."

"Not so much. You're hurt again, and I'm here to help."

Her heart felt as if it had broken into a thousand pieces. The sobs burning deep in her throat erupted, and she clung to her father's neck, burying her face against the rough cotton of his work shirt. "I love him so much," she sobbed, unable to stem her tears. "I'll never love anyone else."

"Sure you will," Ivan predicted, "sure you will."


But she hadn't. No man had ever touched her as Colton McLean had. No boy in high school or college had been able to break through the barriers Colton had built, stone by painful stone.

Now, eight years after he'd left her alone and miserable, silly, futile tears slipped down Cassie's cheeks to fall on to the eiderdown quilt. Regret filled her. Regret for a love that hadn't existed, regret for memories tarnished by Colton's hard heart, regret for the pathetic, lovesick fool she'd once been.

She blinked, then squeezed her eyes shut tight, willing away her tears. She wouldn't cry for him—she wouldn't!

Ignoring the hot lump in her throat, she braced herself for the future. No matter what happened, she'd be strong— stronger than she'd ever thought possible. Because, like it or not, Colton had walked back into her life.

## Chapter Four

Colton stomped on the throttle. The old Jeep leaped forward, its wheels spinning on the gravel ruts that comprised the Aldridge's lane. What had possessed him to drive here? And why, when he'd learned that Ivan wasn't around, had he stayed?

*Cassie.* Always Cassie. Damn, but he wished he could forget her. She'd changed, of course. Her innocence and optimism had matured with her. Though not worldly-wise, she now had a sophistication within her that she hadn't possessed at seventeen. She knew her own mind, said what she thought and had developed a hard-edged sense of humor.

All in all, she'd caught him off guard. He hadn't expected to be attracted to her. In fact, he'd hoped that with time, he'd developed an immunity to her—that his infatuation at twenty-one would seem a simple schoolboy crush.

Unfortunately he'd been wrong. Seeing her now as a beautiful young woman who seemingly could stand up to anyone, he'd been trapped by her beauty. Trapped. Again.

"You've just been cooped up too long," he rationalized, cranking the wheel as he nosed the Jeep onto the highway. The pain in his shoulder flared, and he gritted his teeth. "You need to get out more." *And away from this god-forsaken scrap of scrub brush.*

From the time he'd been a child, he'd known he would leave—that he wanted more than ranching could offer. But for the past six months he hadn't had many options. His wound had required several surgeries to repair the damaged joint and ligaments.

"Soon," he muttered, comforting himself with the thought that he could leave as soon as Denver and Tessa were back.

Unless, of course, this problem with the horse was unresolved. And unless he could not get Cassie Aldridge out of his system.

To change the direction of his thoughts, he snapped on the radio, only to hear a song from the past—a love song that had hit the charts that summer he'd been involved with Cassie—a song that reminded him of her.

Angrily he punched a button for another station and contented himself with listening to the news. The windshield wipers slapped the rain away. The mailbox signaling the turnoff to the ranch flashed in the headlights. Colton slowed, then gunned the engine past the lane. He was too keyed up to go back to the blasted ranch.

He needed a drink, and it was about time he showed his face in town again, anyway. Remembering a local watering hole, he drove down the main street and past a rainbow of flickering neon lights.

The Livery Stable, a weathered plank building named for its original purpose, stood on the far end of town. Colton wheeled into the parking lot, braked, then cranked on the emergency brake and shouldered the door open. Ducking his head against the rain, he plowed through puddles to the front door.

Inside, the interior was hazy with smoke. Customers lined the bar and filled most of the booths. Pool balls clicked, people chatted and laughed, and video games buzzed erratically. Colton strode straight to the bar and recognized Ben Haley, an old classmate of Denver's, who owned the place.

"Well, look who finally showed up," Ben commented. A stocky man with flat features and a cynical smile matched only by Colton's, he motioned to the nearest stool.

"I thought it was about time."

"What'll it be?"

Colton eyed the glistening bottles arranged in front of a ceiling-high mirror. "Irish coffee."

Ben's thin lips twitched. "Irish coffee," he repeated, glancing at Colton's shoulder. "Don't you have enough reminders of that place?"

"I guess I'm just a glutton for punishment." Colton eyed the other patrons as Ben mixed his drink. "Has Ivan Aldridge been in?" he asked.

Sliding a mug across the scratched surface of the bar, Ben nodded. "A couple of hours ago."

"Alone?"

"No—Monroe and Wilkerson were with him. They come in for a couple of beers once in a while."

"Hey, Ben, how about another?" a young, curly-haired man at the end of the bar called.

"Right with ya." He glanced back at Colton. "Glad to see ya around, McLean. Just give me a yell if you need anything."

"I will." Colton stared into the depths of his mug, swirling the hot murky concoction and wondering why, no matter what he did, he couldn't erase Cassie's image from his mind.

\* \* \*

"So McLean's lost his horse again?" Ivan asked the next morning. He kicked out the chair next to him and, cradling a mug of coffee in his palms, grinned widely. "Too bad." Propping his stocking feet on the other chair, he leaned back and eyed his daughter.

"That's what he says," Cassie replied. She flipped pancakes onto a huge platter and watched her father from the corner of her eye. His once-black hair was now steel-gray and thin, his tanned face lined from hours in the sun, and his light brown eyes a little less bright than they had been. Wearing a faded red flannel work shirt and dungarees held in place by red and black suspenders, he warmed his back near the wood stove.

"Serves the whole lot of them right!" Ivan settled back in his chair as Cassie placed platters of pancakes, bacon and eggs onto the gouged maple table.

"You're glad he lost the horse?"

Ivan's grin faded. "I'm glad he's havin' some trouble. No reason for him to be back in Montana as far as I can see."

"He was wounded."

"Yeah, right, got his ass shot up in Northern Ireland—"

"His shoulder."

"Doesn't matter. It's time he took off again. That's what he's good at, isn't it?"

Cassie, feeling a hot flush climb up her neck, sat at the table and stacked hot cakes onto her plate. "I suppose."

"You *know*!" Ivan waved his fork in front of Cassie's face. "He can't be tied to anything. He's been back here six months, and no one in town has seen hide nor hair of him."

"I guess he's been recuperating," Cassie said, wishing it didn't sound as if she was making excuses for a man she detested.

"Yeah, well, he can do it somewhere else."

Cassie smiled wryly. "I'm sure the minute he can, he'll make tracks out of here so fast, all we'll see is dust."

"Can't happen soon enough to suit me!" Ivan declared, spooning two fried eggs onto a short stack of cakes and pouring maple syrup over the whole lot.

"So what do you think happened to Black Magic?"

"Don't know and don't care."

"Dad . . ." Cassie cajoled, probing past the crusty facade of Ivan's surliness. "What do you really think?"

"How the hell should I know? He probably just ran off. The horse isn't dumb, you know." Ivan chuckled. "Maybe Black Magic got tired of Colton McLean and took off for greener pastures."

"Be serious."

"Okay, my best guess is that the stallion was randy, saw some mares and jumped the fence."

"The wires were cut."

Ivan's brows inched up. "Cut?"

"Snipped—just on the other side of the Sage. Where our property butts up to the McLeans'."

"So from that, Colton thinks I had something to do with it?"

"That and the fact that there were tire tracks on the wet ground."

"Big deal."

"Colton seems to think it is. He came over here with his guns loaded."

"Did he now?" Ivan's old eyes sparkled. "I hope you gave him hell."

"Well, I tried to throw him off the property, but that didn't work." She cocked her thumb toward a worn spot under the table where Erasmus lay hoping for a fallen tidbit. "Our watchdog here barked his head off, then turned over and whined for Colton to rub his belly."

Ivan chuckled, though the features of his face had tightened. "I'm sorry I wasn't here," he said. "I'd have given McLean a piece of my mind and saved you the trouble."

"I handled it."

His gaze darkened. "He's a bastard, Cassie. Always has been. Always will be. I haven't forgotten what he did to you."

Cassie's chest grew tight. "Let's not talk about it."

Tenderness crept into the old man's features. "Okay—it's over and done with."

"Right." But Cassie could feel his gaze searching hers.

"Maybe the fence was just broken."

"He didn't seem to think so. I thought I'd go check it out this afternoon when I get back from town."

Ivan shrugged. "Suit yourself. But if I were you—"

"I know, I know. You'd stay away from Colton McLean."

"All the McLeans," Ivan clarified, his expression hardening. "But especially Colton. He's as bad as his uncle was." Then, as if he, too, didn't want to dwell on a past filled with pain and betrayal, he turned his gaze to his plate and tackled his breakfast with renewed vigor.

They finished the meal in silence, Cassie still trying to dispel all thoughts of Colton. "You're on for the dishes," she reminded her father as she set her plate in the sink. "I still have to get ready."

"This is women's work," he grunted, but as Cassie cleared the table, Ivan grudgingly started rinsing the dishes and stacking them in the portable dishwasher that Cassie had purchased with her first paycheck from the veterinary clinic.

"You'll survive," she predicted. "It's time you got yourself out of the fifties."

"I've been out of the fifties longer than you've been alive."

She laughed, glad that the subject of Colton McLean had been dropped. "I have to stop by the Lassiter ranch to look at a couple of lambs, then I'll be at the clinic. I'll be home around six unless there's an emergency."

"I'll be here or over at Vince Monroe's. He's havin' trouble with his tractor and wants me to take a look at it."

"You should've been a mechanic."

"I am," he said, offering her a gentle smile. "I just don't get paid for it."

"I don't know how smart that is," Cassie called over her shoulder as she dashed upstairs. In her room she changed into a denim skirt and cotton T-shirt, dabbed some make-up on her face and ran a brush through her hair. Yawning, she tried not to think about Colton. He'd already robbed her of a night's worth of sleep, she thought angrily, remembering how she'd watched the digital clock flash the passing hours while she'd tried and failed to block Colton from her mind. But his image had been with her—his steely eyes, beard-covered chin, flash of white teeth.

"Stop it!" she muttered at her reflection. She had work to do today, and she couldn't take the time to think about Colton McLean or his missing horse!

"So what did Aldridge say?" Curtis asked, matching Colton's long strides with his own shorter steps as Colton strode across the wet yard to the stallion barn. Sunlight pierced through the cover of low-hanging clouds.

"He wasn't there."

"So you don't know any more than you did last night?"

"I talked to Cassie," Colton muttered, throwing open the door and frowning as he noticed Black Magic's empty stall. A few soft nickers greeted him, and the smell of horses and dust filled his nostrils.

"Did you now? And what did she have to say?"

One side of Colton's mouth lifted. "Not much. She held a rifle on me and ordered me off her place."

"Friendly," Curtis murmured.

"Hardly."

"So you didn't find out anything?"

"Once I convinced her that I'd had enough bullet wounds to last me a while, she finally showed me around the place."

"And?"

"Nothing," Colton said quickly, dismissing the subject of Cassie. He'd thought of little else since he'd seen her, but he wasn't going to get caught up in her again. Not that she wanted him. She'd made it all too clear just how much she loathed him. "Not one sign of Black Magic."

Curtis frowned as he measured grain into feed buckets. "So you think Ivan wasn't involved?"

"I don't know what to think," Colton admitted, climbing a metal ladder to the hayloft overhead. *Damn* the horse. *Damn Denver! Damn, damn, damn!* He kicked a couple bales of hay onto the cement floor and glowered at the empty stall from high above. Why did the damn horse have to disappear now? Using his good arm, he swung to the floor, then slit the baling twine with his pocketknife. "I still have to talk to him."

"What about the sheriff's department? Maybe we should call and tell them what's been going on," Curtis suggested, grabbing a pitchfork and shaking loose hay into the mangers.

"Later—when we know more," Colton said. He'd been an investigative photojournalist for years—lived his life on the edge. He was used to doing things his way and he didn't like the complications of the law. "Not yet. First we'll talk to the surrounding ranchers—see if anyone saw anything. There's still the chance that the horse'll show up like he did before."

Curtis's lips thinned. "If you say so."

"I just think we should dig a little deeper," Colton said. "Give it a couple of days. If we don't find him by the end of the week, I'll call Mark Gowan at the sheriff's office."

"And Denver?"

"Let's not phone him yet," Colton decided, knowing how his headstrong older brother would take the news. "It'll wait until he gets back. There's nothing more he or Tessa could do." He sliced the twine on the second bale. "Besides, I still intend to talk to Ivan Aldridge."

"I don't envy you that," Curtis muttered.

Colton grimaced. He wasn't crazy about facing Cassie's old man again—but it had to be done. As soon as he checked this place again, he would confront Ivan Aldridge and see what the old man had to say for himself.

*And what about Cassie?*

Colton sighed loudly and rubbed the back of his neck. Oh, yes, what about Cassie? There had to be some way to get her off his mind. All night long he'd dreamed of her, imagined the scent of her lingering on his sheets, envisioned the soft, blue-black waves of her hair tumbled in wanton disarray against his pillow, pictured in his mind's eye the creamy white texture of her skin and the soft pink pout of her lips.

Whether he wanted to or not, sooner or later he'd have to face her again.


Cassie slipped the bridle over Macbeth's broad head. A rangy roan gelding with a mean streak, he snorted his disgust and sidestepped as she climbed onto his wide back.

"Come on, fella, show me what you've got," she whispered, leaning forward and digging her heels into his ribs. The horse took off, ears flattened, neck extended, as he galloped over the soggy earth.

A low-hanging sun cast weak rays across the fields, gilding the green grass and streaking the sky in vibrant hues of orange and magenta.

The wind caught in Cassie's hair, tangling it as she leaned closer to the roan's sleek shoulder. Adrenaline pumped through her veins, and the long day at work faded into the background. She'd come home dead tired, found that Ivan was out, and decided to ease the aches from her muscles by riding. Besides, she couldn't help but satisfy her curiosity about Colton and his allegedly stolen horse.

She pulled on the reins, slowing Macbeth at the edge of the woods. As she guided the horse through the undergrowth, she remembered another time she'd ridden this very path—eight years ago—to tell Colton about the baby that hadn't existed.

"It's been a long time," she consoled herself, but she couldn't shake the gloomy feeling as Macbeth picked his way through the shadowy pines.

Before the horse had stepped from the trees, Cassie heard the river rushing wildly. The Sage, engorged with spring rain, slashed a crooked chasm through the wet earth.

The path curved toward the river's banks, and Cassie stared across the wild expanse of water, a physical chasm between McLean and Aldridge properties. Though the river was the natural dividing line, there was a stretch of grassy bank between the swirling Sage and the McLean fence line, where Colton McLean himself was stringing wire.

Wearing mud-spattered jeans and a work shirt that flapped in the breeze, he winced as he stretched the barbed wire taut between red metal posts. His broad shoulders moved fluidly under his shirt, and his jeans were tight against his hips.

He glanced up when Cassie urged Macbeth forward. A cynical smile twisted beneath his beard. "Here to see the scene of the crime?" he shouted.

"If there was one."

"See for yourself." Straightening, he rubbed his lower back.

She did. Her gaze wandered to the far bank where tire tracks were visible in the soggy ground. The fence had been repaired, but Cassie was convinced that Colton could tell that the wires had been cut. It was just too bad he thought her father was involved.

"So your horse hasn't returned?"

"Not yet. I don't really expect him to."

"Last time he did."

"So I heard." Colton ran the back of his hand across his forehead, and his eyes met hers. "Is Ivan home?"

"He wasn't when I got home."

"Tell him I want to talk to him."

"I have."

"And?"

"He thinks you're out of your mind," she said, tossing her hair from her face. "If anyone took your horse it wasn't Dad."

"I wouldn't be so sure of that."

Goaded, she swung off Macbeth's broad back and walked to the edge of the river. The swift current eddied and rushed over fallen trees and huge flat boulders. The air smelled fresh and damp, and if it hadn't been for Colton and his stupid accusations, she would actually have enjoyed being there.

"So why do you think Dad did it?" she yelled as Colton sauntered to his side of the river. Only forty feet separated them, but it could have been miles. "Why not the Lassiters, the Monroes, Wilkersons or Simpsons?"

"Give me a break!"

"They're all ranchers."

"The wires were cut here, Cass. *Here*. The truck took off from Aldridge land!"

"You think! You're not even sure that Black Magic's been stolen."

A thunderous expression crossed his face. "I'm sure all right."

"Then why not someone else? Someone who knew that you'd automatically think Dad was involved?"

"No one else is *your* father," Colton said through clenched teeth. "No one else has a vendetta against the McLeans."

"A vendetta," she gasped, incredulous. "Come on, Colton, you can't believe—"

"What I can't do is deny that a feud ever existed between your family and mine!"

"But a *vendetta*, for crying out loud! I think you've spent too many years dodging bullets and changing the name on your passports!" If it weren't for the river separating them, she would have gone right up to him and slapped his angular, bearded face. "Either that or you've watched too many old movies!"

"Ha!"

"*If*, and I repeat, *if* your horse really has been stolen, any one of a dozen ranchers could've done it! Black Magic's a bit of a legend around here. Anyone who wanted him could've taken him and made it look like Dad was involved. After all, the feud is common knowledge."

"You're grasping at straws, Cass!"

"And you're condemning my father!" Furious, she twisted Macbeth's reins in her fingers and hopped onto the gelding's broad back. "Get real, Colton, or go to the Middle East or some other war-torn place and leave us alone!"

"I intend to," he said under his breath as he watched her dig her heels into the roan's sleek sides. The horse took off with Cassie, her face flushed and furious, clinging to his back. With a clatter of hoofbeats, horse and rider disappeared into the trees. "And good riddance!" Colton growled, stalking back to the fence and ducking under the restrung wires. He snagged his jacket from the post, hooked it over his finger and swore all the way back to the truck.

Why did he let her get to him? Why couldn't he be immune to the mocking glint in her hazel eyes, the soft curve of her cheek, the sharp bite of her tongue? He'd known a lot of women—many far more sophisticated and glamorous than Cassie—yet none of them had gotten under his skin the way Cassie Aldridge had.

Years ago he'd convinced himself he loved her, that they could make a go of it—and she'd lied to him, tried to trap him into marriage.

And yet he was still attracted to her.

"Fool," he ground out, climbing into the cab of the truck. "Damn stupid fool!"

"That's right. Two days ago," Colton said, his jaw rock-hard, his fingers clenched around the telephone receiver. "The horse just disappeared."

"And you think he was stolen?" Mark Gowan asked. He was short and stocky with fiery red hair and a keen mind. Colton had known him for years.

"The wires were snipped. No one here did it."

"Have you talked to Ivan Aldridge?"

"Not yet."

"Maybe he was going to replace the section of fence."

Colton's eyes narrowed. "I'll be sure to ask him when I see him."

"What about neighboring ranchers?"

"Vince Monroe, George Lassiter and Matt Wilkerson swear they haven't seen anything suspicious."

"Okay," the deputy said with a sigh. "I'll be out just as soon as I've made a few inquiries."

"Thanks." Colton hung up and strode out of the den. The house was a mess, he thought, surveying the hallway and kitchen. He hoped that Milly Samms would return soon to clean it up—either that or he'd have to don an apron himself.

One side of his mouth curved into a half smile. He'd never admit it, but he had missed the rotund housekeeper with her constant advice and easy smile. *Watch it, McLean*, he warned himself, *you're getting too comfortable here*.

"Never!" he muttered, shoving open the back door.

Outside, the air was clean and fresh. White clouds drifted in a blue Montana sky. Colton walked directly to the stables.

Fresh paint gleamed, and new windows sparkled. The building had just been rebuilt; the final touches had been completed this past December.

His teeth ground together. The stables represented all that he detested on the ranch. Eight years before, on the night after Colton had learned of Cassie's lies, his mother and father had been killed in a blaze inadvertently set by Tessa Kramer's brother, Mitchell. Denver, trying to save his parents and some of the horses, had been burned so badly he'd nearly died. Despite plastic surgery, Denver would wear his scars the rest of his life.

And so, Colton thought wryly, would he. Though his scars were all internal, they were just as deep and painful.

Leaning against the top rail of the fence, he glowered at the building and didn't feel the wind kick up and ruffle his hair.

All the pain and grief had caused him to hate this ranch and everything about it.

He closed his eyes and shuddered. He'd been out riding that evening, trying to push Cassie out of his mind forever, when the gates of hell had literally opened....

The air was hot, the ground dry. Bees flitted near his Stetson, and flies buzzed around his bay gelding's face. "Come on," Colton growled to his horse, unable to shake his black mood. Cassie's deception was turning his gut even as he tried to forget that she ever existed.

He should be glad, he told himself as the bay sauntered slowly across the dry fields to the river. He stared across that silvery slice of water to the woods and beyond. Aldridge property. Cassie's home. He was better off without her.

But the feelings brewing inside him were far from joyful. Even a sense of relief was missing. In its stead was loss and anger, a deep-seated and hateful anger.

So he wasn't going to be a father; he should be walking on air. No responsibilities, no ties, no *wife*!

*Damn it all to hell!*

More frustrated than he'd been in all his twenty-one years, he climbed off the gelding, kicked at a clod of dust with the toe of his boot and glowered at the Sage. Why had she lied? *Why, why, why?*

The sky turned hazy as diaphanous clouds hid the sun. Colton barely noticed what was happening overhead. His horse snorted a little, then sidestepped nervously.

"Steady," Colton muttered as the first smell of smoke drifted to him. "What's gotten into you?"

Surfacing from his dark thoughts, he froze. A prickle of dread slid like ice down his spine. He noticed for the first time that the day had grown unnaturally dark. The hairs on the back of his neck bristled.

*Fire!*

He whirled. His heart slammed in his chest.

Black smoke surged upward, billowing menacingly to the sky. "God—oh God, no!" Colton cried, jumping onto his horse and driving the heels of his boots into the gelding's sides.

He rode as if the devil himself were following. Slapping the reins hard against the bay's shoulders, swearing wildly, he stared straight ahead. Fire licked upward, crackling and rising in ugly gold flames through the rafters of the stables.

Red-and-white lights flashed; huge fire trucks rumbled up the lane.

The fence was just ahead. "Come on," Colton urged, racing faster, hoping the horse could clear the top rail. But the gelding, once he understood Colton's intention, skidded to a stop and reared, refusing to take the jump.

Swearing, Colton leaped from his back. "Damn coward," he cried, climbing the fence and spying his uncle's old flatbed parked near a dilapidated sheep shed. He wasn't aware that he was running, just that he had to get to the truck.

Breathing hard, he wrenched open the door, climbed behind the wheel and found the keys in the ignition. Colton twisted his wrist, glancing in the rearview mirror at the horror of the fire. "Come on, come on," he said as the old engine turned over, sputtered, coughed and finally caught.

Colton ground the gears and stomped on the gas. Bald tires spun, and the truck shuddered before lurching forward. Colton didn't stop at the gate but drove through, sending boards splintering in both directions. Within seconds he brought the truck to a halt near the house. Sirens wailed, terrified horses screamed and the day had turned to hellish night.

Heart pumping wildly, eyes smarting from the smoke, Colton threw open the door and hurled himself out of the truck, running across the yard toward the flaming stables, stumbling, gasping for breath.

The fire chief barked orders through a bull horn. Men were running everywhere. Horses shrieked in pain and fear.

Tessa Kramer and her brother, Mitchell, were bending over the prone form of her father. Curtis Kramer's hair was singed, and soot streaked his otherwise white face.

"Give us room," a paramedic ordered as he and another man tried to revive the old man. The smell of whiskey on Curtis's breath mingled with the stench of smoke.

"Everybody back off!" the chief ordered.

"What the hell's going on here?" Colton demanded.

The chief ignored him.

Colton stared in horror at the stables. Orange flames shot out of the roof, and heat rippled in sickening waves from the inferno.

Curtis coughed loudly and stirred, his red-rimmed eyes focusing on his daughter. "Tessa, gal?" he murmured, cracking a weary smile.

Colton watched as tears formed in Tessa's eyes. "Thank God, you're all right!" she whispered, wrapping her arms around her father's grimy work shirt and burying her head against his chest. "Did you see Denver—"

"You were with him," Curtis said, and shook his head. "No one—"

"But Denver's in there! So are his parents," she protested, her head snapping up.

Colton's knees threatened to buckle. "Oh, sweet Jesus! No! No!" He stumbled backward, and he had to fight to keep back the blackness that was enveloping him. His head felt as if a herd of wild horses were charging through it.

"Hey, you? Are you okay?" a man shouted.

Stumbling blindly forward, Colton started for the stables.

"It's too late!" Mitchell Kramer yelled. "Colt—stop! Damn him!"

"Stay back!" the chief commanded through the horn. "Christ! Somebody stop him—"

A blast ripped through the stables, and the building exploded in a fiery burst. Glass shattered. Timbers groaned and crashed to the ground. Flames crackled and reached to the sky in death-tinged yellow fingers.

The earth shuddered. Colton's feet were thrown out from under him. He was slammed into the ground, hearing the wail of terrified horses and the screams of firemen. *They were all dead!* Denver, Mom, Dad!

Colton's fingers curled in the gravel. Vomit collected in the back of his throat. Sharp rocks dug into his palms. Deep, wracking sobs tore through him. His family, his entire family had been destroyed by the ranch they'd loved. He pounded impotent fists against the sharp gravel until they bled.

"Come on, son," the fire chief said, offering his hand. "There's nothing you can do here."

He struggled to his feet and blinked against tears and smoke.

"Hey—here's another one!"

Two firemen dragged what seemed to be a lifeless body from the blaze.

"Get the oxygen!"

*Denver!* Colton started forward. The chief's hand curled over his arm. "You'd better wait—"

But Colton didn't listen. He recognized the clothes. But when he was close enough to see Denver's face, he stopped dead in his tracks. His stomach roiled again, and he nearly threw up. Denver's face was blackened by smoke—his hair was singed, and one side of his jaw and cheek had been burned.

"Is—is he—"

"Barely alive! Get out of the way." Dragging Denver, the paramedics headed for the ambulance. "Hold it, Sam!"

Colton started to follow, but the chief reached him again. "There's no room in there!"

Wrenching his arm free, Colton whirled on the older man. His teeth bared, his fists clenched, he growled, "That's my brother, goddamn it, and I don't know how long he's gonna live! Get outta my way!"

"Watch that one—maybe shock," one fireman said to another. "He shouldn't be driving—"

"Frank, Tom, bring that hose over here...."

The chief turned his attention for a second, and Colton jumped into the cab of Uncle John's flatbed, twisted the key and tore out after the ambulance.

"Please, God," Colton whispered in the only prayer he'd ever uttered. "Let him live!"


Miraculously Denver had survived. After several days in a nearby hospital, Denver had been flown to L.A. to face more than one painful session of plastic surgery. And Colton had taken off. His parents were dead; his brother, emotionally crippled, had gone. There was no reason to stay.

Except for Cassie, he thought now as he glowered at the gleaming new stables. In his grief he'd nearly called her. She'd written a note of sympathy, and he, upon reading her kind words, had torn the note into tiny pieces, only to regret it later. He'd reached for the phone, but knew that he was turning to her in grief, not love.

His heart stone-cold, he'd forced himself to push any loving thoughts of her aside. Though a small part of him still cared, he knew that loving Cassie Aldridge was futile.

Without ever looking back, he had packed his bags and taken off.

And now here he was, he thought grimly. And Cassie was becoming as much of an addiction as she'd been all those years before when he'd met her on the sly, lying to his parents and hers just to have a few stolen moments with her.

"Once a fool, always a fool," he muttered, slamming his hand against the fence. Pain shot through his shoulder, and he winced. As soon as Denver and Tessa returned, he was out of here. This ranch meant nothing to him. Nothing but the smoldering ashes of a past based on lies and sorrow.

Cassie grinned as Beth Lassiter Simpson, nearly seven months pregnant, carried a squirming cocker spaniel puppy into the examination room. Beth's face was framed in soft brown curls. She'd been Cassie's best friend since high school.

"So this is Webster?" Cassie asked, glancing at the pup's chart.

"In the flesh."

"Okay, let's see how he's doing." Cassie took the blond bundle of energy from Beth's hands and settled him onto the stainless steel scales.

Beth's four-year-old daughter, Amy, slid into the room. Her hair was a mass of fiery red curls, the skin over her nose sprinkled with tiny freckles. Amy's huge brown eyes rounded as she stared at Cassie. "You gonna give him a shot?" she asked anxiously.

"A vaccination," Cassie replied with a grin as she took the dog's temperature. "He won't even feel it."

Amy's lower lip protruded. "I *hate* shots."

"So do I," Cassie said, recording the pup's weight and temperature before slipping her stethoscope into her ears. The poor animal was shaking, his heart pounding like a jackhammer.

Throughout the examination Amy watched Cassie suspiciously. When Cassie pulled the flap of skin behind Webster's neck and slipped the needle beneath the pup's fur, the little dog didn't so much as whimper.

But Amy gasped, her chubby hands flying to her eyes. "I can't look," she whispered to her mother.

"That's it!" Cassie tossed the disposable needle into the trash. "He looks great!" She held the puppy out to Amy, who opened one untrusting eye.

"For real?"

"For real! Take him into the reception area. Sandy, the girl behind the desk, might just have a dog biscuit for Webster and a sucker for you."

"What kind?" Amy asked, already heading for the door.

"Any kind you want."

Grinning from ear to ear, Amy hauled the wiggling cocker pup through the door.

"You have a way with animals—and kids," Beth said.

"I like them both," Cassie admitted. She stuffed her stethoscope into the pocket of her lab coat and leaned against the scales.

Beth grinned. "So do I—most of the time."

"You'd better," Cassie replied, glancing pointedly at Beth's protruding belly.

"Don't tell me! I already know I'm going to have my hands full." She gathered up her purse and glanced at Cassie. "I suppose you've heard that Denver McLean's horse is missing."

Cassie nodded. Beth was the one person other than her father and Colton who knew how much she'd once cared for Colton.

"Colton stopped by yesterday. He was fit to be tied!" Beth declared.

"I know. He seems to think the horse was stolen."

"You've seen him then?"

"Oh, yes," Cassie said with a small smile. "He's even better-looking now."

"Is he?"

"Didn't you notice?"

Cassie shrugged, though she'd noticed all right. Who wouldn't? Even if the man was a bastard, Cassie understood what Beth was trying to say. Colton was still incredibly male, virile and sexy. Cassie compressed her mouth into a tight line, and drew her brows together.

"Who do you think would have the gall to steal Denver's horse?"

"Who knows?" Cassie replied, thinking again of Colton's angry accusations. At least it seemed that he hadn't spouted off to Josh and Beth about her father. "If you ask me, the horse probably just wandered off."

"Try to convince Colton of that," Beth teased.

"I have. He didn't buy it."

"Well, maybe Black Magic will just turn up like he did last year."

"I hope so," Cassie whispered. If the horse showed up again, it would make things so much easier.

"I'll see you later," Beth called, collecting her spritely daughter and excited pup in the reception area.

"In just about six months," Cassie replied.

Beth shook her head. "Let's not wait that long. We could have a social life that doesn't revolve around rabies vaccinations, you know. I'll have you over for lunch *before* number two is born.''

''And I'll hold you to it.''

''Good!'' Beth grinned, snapping a leash onto Webster's collar.

''Is that it?'' Cassie asked Sandy as the door clicked shut.

''Until tomorrow at nine,'' Sandy replied.

Rotating the kinks from her shoulders, Cassie slipped out of her lab coat, threw it in the laundry basket and washed her hands before walking through the labyrinth of metal cages in the back of the clinic.

At the first cage, Cassie bent on one knee and peered inside. The Monroes' German shepherd was lying listlessly on the floor, recovering from tendon surgery. She slipped her hands into the dog's cage to pat his broad, graying head. He rolled glazed eyes up at her, and his tongue lolled from his mouth. ''Hang in there,'' Cassie whispered with an encouraging smile. ''You'll be a new man in the morning.''

She passed several other cages, eyeing the Fullmers' Siamese cat and the Wilkersons' pet hamster. Everything was quiet as she turned off the lights.

Outside, lacey clouds gathered over the surrounding hills. An early spring breeze caught in her hair and tossed the bare branches of the old maple near the clinic's parking lot. Cassie climbed into her car and shoved it into gear.

Her thoughts wandered back to Colton and the empty years when he'd been gone. She'd been devastated, of course, but her father had helped her, and she'd thrown herself into her studies at the university, eventually gaining a partial scholarship to veterinary school.

She'd made friends and dated, but never had she ever let anyone close to her again. She just hadn't met anyone who held a candle to Colton. ''Idiot,'' she muttered between clenched teeth.

Why, now? she wondered. Why, after eight years, after enough time had passed that she'd been sure she was over him, did he have to show up?

## Chapter Five

Cassie ran the currycomb over Macbeth's shoulder and was rewarded with a snort and kick that barely missed her shin. "Miserable beast," she muttered, slapping his rump playfully. She loved Macbeth and his surly temperament. "Okay, go on!" She unsnapped the lead rope, and Macbeth bolted for the far side of the paddock where he promptly lay down and rolled in the dirt beneath a single spruce tree. "Oh, great," Cassie murmured, seeing her hard work destroyed in an instant.

Long shadows crept across the land, and the sky had turned a dusky blue with the coming of night. "Why do I bother?" Cassie wondered aloud as the horse, his hide dulled by dust and dirt, scrambled to his feet and shook his head.

"You're wretched, you know that, don't you?" Cassie laughed as she washed her hands under a faucet near the barn.

She was just wiping her fingers dry on the back of her jeans when she heard the sound of a vehicle thundering down the lane. She didn't even have to look. She'd been expecting Colton for three days. "Here we go," she muttered under her breath, bracing herself as the engine died and she spied Colton behind the wheel.

Climbing out of the Jeep, Colton hesitated when he saw her. "Is Ivan home?" he asked, closing the door behind him.

"In the house."

"Good. I need to talk to him."

"So you've said."

He cocked one of his roguish brows in amusement. "No arguments from you?"

"Would it change things?"

"No—"

"Then what would be the point?" she countered. "There's no use wasting my breath." Without another word she led him through the back door. Ivan was in the living room, scanning the paper. "We've got company," she announced, trying to ignore the fact that her stomach was twisting in knots. Just being in the same room with her father and Colton brought back unwanted memories.

Ivan glanced up, his gaze clashing with Colton's. With deliberation he laid the paper aside and stood. "I've been expecting you," he said slowly. "Seems as if you've been spreading rumors around town about me."

"I just asked some questions."

Cassie's eyes widened. "You've been telling people in town that you think Dad is behind Black Magic's disappearance?"

"Of course not," Colton said through tight lips as he swung his gaze to her father. "But I did want to find out what you know about it."

"Nothing," Ivan snorted.

"The wires were snipped on the fence between your property and mine."

"Big deal," Ivan muttered, scowling. "If you've come here to accuse me of taking your horse, just do it, get it over with and leave. Or go talk to someone at the sheriff's department."

"I already have."

"And what did he say?"

"Mark Gowan's checking into things."

"Good. Then maybe he can clear up the big mystery. But if you ask me, you and your hands just got careless, McLean, and that damned horse of yours wandered off."

"No way."

"Then ask Kramer. Wasn't it his son who started the fire?" Little beads of sweat dotted Ivan's upper lip, and he was so angry his entire body had begun to shake.

Beneath his beard, Colton blanched. "That's over."

"Oh, right. So now you and the Kramers are one big happy family?"

The younger man's lips thinned. "Careful, Ivan," he warned.

"Look," Cassie interjected, "you came over here to say something to Dad. If you're done accusing, then get down to business, and when you're finished, leave."

Colton's eyes moved from Ivan to Cassie. "All right. Let's talk about the fence."

"Cassie says you claim it was cut."

"It was."

"And you think I did it."

"Or know who did."

"You're barking up the wrong tree, McLean," Ivan growled. Bending near the fireplace, he tossed a mossy log onto the fire in the grate, turned his back on Colton and prodded the log with a poker. "If someone did take your horse, and I'm not saying they did, they must've come onto

my property through the north gate that leads to the road—
the one we use for the hay baler and combine.''

"I know which gate you're talking about."

"Good." Ivan dusted his hands and straightened slowly.
"Why would anyone else go through your land?"

"Ah, motive," Ivan said, rubbing a crick in his back and
glowering. "I suppose I've got the best one, don't I? After
all, it was my wife your uncle used, my daughter you dal-
lied with—"

"Enough!" Cassie shouted, the old wounds bleeding.

Colton sucked in a swift breath. He clenched his fists, and
he took a step forward before getting a grip on himself.
"Let's leave Cassie out of this," he said through teeth that
barely moved.

"Seems you forget quicker than I do!"

Colton bristled defensively. "What happened between
Cassie and me hasn't got anything to do with this."

"Bull!"

Colton's storm-gray eyes darkened with a private agony.
Was he still hurting, too? Cassie wondered. But if so, why
the witch-hunt?

"You think I would steal your horse, then leave tracks all
over my property?" Ivan tossed back. "What do you take
me for? I've been burned too many times by the likes of you
to take a stupid chance like that!"

"I thought you might like to rub it in."

"Stop it," Cassie cut in. "Everyone's had their say."

Colton slid a glance her way. "So now it's over, eh?"

Deep inside she quaked and her voice shook. "It's been
over a long time." She stared straight into his eyes, hoping
she didn't look as vulnerable as she felt.

"Go home, McLean," Ivan suggested, seeming suddenly
tired and worn, "before I lose my patience altogether."

"I won't let this lie," Colton warned.

"Fine, fine, waste your time and your breath," Ivan suggested. "But don't waste mine."

Colton strode out of the house, and Cassie was right on his heels. Too many buried emotions kept churning to the surface, and she couldn't just watch him leave.

"Your father knows more than he's willing to tell," Colton muttered.

"No way."

"Why not?" He reached the Jeep but didn't climb inside. Instead he faced her, his expression blank, his eyes guarded.

"My father has nothing to hide, Colton. He's just an old rancher trying to scratch out a living. He doesn't have time for junior high pranks."

"Taking a valuable stallion isn't a prank! It's a crime."

"Go home, Colt."

But he didn't move, and his eyes raked over her. "You've changed, Cass," he observed.

"So have you. What happened to you, Colton? Just what happened to you? For months you've been holed up in the McLean house like some kind of recluse, and now, now when it looks like you're finally getting well, you come over here with accusations that just don't make any sense!"

Colton's jaw slid to one side. "Maybe I've just gotten smarter."

"Smarter or more bitter?"

"Probably a little of both. But then I have learned a few things in the last eight years."

"Such as baiting old men and accusing them of lies?" she lashed out.

He gritted his teeth. "I just wanted to hear what Ivan had to say for himself."

"But you don't believe him."

"I've heard lies before."

The vicious words stung like the bite of a snake. "I never lied to you, Colton, but then you didn't stick around long enough to find out, did you? You believed what you wanted to believe! That way your conscience was clear!"

"*My* conscience?" he repeated incredulously as he reached for the door of his Jeep. "My conscience? I was just along for the ride—remember?"

Cassie wished the tears behind her eyes would go away. "What I remember, McLean, is that you ran—away from me, away from any responsibility, away from any ties. For that, I suppose, I should thank you!"

He whirled, and the hand that had been poised over the handle of the Jeep's door clamped around hers. "I was going to do my duty, Cassie," he growled, his gray eyes flaring dangerously. "But I wasn't about to be conned, just like I'm not going to be conned again."

"I loved you, Colton."

"You didn't know the meaning of the word."

Inside she ached, but she wouldn't give him the satisfaction of knowing how deep her scars ran. Her throat was thick, her eyes moist, but she held back her tears and tossed her hair out of her face to glare furiously at him. "At least I was with you because I wanted to be—not because of some warped sense of 'duty' as you called it!" Her heart was pounding, but she kept her voice cold. "I wanted you and I wanted your child. I cried myself to sleep so many nights, I can't even remember how many there were, but it's over. It's been over a long, long time. So let go of me and go back to your house where you can brood and plot and try to think up paranoid schemes where my father is out to get you!"

He dropped her hand as if it were hot. Some of the color seeped from his face. "That's twisted."

She knew he was right, but didn't let up. She couldn't. Afraid that he might see through her defenses, she said, "Probably. But then, I had a good teacher."

His breath hissed between his teeth, and his jaw slackened. "Did I hurt you that much, Cass?"

Her heart turned over, and for an insane instant she wanted to throw her arms around him. Instead, she bit out, "You only hurt me as much as I let you. That was *my* mistake, not yours.'' Then, before she said anything that might betray her true feelings, she stepped back and folded her arms over her chest and didn't move until he'd driven down the lane and the sound of the Jeep's engine had faded into the dusky twilight.

Colton sank into the blackest mood he'd been in since he'd awoken in that hospital room in Belfast with tubes attached to his wrist and the pain in his shoulder racking his body. He tried and failed at shoving thoughts of Cassie and her father from his mind. He drank more than he should have, wandered around the empty farmhouse and spent too many hours near the roaring Sage River, staring at the damned Aldridge property beyond.

Gruff with the hands, rude to Curtis, he discovered that almost everyone on the ranch granted him wide berth. Good! He didn't care. All he wanted was to find the bloody horse and for Denver and Tessa to cut their trip short and return.

Two days after his confrontation with Cassie and Ivan, Colton stepped off the back porch and spied Curtis on his way from the stables. But before he reached Colton, Curtis stopped dead in his tracks. ''Well, I'll be damned!'' he muttered, his old eyes squinting toward the distant hills.

Colton followed the old man's gaze. Morning mist rose from the grassy fields, and the highest peaks of the mountains, snowcapped and craggy, were gilded by a bright Montana sun. In a field near the foothills, a solitary black horse stood, head raised, mane and tail fluttering in the slight breeze. Colton's eyes narrowed. ''Is it Black Magic?'' he asked, running across the yard.

''Or his twin.''

They didn't waste any time. Together Curtis and Colton climbed into a truck and maneuvered through the series of gates to the most westerly field, where the stallion, ears pricked forward, coat gleaming, picked at a few spring blades of grass.

"Where've you been?" Colton asked as Curtis clipped a lead rope on Black Magic's halter.

"And what've you been doin'?" Curtis ran expert hands along the horse's sides and legs, then looked into his eyes. "He looks good," the old man said with a relieved sigh, his gnarled fingers stroking Magic's shoulder. Curtis studied the horse. "Good thing we didn't call Denver. He and Tessa would've worked themselves up over nothin'."

"Right." But Colton was still uneasy. True, the stallion looked none the worse for wear. His charcoal coat was glossy beneath the morning sun, his eyes held the same fire Colton remembered, and he butted Colton playfully. "How the hell did you get back here?"

"Beats me," Curtis said under his breath. "But if I were you, I'd count my blessings."

While Curtis drove the pickup back to the yard, Colton walked the stallion to the stables. Black Magic pulled and tugged at the lead, mincing and sidestepping. "You're full of it, aren't you?" Colton remarked as he closed the final gate and led the horse into the stallion barn.

Curtis was already waiting. The floor of Black Magic's stall was covered with fresh straw. Oats had been spread in the manger. Curtis finished drawing a bucket of fresh water and offered it to the stallion before locking him into the stall. "Okay, now that he's back where he belongs, tell me where you think he was."

"I wish I knew," Colton said with feeling.

Curtis ran a leathery hand around his neck. "I'll still stake a month's wages on Aldridge. You probably scared the bejeezus out of him the other night and he thought he'd better cover his backside. If you ask me, Ivan Aldridge brought our boy, here, back."

Colton's eyes never left the stallion. "Is this exactly what happened last year?"

"About. But he was gone longer."

Puzzled, Colton asked, "Why would Ivan Aldridge have taken the horse last year? If he's got any gripe against the family, it's with me, and I wasn't even around."

"He didn't much like John. It happened before his death." Curtis lifted a shoulder. "He hates the lot of you, you know."

It was a simple enough explanation, but not good enough.

"You just wait. I bet the foals born on the Aldridge spread this year look a lot like this guy." Curtis petted Black Magic's muzzle.

"Then I suppose we'll just have to wait and see, won't we?" Colton's gaze swept the stables before landing on the empty stall next to Black Magic's. "Maybe I'll sleep out here tonight."

Curtis's faded eyes darkened. "You think he'll be taken—again?"

"I don't know," Colton replied, unable to shake the restless feeling that things still weren't resolved. Just because the stallion was back didn't mean whoever was behind the theft wouldn't try something else. "But I don't want to take any chances."

Curtis eyed the empty stall. "It won't be very comfortable."

"I've been in worse places."

"And look what it got you."

"I'm *not* losing this horse again."

Curtis forked some hay into Black Magic's manger. "Do whatever you want."

*It's not what I want,* Colton thought unkindly. But it had to be done. He wasn't about to explain to Denver that he'd lost his prize stallion twice in a few weeks. "Stay with him until I get back."

"Whatever you say."

His mind racing for a possible explanation to Black Magic's disappearance, Colton saddled up Tempest, a sorrel stallion without much personality. Reasoning that the only gate to the field in which Black Magic was found was near the house, Colton decided to check the fence line. Either the stallion had jumped the fence, walked right through the main yard and opened the gate himself, or the fence had been cut again.

"Come on, Tempest, let's figure this out," he muttered as he swung into the saddle. Pain pierced his shoulder, and the stallion sidestepped gingerly.

Colton held the sorrel to a quick walk, his gaze following the four strands of barbed wire encircling the field in which Black Magic had been grazing.

The fence was intact. Not one strand had been clipped. Nor had any of the sections been replaced. All the barbed wire was the same dull brown that sectioned off the fields surrounding the ranch. "So much for that theory," Colton grumbled.

By the time he unsaddled Tempest, Colton didn't know any more than he had when he'd left. It seemed as if he was all out of options. If he had to sleep in the stables in a sleeping bag, so be it. Just so long as when Denver returned, Black Magic hadn't disappeared again.

"Find anything?" Curtis asked as Colton tossed a worn sleeping bag onto an army cot he'd positioned in the empty stall next to Black Magic's.

"Nothing." Colton shook his head, baffled.

"If only he could talk." Curtis leaned one arm over the box door and stared at the nervous black stallion.

Colton rubbed his jaw and scowled into the stall that was to be his bedroom for the next couple of weeks.

Was Aldridge behind the horse's disappearance? Or was he just a convenient scapegoat? Could someone else have taken him—Matt Wilkerson or Bill Simpson? Had Denver or John made some enemies that no one knew about? Or, had Black Magic found a hole in the fence and wandered through?

"No way!" Colton decided, slapping the top rail of the box. Black Magic snorted, his ebony coat gleaming in the dim light of the fluorescent bulbs.

Colton knew that the best course of action was just to hold tight until Denver returned. The horse's disappearance, now over, wasn't any of his business. His older brother could deal with it.

And yet, a part of him was still intrigued. Years of unraveling mysteries and living on the edge in some of the most dangerous political hot spots in the world caused his suspicious mind to leap ahead to every available conclusion. He'd find grim satisfaction in exposing the culprit, should there be one.

Thoughtfully he rubbed his chin again, his beard scratchy and rough. And what if that culprit turned out to be Ivan the Terrible? What then? How would he break the news to Cassie? Instead of experiencing triumph and satisfaction, he just might feel guilty as hell.

Angry with the turn of his thoughts, he kicked the wall. A water pail jangled, and several horses snorted and whinnied. Colton barely noticed. His thoughts were too dark. Whether he liked it or not, Ivan Aldridge was Cassie's father and had stood by her when Colton had taken off. Not that she didn't have it coming, he reminded himself, then strode out of the stallion barn to the late morning air.

A small flock of crows cawed loudly and flapped their shiny black wings noisily. "Yeah, yeah, I know," Colton growled, glad to have something at which to vent his frustrations.

He didn't want to think about Cassie or her old man. Too many emotions he'd rather forget kept surfacing. And the fact that she lived just down the road brought temptation much too close. He'd like to see her again; he couldn't even deny it to himself. He'd lain awake more nights than he wanted to admit fantasizing about her. But he'd be damned if he'd get caught in her sweet trap all over again! No, at the soonest opportunity he was making tracks out of this desolate, windswept country, and he was leaving all thoughts of Cassie behind!

Cassie parked near the garage and frowned when she recognized Vince Monroe's green Chevy. In the past few years Ivan and Vince had become friends—helping each other with odd chores—and though Cassie didn't hold Vince in very high esteem, she kept her thoughts to herself. Her father needed help on the ranch, more help than she could give, and Vince Monroe had broad shoulders and a strong back. The fact that he was Jessica's father shouldn't be held against him, Cassie supposed ungraciously as she hauled two bags of groceries from the car. After all, what had happened between Colton, Jessica and Cassie was long over.

She kicked the car door shut with her foot, then nearly tripped on Erasmus, who had bounded down the steps to greet her.

"You should be careful," she warned the old dog as she backed through the kitchen door and set the ungainly sacks on the kitchen counter. Bending on one knee, she scratched Erasmus behind his ears. The old dog whined in ecstasy, rolling over on his back and exposing his belly. "Glutton," Cassie teased.

"I thought I heard you drive in." Her father, followed by Vince Monroe, walked stiffly into the kitchen. The television was still blaring from the living room, and Cassie made out the sounds of a pre-game talk show. "I was just telling Vince that it was about time for you to show up."

"Glad you missed me," she quipped.

Grinning, Ivan settled into his favorite chair near the wood stove.

As she began unpacking groceries, Cassie silently evaluated the two men. Her father and Vince were as different as night and day. Where her father was lean to the point of being gaunt, Vince was robust and supported a belly that stretched his belt to the last notch. Her father's hair had turned steely and thin, but Vince's sandy hair was thick and vital, his blue eyes still bright and quick. Cassie had the feeling that Vince Monroe didn't miss much. She'd often wondered if he'd known of her involvement with Colton. As Jessica Monroe's father, he must've realized that his daughter and Cassie had once vied for Colton's affections. Or maybe he didn't. Maybe he wasn't that involved in his daughters' lives.

"I suppose you've heard the news," her father said, grinning widely, his eyes twinkling.

"What news?"

"McLean's Black Magic reappeared. According to Vince, here, Curtis Kramer found him in one of the main pastures."

"But—"

Vince shook his head and chuckled. "The same thing happened last year, you know. The stallion was gone for a few weeks and just showed up again. Old John was fit to be tied!" Vince hooted at the memory, and Ivan chuckled.

"That doesn't make sense," Cassie said, her thoughts tangled in emotions that should have been long dead. "Colton wouldn't make this kind of mistake—he wouldn't have come charging over here like a mad bull, making all sorts of accusations if the horse had just wandered into the wrong field...."

"Boy, I would've loved to have been a fly on the wall when McLean found his horse," Ivan muttered, reaching for the old coffeepot on the stove and pouring himself another cup. "Serves him right. How about a cup?" he asked his friend, but Vince spread his big hands and shook his head.

"How'd you find out about this?" Cassie asked.

Vince set his empty cup in the sink. "I ran into Bill Simpson in town today. He'd been over to the McLean spread and talked to Curtis Kramer. Simpson says McLean and Kramer are still scratching their heads over it."

"You know, everyone at the McLean ranch is sure he was stolen. Some big conspiracy or somethin'. Only thing they can't explain is why anyone would bother taking the horse just to return him." Vince chuckled deep in his throat. "If you ask me, Colton McLean had one too many shots taken at him. Maybe one grazed his head."

Cassie stiffened, but she didn't jump to Colton's defense. After all, he thought her father was involved. "Where was Black Magic all this time?"

"No one knows—probably with the wild horses," her father said.

Cassie didn't know whether to laugh or cry. She was relieved that Black Magic was safe, but also felt a small triumph. Though she told herself that she had outgrown her need for vengeance, she knew she would feel a warm glow of satisfaction in telling Colton just what she thought of him. She'd love to watch him eat crow! "So the horse was on McLean land the entire time?"

"No one knows for sure."

"What about the snipped fence?"

"Beats me. McLean probably made it up," Vince said as he reached for his hat and rammed it onto his broad head. "Thanks for your help with the tractor," he said to her father. "I owe you." With a wave, he was out the door and down the back steps.

Ivan eyed his daughter. "So what do you think about Colton losing his horse?"

"I don't know," she murmured, watching through the window as Vince's truck lumbered down the lane. "But I bet there's more to it than we know."

"Well, it doesn't matter," Ivan decided, dismissing the subject. "He's got his horse back and he'll leave us alone."

Cassie wasn't so sure. Colton had dragged her into this mess, charged her father with horrid accusations, then stormed out. Surely he wouldn't expect her to ignore the fact that he'd been wrong.

Cassie closed the cupboard and folded the empty sacks. "I think I'll go talk with Colton and see what he has to say for himself," she said, almost to herself. She knew she was playing with proverbial fire, but the idea grew on her. She could almost taste the sweetness of Colton's apology.

"Maybe it would be best to leave well enough alone," Ivan suggested. He wedged off one boot with the toe of the other.

"Like Colton did?" she responded, angry all over again at the gall of Colton McLean. "Maybe you've forgotten, Dad. He came busting over here and practically accused you of being a horse thief!"

"Well, he was wrong, wasn't he? I guess he'll have to live with that." Ivan chuckled.

"And I guess I'm going to give him a piece of my mind!" Cassie relished the idea more and more. "I'll be back later."

"Cass..."

She heard her father call her name as the screen door banged behind her, but she didn't care. For the past few days she'd been walking on eggshells with Ivan. He'd been touchy after his meeting with Colton. She'd caught him sitting in the dark, brooding. But now it was over. Now it was time to set the record straight!

After all, she reasoned as she shifted the gears of the old Dodge truck, Colton McLean owed her an explanation. Her fingers curled tight over the steering wheel, and she squinted through the grimy windshield against the final blaze of a dying sun.

She couldn't wait to hear what Colton had to say for himself, but her stomach churned at the thought of facing him again. There was something powerful and potent about Colton—something she could never ignore.

The wheels of the truck ground to a stop as she parked beneath a single oak tree near the front of the McLean house. Pocketing her keys, she swallowed hard, and without taking the time to second-guess herself, marched briskly up the brick path to the front door.

The McLean house was everything the Aldridge home was not. Freshly painted a light gray with slate-colored trim and blue shutters, it stood on a hill in the center of the ranch. A wide veranda flanked the house on three sides, and a sun porch had been built off the back. The yard was kept up and trimmed, even in Tessa McLean's absence.

Cassie didn't waste any time. She climbed the worn steps and knocked loudly on the front door. There she waited, crossing her arms under her breasts and wishing she knew what she was going to say to Colton when she came face to face with him.

Within seconds she heard the scrape of boots.

Her heart began to slam against her ribs.

The door swung open, and Colton himself, stripped bare to the waist, eyed her. His muscles were firm and sleek under skin that was surprisingly dark. Several ugly scars criss-crossed in a purple webbing across his shoulder. A white towel was slung around his neck, and from the dabs of foam near his temple and the fact that his chin was buck naked, she knew he'd been shaving.

Her throat tightened. His skin, recently covered with a dark beard, was now pale but firm. Thin, defined lips curved slightly at the sight of her, though the line of his jaw remained rigid.

"Well, Cassie," he drawled, crossing his arms over his naked chest and leaning the battle-scarred shoulder against the doorjamb. "You're the last person I expected to see. Don't tell me—this isn't a social call. Right?"

Her throat so tight she could barely speak, she stared at him. Without the beard he looked exactly like the young man she'd loved so fervently all those years before. "I—I, uh, heard you found your horse." Dear Lord, why was her voice so soft?

Colton's grin widened. "Good news travels fast."

"And he was right in the middle of your ranch?"

"Approximately," he agreed, amusement plain in his gray eyes.

"So he wasn't stolen after all?"

"Oh, he was stolen, all right. Whoever took him decided to put him back."

"That's crazy!"

Colton tugged thoughtfully on his lower lip. "Maybe they were running scared."

"You *think*."

"I wasn't here, but Curtis is convinced the same thing happened last year."

"Curtis could be wrong."

"I doubt it. Someone 'borrowed' the horse—either for free stud fees or just to get under my skin. Anyway, it won't happen again."

"Why not?"

One side of his mouth lifted, and he snapped the towel from around his neck. "I'll show you. Just give me a minute."

"You don't have to..." But he had turned, disappearing into the house.

Cassie waited, listening to the sound of his retreating steps and feeling like a fool. She'd raced over here fully intent on giving Colton a little of his own back. But seeing him stripped to the waist and beardless, she'd been nearly tongue-tied, and the fire that had propelled her over here had been doused by the water of bittersweet memories.

Fingering the rail surrounding the porch, she told herself she should leave, that being alone with him was doing more damage than good, but she didn't want to take the coward's way out. Just as anger had forced her over here, pride kept her from running away.

At the sound of his returning footsteps, she stiffened.

"Okay, let's go," Colton said, striding across the porch. He was stuffing his wounded arm through the rolled sleeves of a loose blue work shirt. He winced at the effort while the tails of the shirt flapped in the breeze.

"Go where?"

"I thought you'd like to see what all the fuss was about." Before she could protest, he took her hand, led her down the porch and around the side of the house.

"Maybe I should just go."

"I don't think so. You came over here to bait me, didn't you?"

"I thought you might apologize."

"Apologize?" he repeated, then laughed. "For what?"

"Let's start with accusing my dad of being a horse thief!"

"The jury's still out on that one."

She yanked hard on her hand, but his fingers only tightened. "You're out of your mind!"

"So you keep saying."

He was walking so fast, she had to half run to keep up with him. Her black denim skirt billowed, the soles of her boots crunched on the gravel. They crossed the yard and headed straight for the stables. Colton shouldered open the door and pulled Cassie into a darkened interior filled with the scent of horses and dust, oil and leather. Stallions snorted and rustled in stalls as they passed, but Colton didn't stop until they came to an end stall.

She recognized Black Magic instantly. Denver's prize quarter horse stallion was the most famous horse in the county—possibly the state. Magic's glossy coat gleamed almost blue beneath the lights, and his only marking, a jagged white blaze, slashed crookedly down his nose.

"This is Black Magic," Colton said grandly, dropping Cassie's hand and eyeing the horse as if he didn't much care for him.

"We've met before." Cassie couldn't keep the sarcasm from her voice.

"Well, take a good hard look at him, Cass. Because no one on the ranch has laid a hand on him since he got back."

"So?"

"So how do you explain that a horse who was supposed to have been wandering around the ranch in the hills for the better part of a week is in such good shape? Shouldn't he be filthy? It's been raining and yet he hardly has any mud on his coat. And he's obviously not starving. In fact," Colton said, nodding to himself, "I'd say Magic here looks better now than when he was taken."

"Which proves someone took him to use him as a sire," she mocked, blowing a loose strand of hair from her eyes.

"Bingo!"

"But that doesn't wash, Colton. Even if your theory were true—and I'm not saying it is—the thief couldn't claim that your horse was the sire to any of his foals. They wouldn't be any more valuable. So what would be the point?"

"Better offspring. And you're wrong about the value." Colton slid a knowing glance her way. "What's the name of your father's best stud?"

"Devil Dancer."

"And is he a black horse?"

"Yes, but—"

"Just suppose that Devil Dancer's foals turn out to be the best horses you've ever raised. Better than you expected. Better than both the sire and the dam. Not only would the foals be worth more, but Devil Dancer's stud fees would go up."

Cassie almost laughed out loud. The idea was too absurd. "You're really reaching, McLean," she challenged, shaking her head. "Why would anyone, especially Dad, go to all the trouble?" She saw his eyes darken, and she knew. The feud. Of course. Always the feud. "I thought I already told you that what happened in the past is over, Colt," she said, unable to let the subject drop.

"Is it?" His gaze moved from the horse to her, insolently sliding from her crown to her toes. Suddenly the dimly lit barn seemed intimate and sultry, warmer than it had been.

"Of course."

"Then why're you here?" He leaned one of his hips against the stall door, waiting.

"Two reasons," she said, feeling a ridiculous need for honesty. The musty room seemed to close in on her, and she shifted her eyes away from Colton. "First, and I'll admit it, I wanted to gloat."

From the corner of her eye she noticed that one of his dark brows was cocked in interest.

Her pulse leaped crazily. Coming here was a mistake, a serious mistake. She knew that now, but she was trapped, and in all honesty she didn't know if she would run from him if she could. "Believe it or not, Colton, you bring out the worst in me. You came storming over to my house, ranting and raving, parking your backside in the middle of my kitchen, claiming that my father had done you dirt. And I wanted to see how you'd like it if the tables were turned." She clenched her fingers around the top rail of Black Magic's stall. Suddenly self-conscious, she thrust her hands into her skirt.

"And the other reason," he prodded, his voice low.

"The other reason." She licked her lips and plunged on. "It's time everyone forgot there ever was a feud and buried the past." She tilted her face up mutinously and met the questions in his eyes with the cool fury in hers.

"Tell that to your father."

"My father had nothing to do—" she started before his hard brown hand caught her wrist.

"Drop it, Cass," he suggested, gray eyes blazing.

"What's gotten into you?"

He gritted his teeth. He wanted to tell her. Oh, God, how he wanted to tell her that she'd gotten to him again despite all those damned promises to himself. The scent of her hair, the challenge in her eyes, the thrust of her small chin all beckoned him in a primal way he detested. "I don't want any more foul-ups, Cass," he said, his teeth clenched, his fingers curling possessively over her small wrist."

"Meaning?"

"That I don't want to lose Black Magic again!" He cocked his head to the stall next to the black stallion's box, indicating the cot and sleeping bag. "And I intend to make sure it doesn't happen."

A dimple creased her cheek. "Dedicated, aren't you?" she mocked.

"When I have to be."

"Is that right?" she baited, thinking back to a time when she'd needed him and he'd abandoned her. "You couldn't prove it by me!" She yanked her arm free and started out of the barn, away from the intimacy, away from him. She opened the door, but he caught up with her, slammed the door shut with the flat of his hand and grabbed her shoulder, spinning her around. "Let go of me, Colton!" she snapped. Her back was pressed hard against the door.

"Not until you hear me out." His voice had turned softer, the angle of his jaw less harsh. His stubborn gray gaze delved deep into hers. "I didn't mean to insinuate that I didn't care for you."

What she read in his gaze made her sick inside. Pity. He actually *pitied* her! "Don't worry about it."

"But I do, Cass."

"Why?"

"Because we were both young and made mistakes."

"My only mistake was that I loved you, Colton," she said, her voice surprisingly calm. His face was so close she could smell the lingering scent of shaving cream on his skin. "But you taught me how foolish that one emotion can be, didn't you?"

"I never lied to you," he reminded her.

The ache within stretched wide, hurting all over again. "You lied to me every time you held me," she whispered, her heart shattering into a thousand pieces. "Every time you kissed me, every time you pretended to care!"

"I never pretended, Cass," he said, the fingers on her shoulder firm but gentle, the cynicism in his eyes fading in the half light of the barn.

"Liar!" she declared, blinking rapidly, then she stumbled backward, groping for a way to escape. Being here with him, alone in the shadowy barn, was a mistake. Her feelings for him were too deep, the wound of his rejection, though eight years old, still raw and bleeding.

She found the handle and yanked hard, slipping through the narrow opening and taking in deep lungfuls of fresh air.

"This isn't finished, Cass." Colton's voice, barely a whisper, reverberated through her soul.

Forcing herself to walk when her legs wanted to run, she strode to the old truck, climbed inside and turned the key with shaking fingers.

The old engine sparked to life. Cassie cranked the steering wheel and shoved the gears into reverse. She caught a glimpse of Colton standing in the doorway to the barn. Hands planted on his hips, shirttails flapping in the breeze, he glared at her. His face was set once again in a hard, impenetrable mask, his expression cold and distant.

Cassie rammed the truck into first and took off. Gravel sprayed from beneath the tires, and she didn't dare look back in the rearview mirror—afraid that if she did, she might lose her heart all over again to a man who could change from warm to cold as quickly as the winter wind could change directions.

## Chapter Six

Colton's shoulder throbbed. After several nights of sleeping on the army cot, his cramped muscles rebelled and he wondered if standing guard over Black Magic was worth the effort. "This is all your fault, you know," he grumbled to the stallion, throwing wide the outside door.

Black Magic bolted out the door and tore through the rain-sodden fields, kicking and bucking beneath the gray spring skies. His ebony mane caught the wind, his tail unfurled. He seemed more colt than stallion as he raced from one end of the field to the other, whistling sharply to the horses in a nearby pasture.

"Show off," Colton muttered, feeling a grin tug at the corners of his mouth despite his bad mood as he strode to the house.

In the kitchen Colton put on a pot of coffee, then headed upstairs. Stripping away his grimy clothes, he glanced in the mirror, then massaged his strained muscles. He stood for twenty minutes under the steamy hot spray of the shower, and slowly the ache in his shoulder subsided.

By the time he'd shaved and dressed, he felt almost human again. Almost, he thought with a grimace, his thoughts turning as they had of late, to Cassie. "Forget her," he ordered the brooding man in the mirror, and knew it was an impossible task.

Growling to himself, he sauntered downstairs and poured himself a cup of strong coffee. Cassie's accusations hung over him like a pall these past few days. Despite all his arguments with himself, his conscience had begun to bother him. Maybe he had been too hasty in his accusations. Perhaps he'd jumped to the wrong conclusions. Maybe, just maybe, he'd been wrong about Ivan Aldridge.

And maybe he hadn't.

But it didn't help to keep the old rift festering, his guilty conscience prodded. He sipped from his mug, ignored the mess that had accumulated since Denver and Tessa had left for L.A., and slapped a couple of pieces of bread into the toaster. As he waited for his toast, he actually toyed with the idea of driving over to the Aldridge ranch and squaring things with Ivan. He probably owed the old man that much.

Colton didn't believe in making excuses or kidding himself. Deep down, he knew the reason he was considering a visit to the Aldridge spread was Cassie. He wanted to see her again. It was that simple . . . and that complicated.

The phone rang loudly, interrupting his thoughts. He snatched the receiver.

Denver's voice boomed over the wires. "So you are still there," he joked. "Tessa and I had a bet."

"Who won?" Colton asked.

"Tessa. I thought by now you would've gone stir crazy."

"Not quite," Colton drawled, grinning to himself and gazing out the kitchen window to see Black Magic grazing near the fence. "About time I heard from you."

"We've been busy."

"Have you?" Colton couldn't hide his sarcasm.

"Yep. But it won't be long now. We'll be back in less than three weeks."

It sounded like an eternity. Restlessly Colton scraped the nail of his thumb against the wall. "I'll try to hold it together till then."

"Have you had any trouble?"

Colton's eyes narrowed on Black Magic, and he considered telling his brother the truth. But what would be the point? Worrying Denver wouldn't bring him home any quicker. In fact, it would only serve to make his brother angry and nervous. And Denver's temper was as quick to flare as his own. "Nothing I can't handle," he said evasively before hanging up.

He finished his coffee, dashed the dregs down the sink, then strode outside. Clouds rumbled across the sky, and the wind had picked up, whistling through the branches of the oak and pine trees near the barns. He glanced at the Jeep, thought about driving over to see Cassie, and fought like hell to avoid that particular temptation.

Ramming his hands into the back pockets of his jeans, he took off across the yard. The rest of the day he threw himself into his work, repairing broken boards and sagging beams. As his hammer slammed nails into the wood, he tried and failed to shove Cassie Aldridge out of his mind.

"Okay, that's it—the last of today's walking wounded," Sandy said, turning the lock of the front door behind a border collie that walked with a pronounced limp from a mending leg.

"Thank goodness!" Cassie quickly cleaned the examination room, then stripped off her lab coat and dropped it into the laundry bin.

In the back room, Craig Fulton the veterinarian she worked with, was closing the final cage on a fat gray tabby. Craig was a short man with thick brown hair, freckles and oversized features in a round face. A bachelor since his divorce three years before, Craig had offered Cassie a job as soon as she'd graduated. His clothes were always a little rumpled, and his thick wire-rimmed glasses tilted slightly to one side.

"It's been a long one, hasn't it?" he said with a tired smile. He'd spent most of the day driving from one ranch to another, examining sheep, cattle and horses.

"Maybe things'll quiet down for the weekend."

"Sure." Craig chuckled. "Just remember, you're on call."

Cassie laughed. Though they took turns answering emergency calls on Saturday and Sunday, invariably they each worked part of every weekend. "I won't forget," she promised as she slung her jacket over her head and shouldered the door open.

Outside, rain poured from a darkening sky. Hunched against the wind, she dashed through the uneven parking lot, skirting the biggest puddles as she hurried to her white pickup. She flung open the door and started to climb inside, then pulled up short. There, slouched insolently against the worn seat on the passenger side, his legs sprawled in front of him, his wet Stetson shoved back on his head, was Colton McLean. "What're you doing here?" she asked.

"Waiting for you."

"Seems you've been doing a lot of that lately."

"Probably too often," he admitted, his sensual lips curved in a self-deprecating grin. "You'd better get in before you get soaked."

She didn't move other than to drop her shoulders. Oblivious to the rain collecting in her hair and sliding down her neck, she glared at him. "*Why* were you waiting for me?"

"The storm broke and I decided I'd rather be dry than wet."

"But you can't just climb into my truck and—"

"You don't lock your pickup any better than you lock the back door," he said. "Come on, get in." He stretched, reaching across with his hand, and his eyes were surprisingly warm. "I won't bite—I promise."

She almost laughed. "I'm not afraid of you, Colton. Bite or not." Ignoring his hand, she climbed into the cab and settled behind the steering wheel. "Don't you have some horse to protect or something?" she needled. "Why, right this very minute someone could be sneaking off with Black Magic to God-only-knows where."

His smile widened. "I guess I deserved that."

"And more."

"I did come on a little strong."

"That's putting it mildly."

Colton shoved his hat further back on his head. A dark swatch of hair fell over his brow. "I didn't come here to argue."

"Good. Now we're getting somewhere," she mocked. "Why are you here?"

"To invite you to dinner."

"You expect me to go to dinner with you?" she asked, stunned. "You're kidding, right?"

"Nope."

"But—"

"Look, Cass, I know I've been a first-class jerk," he admitted. "But I had my reasons."

"And now they've changed?"

"I thought about what you said, that's all. The horse is back, there's no harm done, and I—" his face changed expression and his eyes darkened a bit "—and I'd like to take you to dinner. Think of it as my way of apologizing."

"I didn't know you knew how."

"Maybe I don't. Seems I'm having one helluva time convincing you."

Suddenly the cab felt close. The windows, streaked with rain on the outside, had fogged on the inside, closing Colton and Cassie from the rest of the world. She felt like biting her lip, but didn't. "What would be the point?"

"Believe it or not, we might just have a good time."

Cassie nearly choked.

"And I'd like to spend some time with you," he admitted with a sigh. There was more to it, of course. Colton had argued with himself all day, knowing that being with her again would tangle him up in an emotional rope he wasn't sure he could unknot.

Cassie watched his fingers drum against his knee, saw the dark hair that covered the back of his hand. Her pulse jumped, though she forced herself to ignore it. "I don't know if I can—"

"Is your dad expecting you?"

"No." She shook her head. "He's used to me working late."

"Then why not?" he asked, a small smile teasing his lips again. She caught a glimpse of his sensual mouth, felt her heart flutter, then turned her gaze to the keys in her hand.

"I guess there's no reason," she admitted, jamming the key into the ignition. "Where to?"

"How about Timothy's?"

Her throat tightened. Timothy's was a small, intimate restaurant on the far side of town. She and Colton had been there together years before. "Sure," she said casually. "Why not?" She flicked on the engine, and the old truck roared to life. Her eyes sparkling, she asked, "Need a lift— or would you rather take your Jeep?"

Colton actually chuckled. "I'd rather ride with you."

"Would you?" She couldn't help but smile. "That's a turn around."

"Maybe not, Cassie," he muttered to himself.

Her hands were shaking as she drove out of the parking lot and eased into the gentle flow of early-evening traffic. The wipers swished rain from the windshield, and Cassie squinted against oncoming headlights.

Colton slouched even lower, and she could feel the weight of his gaze upon her as she drove. She refused to glance in his direction, forcing herself to stare at the shimmering road ahead, concentrating on the traffic.

Timothy's was perched on the banks of the Sage River, near the famous falls for which the town was named. Originally a flour mill, the rambling building was constructed of river rock, mortar and dark cross beams. Near the front door an old waterwheel still creaked and turned, with water splashing over its time-worn planks.

She climbed out of the truck and marched toward the restaurant, all too aware of Colton beside her. He didn't touch her, didn't so much as brush her arm, but she was careful to keep the distance between them wide as they hurried up the slick brick path to wide double doors.

Inside, a huge foyer was lit with flickering sconces and wagon-wheel chandeliers. The stone walls rose three full stories to an arched, beamed ceiling. The floor was smooth stone, and burgundy cloths covered the tables. Kerosene lanterns adorned each table, the quivering flames providing intimate illumination.

"I haven't been here in years," Cassie admitted, following a waiter to the back of the building.

Their table was private, near a huge bank of windows overlooking the swollen Sage River as it tumbled wildly over the falls. Filled with spring rain and the runoff from the mountains, the green water churned in frothy torrents, cascading over steep rocks, crashing some forty feet below to swirl in a swift current. Cassie, aware of Colton, stared through the glass.

"What would you like?"

*To run away from here—from you.* "Anything." She forced her gaze to his.

When the waiter reappeared, Colton ordered for them both, then settled back in his chair.

Nervous, Cassie sipped from her water glass. Pretending interest in the wine list, she was able to avoid his eyes. Obviously he wasn't going to make this easy.

"So," she ventured, trying to appear calm, though a nervous sweat had dampened her skin. "What changed your mind? It must've been something earth-shattering for you to think you should apologize."

"It was."

The waiter brought their orders—crisp salad, fresh trout, steaming vegetables and a basket of sourdough bread. Once he disappeared again, Colton ignored his food. "You changed my mind, Cassie," he said.

Her eyes flew to his, and he held her gaze, though she could swear his face had turned a darker shade. "Me?"

"All that self-righteous indignation the other day."

"It got to you?" She could barely believe her ears.

He lifted a shoulder. "I guess."

"So you think Dad's innocent?"

Colton frowned. "I wouldn't go that far," he hedged, "but whatever happened with the horse, it's over. As far as I can see, other than that I was made to look like a fool, there was no harm done."

She eyed him thoughtfully. "You expect me to believe you?"

"Believe what you want, Cass," he said with a sigh. "I just thought that instead of working so hard at fighting, we should try to be civil to each other."

Her throat was suddenly dry. "Why?"

"It's long overdue."

Colton picked up his fork and cut into his fish, but Cassie ignored her meal. "So this is your grand gesture to end the feud, is that it?"

He shook his head. "Unfortunately I don't think I can do that," he admitted. "But I'd just like to start over with you."

*Start over.* Cassie looked away. If only they could roll back the years and erase the pain that kept them apart. She tried to swallow a bite of bread, but it seemed stuck in her throat.

"I think we got off on the wrong foot the other night."

"You think right," she finally replied, trying to remember that she was supposed to detest him. "I'm not crazy about my family's name being dragged through the mud."

"Neither am I," he said, his temper evident in spite of his efforts to remain calm. "And I'm not thrilled about looking like an idiot! Any way you cut it, the horse was stolen while I was in charge."

"*Maybe.*"

Colton had trouble hanging on to his patience. "Anyway, as I said, it's over. Let's forget about Black Magic."

"Amen," Cassie whispered, wishing she could close the door on their past as easily. She toyed with her food, barely tasting it, watching Colton surreptitiously and wishing that all the questions raging in her mind would vanish. "You know," she finally said when the silence stretched long between them, "I didn't think I'd ever see you again."

He shoved his plate aside. "Sometimes things don't go as you plan."

"Would you have come back on your own?"

"You mean, if I hadn't been forced?" he asked, rubbing his shoulder unconsciously. "I don't know. Probably not. There's nothing here now," he said, unwittingly cutting her to the bone. He thought aloud. "Mom and Dad were killed in the fire, and Uncle John died last year. I suppose I might have come back to see Denver once in a while, but I'm not sure about that. In case you don't remember, we haven't always seen eye to eye."

"I remember," she said softly, the memory of Denver intruding upon them at the lake all too vivid. Despite the years that had passed, her cheeks felt hot. "But you own part of the ranch now. John left half of it to you."

Colton's lips curled at the thought of his wayward uncle. "It was just the old man's way of trying to tie me down. He knew I didn't want anything to do with the ranch, not after the fire. Neither did Denver. But, at least in my brother's case, it looks as if good old Uncle John won. Denver's settled down and become a family man."

"The ultimate sell-out," Cassie observed, forcing a cool smile she didn't feel.

"Not if it's what he wants."

"And what is it you want, Colton?" she asked, afraid she'd never have the opportunity to question him again. "Danger? Thrills? What?"

"Why do you care?"

"It's something I've always wanted to know," she admitted. "Because all your life it seems that you've either been running from, or racing to, something. I just wondered what it was."

The smile that had touched his eyes faded, and his lips thinned a little. "You never did understand me, Cass."

"Because you never let me."

They were suddenly alone, just the two of them in this crowded room. The quiet conversation and soft clink of silverware dissolved. Cassie heard only the sound of her own breathing and the loud thudding of her heart.

Colton drew in a swift breath, looked as if he was about to say something, but held his tongue.

The long, silent seconds ticked by until the waiter deposited their check on a corner of the table.

As if thankful for the intrusion, Colton snatched up the ticket, reached into his wallet, peeled off some bills and stood in one single motion. "I think it's time to go."

"Past time," she agreed sadly.

They drove back to the parking lot of the clinic where Colton's truck sat beneath the barren branches of a young maple tree. Cassie flicked off the engine and waited. "I guess I should say thank you," she said, sliding Colton an uneasy glance.

"You don't have to." He reached for the door.

"No—" without thinking, she placed a restraining hand on his shoulder "—I want to. Thanks."

Colton winced, and belatedly she realized she'd gripped his injured muscles. She tried to draw away, but he stopped her with his free hand, enfolding her fingers as his eyes met hers. "It's okay," he assured her. "And as for dinner, you're more than welcome, Cass. Maybe we should consider this the beginning of the end." When she didn't reply, he glanced down at her hand, still resting lightly, teasingly against the soft leather of his jacket. "The end of the feud."

"I think it'll take more than one meal," she said, grinning despite the tension she felt in the small, confined space. She slithered her hand away from his and saw his Adam's apple bob as he swallowed.

"Probably." His eyes locked with hers for an instant, and Cassie's veneer of self-control slipped. She realized in that one sizzling glance that Colton wasn't as immune to her as she'd thought. She recognized the shading of his gray eyes, the slight flare of his nostrils, the restraint in the skin stretched taut across his features. Though they weren't touching, their bodies separated by inches of worn upholstery, Cassie could feel the heat in his stare, noticed the scorch of desire in the twist of his lips.

"I—I'll see you later," she said, willing her voice to remain steady.

"Right. Later." Colton grimaced, and again he reached for the door. This time, however, he swore, and instead of lifting the handle, he twisted back, caught the back of Cassie's head in one hand and pulled her face to his.

Cassie gasped but didn't have time to resist. His lips found hers, and she felt the warm, insistent pressure of his tongue against her teeth. Her mind spun out of control, her pulse began to thunder, and she closed her eyes, allowing herself this one, tiny taste of pleasure. She knew that Colton didn't care for her—no more than he had all those years ago—and yet she couldn't stop herself from tasting him, feeling him, enjoying the bittersweet pressure of his mouth against hers.

His hand became tangled in her hair, and he groaned. When he finally dragged his mouth from hers, he stared at her through passion-glazed eyes. "Some things never change," he whispered raggedly before unlatching the door and sliding outside. "Good night, Cass." Without waiting for a response, he slammed the door shut and turned his collar against the wind. He strode across the parking lot, mentally kicking himself. Why had he kissed her? Why? *That* was a dumb move.

He yanked open the door of his truck, climbed inside and thrust his key into the ignition, swearing under his breath. If he thought kissing Cassie would convince him that it was over between them, he'd been wrong. Dead wrong.

"Fool," he ground out, flicking on the ignition. "Goddamned fool!" He glanced in the sideview mirror and watched as Cassie pulled out of the lot.

What would it be like to spend a night with her? A weekend? One kiss had only whetted his appetite for more. Would a weekend in bed satisfy him—fill his need so that he could forget about her? Or would being with her become an addiction—the more time he spent with her, the more he craved?

"Don't even think about it!" he growled. The woman was trouble. Big trouble. And for once in his life, Colton intended to keep himself out of trouble.

Her father was in the living room watching television when Cassie walked quietly into the house. She could hear the laugh track from a weekly sitcom and Ivan's soft chuckle.

She could tell he'd eaten, as she glanced around the kitchen. Though most of the evidence wasn't in sight, as he'd washed his dishes, she noticed the leftover chicken he'd forgotten to wrap and place in the refrigerator.

" 'Bout time you showed up," he said when she hung her coat in the hall closet and poked her head into the living room. "Where ya been? Emergency?"

"Not this time."

He glanced up. His reading glasses were perched on the end of his nose, his stocking feet propped on an ottoman. Only one lamp was lit, and the morning newspaper was scattered across an end table with one page folded to a half-finished crossword puzzle.

Cassie decided to come clean. Three Falls was a small town, and it would be better for Ivan to hear the truth from her before someone else spread the news. "I had dinner with Colton."

Her father's bushy brows rose. "Did you now?"

"Uh-huh. He was waiting for me when I got off work, and we drove over to Timothy's."

"Any particular reason?"

Anticipating a battle, Cassie drew in a long breath. "Believe it or not, it was his way of apologizing." She dropped onto the couch beside her father and grabbed the paper with the puzzle.

"McLeans don't apologize."

Cassie grinned. "Well, it was tough. Colton's not very good at it, but he seemed sincere."

"Bah!"

"Prevaricator."

"What?" He twisted his head around, looking at her as if she'd lost her mind.

"Eighteen down—liar. It's prevaricator." She handed the folded newspaper to her father, who scribbled in the answer.

"Just don't go trustin' Colton," Ivan said, glancing up at her before filling in a few more letters.

"Because he's a McLean?"

"That's a good reason."

"Dad," she said gently, "don't you think it's time to end all this nonsense about a feud?"

"Never!"

"But John's dead now."

"That doesn't change what he did," Ivan muttered, his color rising. "And as for Colton, he's very much alive and he's as bad as his uncle. I haven't forgotten how he treated you."

"Neither have I," she admitted, combing her hair back from her face with unsteady fingers. "But I've decided not to dwell on it."

"That's good."

"And I'm not going to act like Denver and Tessa and Colton are a bunch of pariahs."

"I've got nothing against Tessa Kramer," Ivan said quickly. "She's just a fool who lost her heart to a McLean. But Denver and Colton, I've got no use for them. Neither one of 'em would be here if they had their choice. They both made it clear to God and everybody around just what they thought of ranching. Too good for it, you know."

"Denver's back for good."

"Well, who needs him? As for Colton, he's just biding his time until he can leave, and I say the sooner the better." He thrust his jaw out angrily before he looked up, his weathered face softening. "Colton hurt you once, Cassie. But you're a smart girl. You wouldn't let it happen again, would you?"

"Of course not!" she snapped quickly.

"Good." He slapped the newspaper down. "Now, have you had dessert? How about a dish of ice cream?"

"I'm not really hungry."

"Well, I am, so you may as well join me." He straightened, rested a big hand on her shoulder a second, then made his way to the kitchen.

Cassie flung herself back against the cushions of the couch. Her father was right, of course. Colton McLean had only caused her heartache and grief, while her father had been strong enough to help her pick up the pieces of her life and put them back together. Ivan had done everything he could to help her—borrowed money to help send her to college, encouraged her to go on to veterinary school and had even suggested that it was time she moved out—found an apartment in town. He'd been absolutely wonderful—and he'd been burned twice at the hands of the McLeans. She wouldn't let it happen again.

Cassie thought about her mother—beautiful, raven-haired Vanessa. Without a backward glance Vanessa Shilcoat Aldridge had left after her disastrous affair with John McLean had become common gossip. She'd returned to South Carolina where she'd found herself a wealthy doctor, remarried within a year and subsequently borne three children—Cassie's half brothers and sister, whom she'd never met.

Cassie never saw her mother, nor had she heard from her. Not a card at Christmas, never a call on her birthday. No, Vanessa would never look back. Cassie knew that she and her father had ceased to exist in her mother's mind.

Blinking against tears she'd sworn never to shed, Cassie tried not to think about her mother. Who needed Vanessa anyway? She and Ivan had done all right without her. But the weight in her heart felt like a stone.

"Rocky road or butter brickle?" her father called from the kitchen.

"Really, Dad, I'm not—"

"Oh, hogwash!" He chuckled and returned to the living room, carrying two huge bowls filled with both kinds of ice cream and oozing chocolate syrup.

"I'll get fat," she warned him.

"You?" He glanced down at her lithe body and handed her a dish. "No way! You're built like me. Now, come on, eat up and help me with this damned puzzle.'' He dropped back to the couch, studied the paper again and asked, ''What's an eight-letter word that starts with *b*, ends in *a-l* and means trick? The third letter's a *t*.''

''*B*, blank, *t*, blank, blank, blank, *a*, *l*?''

''Right,'' her father grunted.

Cassie thought for a minute, deliberately scooping up a spoonful of her father's gooey concoction. But she paused midair as the word hit her. ''What about betrayal?''

''Betrayal...it fits.'' His lips flattened over his teeth as he scribbled the letters. The only sound was the scratching of his pencil and the barely perceptible chatter of the TV program in progress.

Prevaricator. Liar. Trick. Betrayal. The words rushed through her mind, though her father didn't say anything.

Cassie turned her attention to the television set. She'd thought enough about lying and betrayal and loneliness for one night.

''You know, you're the ugliest beast I've ever slept with,'' Colton grumbled to Black Magic. He petted Magic's velvet-soft muzzle only to have the horse toss back his head and snort indignantly. ''Yeah, well, I don't like it any more than you do.''

Colton hung his damp Stetson on a nail pounded into one of the rough-hewn posts supporting the hayloft. Sighing, he sat on the edge of the cot and pushed off one boot with the toe of the other.

He listened to the sounds of the wind whistling in the rafters and the rustle of hay as the horses settled in for the night. There were snorts, chewing noises and a quiet dry cough. Outside, the wind shoved a branch against the building, but Colton didn't hear or see anything out of the ordinary.

Guarding the stallion might well be a waste of time, he thought, as he lay back on the sleeping bag, staring up at the floor of the loft and shifting so that his weight wasn't on his bad shoulder. If that were the case and Magic was safe, there was no reason Colton couldn't sleep in the house in a warm, clean bed instead of camping out here.

"You're just getting soft," he growled to himself, realizing that for the first time in eight years the old ranch house seemed a haven.

It was time to move on, get out of this place before he became complacent and self-satisfied. He considered his life beyond the ranch, remembering foxholes in Afghanistan, the hot, damp jungles of Central America, the blackened rubble of hideouts in war-ravaged Beirut. Why, he wondered, when he'd lived on the edge so long, had it begun to lose its appeal?

## Chapter Seven

Beth Lassiter Simpson wasn't one to take no for an answer. And she wasn't taking Cassie's "no" seriously. In Beth's condition every meal was important, and a lunch that could combine friendship, gossip and food was an event. "Come on, you promised," Beth insisted, shifting her ungainly weight from one foot to the other. Planted in the reception area of Three Falls Veterinary Clinic, she crossed her arms over her protruding abdomen and stuck her lower lip out in a childish pout.

Cassie couldn't be tempted, at least not now. "I'm sorry, Beth, I'd love to, you know that. But I can't. Not until Craig gets back from the Wilkerson ranch."

"And when will that be?"

"Probably not more than an hour," Cassie said, glancing at her watch and frowning.

"Good. Then I'll wait," Beth decided. "I have a few errands to run and I'll meet you at The Log Cabin at one-thirty." She must have seen the hesitation in Cassie's eyes.

"Come on, Cassie, you've got to eat anyway, and how often is it that I'm in town without Amy? Think about it. In a few more weeks I'll have another baby and it will be *ages* before we can have lunch together!"

"All right, all right," Cassie agreed, holding her hands up, palms out, in mock surrender while mentally crossing her fingers. "But if I don't show, it's because Craig got held up." Cassie was worried. Craig had left early this morning, driving over to a ranch on the outskirts of town. The rancher suspected one of his horses had come down with equine influenza, which may have developed into pneumonia.

Beth's eyes twinkled. "If you don't show up, I'll come looking for you!" With a giggle, she breezed out of the complex, leaving Cassie to deal with two cases of feline leukemia and a pet rat with a growth on its leg.

Two hours later Cassie was seated at a corner table in the main dining room of The Log Cabin, a house-turned-restaurant that specialized in hearty man-sized meals. Brass lamps hung from the ceiling, and blue-and-white checkered cloths covered the tables.

Beth shoved the remains of her spinach salad aside. "You'll never guess who I saw today!" Her eyes shone with a private secret.

"I couldn't begin to," Cassie admitted.

"Ryan Ferguson! He's back!"

Cassie glanced up sharply and ignored the uneaten half of her sandwich. "But I thought he swore he'd never set foot in Three Falls again."

"Well, he lied. I saw him at the bakery this morning. Amy and I went in to buy some donuts and there he was, big as life, drinking coffee and talking to Jessica Monroe!" She motioned to the waitress, ordered a fattening, sinful dessert, then glanced back at Cassie. "The way I heard it, Denver McLean fired Ryan last winter. Caught him stealing supplies or something."

Cassie remembered the rumors but didn't put much stock in them. After all, she'd been on the unkind side of gossip more than once in her life. "I guess no one knows but Denver."

"And Ryan," Beth pointed out. "You know, I bet he's only daring to show his face because Denver's in L.A.!"

"Ryan has family here."

"Just a sister," Beth said. "And the way I understand it they don't get along."

"That could be just talk. Maybe he's only visiting."

Beth pursed her lips together and shook her head. "Nope. I talked to Jessica about him after he left the bakery. She said he was asking about work."

"You think he's back to stay?" Cassie was surprised. After Denver had accused him of stealing and fired him, Ryan hadn't bothered defending himself and had simply left town.

"Who knows? According to Jessica, Ryan stopped over at her dad's ranch earlier this week, looking for a job." Beth's eyes narrowed. "If you ask me, Ryan could've taken Black Magic—just to get under Denver's skin. It would be like him, too—to wait until Denver was gone!"

"Then why would he stay?"

"Just to see Denver's reaction."

Cassie wasn't convinced. "Seems farfetched to me."

"Maybe," Beth agreed. "Lots of people around here would like to get back at the McLeans. Nobody much liked John." Her lips pursed. "He made more enemies than friends, and even though he's gone, Denver and Colton haven't won any popularity contests around town, either. Both of them turned their backs on Three Falls, then showed up again once John died and they inherited the place. It looks pretty mercenary to some of the ranchers who stuck it out through the bad years."

"Some of the ranchers—meaning Josh?" she asked, mentioning Beth's husband.

Beth shook her head. "No, Josh likes Colton and Denver, but his father Bill, and my dad never had any use for either of the McLean boys."

"Neither does mine," Cassie admitted, wondering just who disliked Denver and Colton enough to risk stealing their horse. This was more than a practical joke—taking a valuable stallion was a criminal offense, and Cassie didn't doubt for a minute that, if given the chance, Colton would press charges.

Beth grinned as the curly-haired waitress deposited a huge wedge of chocolate mousse pie covered with a cloud of whipped cream in the center of the table. "This looks positively decadent," Beth murmured, handing one of the long-handled spoons to Cassie. "Come on, help me out."

Cassie sighed theatrically, but her eyes crinkled at the corners. "First Dad, now you," she murmured, but plunged a spoon into the pie anyway. "I haven't eaten so many calories in an entire month as I've consumed in the last two days."

Beth's lips curved upward. "You could use a few pounds." She took another bite, then said, "I heard you had dinner with Colton last night."

Cassie's brows shot up. "How'd you find out?"

"Josh's brother was there with his wife. They saw you together at Timothy's."

"Colton dropped by after work and twisted my arm," Cassie explained. "Kind of like you did today."

"And so how was Colton? The same as ever? Restless and mysterious?"

"Conciliatory," Cassie said, thinking. "A little on the mellow side."

"That's not the Colton McLean I remember."

"Me, neither," Cassie admitted. "But it was nice."

"So you two ended the feud in one date?"

"It *wasn't* a date."

Beth polished off the last dollop of whipped cream. "If you say so." She leaned back in her chair, linked her hands around her protruding abdomen and sighed happily. "Does he still think someone took his horse?"

"Oh, yes," Cassie replied, nodding. "He's convinced."

"But you don't think so?"

"I don't honestly know. I'm just glad Black Magic is back where he belongs and Colton is off my dad's back.

Colton's watch over Black Magic didn't turn up anything suspicious. In fact, all he got for his efforts was a sore shoulder and a bad disposition from several nights of little sleep.

For years he'd existed on two or three hours' sleep at a stretch, always wary, always concerned that he might wake up with a knife against his throat or the muzzle of a gun in his back. And yet, since he'd been back in Montana, the hours of physical labor on the ranch made demands on his body that five hours of sleep each night couldn't replenish.

"It'll get better," he told himself, but secretly wondered if the reason he was tired all the time was that his nights were filled with wild dreams of Cassie—startling, vivid images that he couldn't erase from his mind. He'd wake up burning for her, wishing there were some way to douse the fire searing through his mind and body.

Short of finding a woman, he had no cure. As he saw it, he had two options. Chase her down and start rebuilding a relationship or find someone else.

"Fat chance of that," he told himself, knowing that as long as Cassie was nearby, no other woman would do. He jammed his pitchfork into a bale of hay, then made his way outside. It had been two days since he'd seen Cassie, and it seemed a lifetime.

Glancing around the sun-dappled fields, he felt a kinship with this land he hadn't experienced in years. Swollen-bodied mares grazed, picking at grass. Red Wing and

Ebony, Tessa's favorites—the pride of her small herd—moved slowly with the rest of the mares. Colton hoped they wouldn't foal until Tessa and Denver returned, as Tessa had been anticipating the birth of her prize stallion, Brigadier's offspring, for months.

In another field, yearlings cavorted, kicking up their heels and playfully nipping one another's necks.

No, this place wasn't so bad if you could stand the lack of excitement, he decided as he strode to the Jeep. It was fine for Denver. His older brother had changed over the years. But Colton hadn't, and if it weren't for Cassie there wouldn't be anything for him here.

The turn of his thoughts worried him. Admitting that Cassie was more than a passing attraction bothered him. But there it was. Colton believed in "calling 'em as he saw 'em," and unfortunately he was forced to recognize the simple and annoying fact that Cassie Aldridge had gotten to him all over again. A restlessness overcame him—the same restlessness he'd experienced every night since that evening when he'd first seen her again.

"Idiot," he muttered, striding across the yard and up the steps of the back porch. He flung open the back door and stopped dead in his tracks.

In the kitchen, an old apron tied around her thick waist, Milly Samms was polishing the stove. Her steel-gray hair had been freshly permed, and she bit her lower lip as she worked furiously. She glanced toward Colton, then stopped, her mouth dropping open. "Well, look at you," she said, a wide smile cracking her round face. "I barely recognized you without your beard!"

"I got tired of it," he said, eyeing her as she continued her work at a fever pitch. "I thought you weren't due back for another week."

The housekeeper nodded. If she noticed his impatience, she didn't comment. "I wasn't. But I heard about Black Magic and decided to cut my vacation short."

"He's been found."

"That's what Curtis said, but I didn't want to let Denver and Tessa down."

Colton grinned in amusement as he hung his hat near the back door. "We were surviving."

With a frown, Milly motioned to the cluttered counters and spotted wood floor. "Looks like you could use a little help—a woman's help. Tessa spent all last fall remodeling this house, the least you could do is keep it up while she's gone."

"I'll remember that," Colton replied, noting the freshly painted cupboards, tile counters and polished oak parquet floor. Between his sister-in-law's hard work and Denver's financial help, the old farmhouse had taken on a fresh luster.

"Do!" Milly said with mock severity as she placed a cup of coffee on the counter near Colton. "So tell me all about Black Magic. The way I heard it from Madeline Simpson, you think he was stolen again."

"That's right," Colton allowed, blowing across his cup before explaining the events of the past three weeks. Milly didn't stop scrubbing and shining every pot and pan in the house as well as the countertops, refrigerator and light fixtures. She listened to him, interjected her own two cents when appropriate and never once sat down.

"Well, all's well that ends well," Milly finally said when Colton had finished. She washed her hands for what had to be the tenth time, then wiped them on her apron.

"If it's ended."

"You don't think it'll happen again!"

"I hope not, but we don't know for sure, do we?" he replied, his eyes narrowing.

"I suppose not," Milly said absently. She stood in the middle of the kitchen, surveying her work. The appliances and brass-bottomed pots gleamed. "But I wouldn't be thinking Ivan Aldridge was behind it, you know."

Colton raised a skeptical brow.

"It could've been anyone around here. There's a lot of good will and friendliness in ranching," she said thoughtfully as she poured herself a well-deserved cup of coffee and added a spoonful of sugar. "But there's a lot of jealousy and envy, too. All the ranchers in these parts lost money a few years back. Winters were bad, crops ruined and some of the stock froze to death. But this place—" she gestured grandly to the house and beyond, through the fields "—managed to get by. Barely, mind you. When Denver returned, he was fit to be tied—claimed Tessa and Curtis had run the ranch to the ground. But he soon found out that she'd turned the corner, forced McLean Ranch into the black when some of the other ranchers, Bill Simpson, Matt Wilkerson, Vince Monroe and the like, were having trouble keeping the banks from foreclosing."

"Seems as if they all made it," Colton observed.

Milly frowned. "By goin' further in debt."

"Including Aldridge?"

She shrugged her big shoulders. "Don't know, but it wouldn't surprise me. Cassie got herself through college and veterinary school somehow, and that's not cheap!"

"Curtis seems to think Aldridge is the most likely suspect."

Milly's steely brows quirked. "So now you're listening to a Kramer!"

"He's family."

"You didn't always think that way."

"I was wrong," Colton admitted, thrusting his jaw out a bit.

"Yes you were, and you might be again. Just because there was a feud between the families, doesn't mean that Ivan's going to do something about it. Leastwise not anymore. And as far as what Curtis thinks..." She snorted. "He's as stubborn as a bull moose." Colton thought she was so agitated that she might spill her coffee as she raised it to her lips and took a sip. "Well," she finally conceded, "I suppose we're all entitled to our opinion."

"Even me?" Colton asked, his eyes glinting with amusement.

"No, you're the one person on this ranch that doesn't count," she teased, then chuckled to herself. "By the way, I found something earlier—now where'd it go?" She reached into the closet and pulled out a shoulder bag containing his 35-mm camera with a wide-angle lens. "This yours?"

Colton nodded, accepting the bag.

"It was in the den beneath a stack of newspapers a mile high! Thought you might be lookin' for it."

"Haven't had much use for it here."

"Why not? Seems to me you can take pictures of anything." Her old eyes twinkled. "You don't have to limit yourself to war and political scandals and all the rest of that nonsense."

"Nonsense, is it?"

"If you ask me."

He slung the strap of the bag over his shoulder. "I guess I'm just not into pastoral scenes."

"Maybe it's time you changed. Slowed down a bit. Before the next bullet does more damage than the last one."

"It won't," he assured her, setting his empty cup in the sink. "Thanks for the coffee."

"Anytime."

With the same restless feeling that had followed him in, Colton shouldered his way through the door and walked outside. He considered Milly's advice, discarded most of it, but couldn't help wondering if she were right about Ivan. How much simpler things would be if Aldridge weren't behind Black Magic's disappearance. How much easier his relationship with Cassie would be.

Loading his camera without thinking, Colton lifted it, staring through the lens and clicking off a few quick shots—

Len, tall and rawboned, the epitome of the twentieth-century cowboy, working with a mulish buckskin colt; Curtis leaning against the top rail of the fence, smoking and eyeing the surrounding land; the sun squeezing through thin white clouds. Snap. Snap. Snap.

And yet his mind wasn't focused on the image in the lens; his thoughts kept wandering to Cassie. He forced himself to concentrate. Snap. He caught Curtis leading Black Magic outside. Snap. A shot of the horse yanking on the lead rope and rearing against a backdrop of late afternoon sky.

The clicking of the shutter sounded right. The view through the lens looked right, and yet, something was missing—something vital—that surge of adrenaline he'd experienced so often when he'd stared through the eye of the camera.

"Hell with it," he muttered, savagely twisting on the lens cap and shoving the camera into its case. Without considering the consequences of what he was doing, he shouted to Curtis that he'd be gone for part of the evening, advising the older man to lock Black Magic in his stall. Then he strode angrily across the yard to his Jeep. He jammed his key into the ignition and growled an oath at himself. Tonight, come hell or high water, he was going to see Cassie again.

She saw him coming. Pale sunlight glinted against chrome and steel. Tearing down the narrow lane, the motorcyclist bore down on her. Yanking hard on the steering wheel, Cassie felt the old truck shimmy, its wheels bouncing on the uneven ground as she made room. The motorcycle sped past. The driver, dressed in black from helmet to boots and huddled over the handlebars, didn't glance her way as he drove recklessly on the narrow lane leading from the Aldridge house.

"Damned fool!" Cassie muttered, her heart pounding as she stared into the rearview mirror and watched as the motorcycle disappeared around the bend.

She eased the truck back into the twin ruts of gravel that comprised the lane and drove the final quarter-mile to the house. Her heart was still thundering wildly when she parked her pickup near the garage. "Who was that?" she demanded, hopping out of the cab and spying her father in the door to the barn. Erasmus yelped at the sight of her and bounded over, whining and wiggling at her feet.

"Ferguson," Ivan replied.

"Ryan Ferguson? What was he doing here?" Bending down, Cassie scratched the old dog behind his ears. "He drives like a maniac!"

"He was looking for work." Her father wiped his forehead with a handkerchief and stuffed it back into the pocket of his overalls. "I hired him."

"You did *what*?" she fumed, still shaking from the close call. "He nearly ran me off the road!"

Ivan's eyes filled with concern. "Did he?"

"Didn't you see it!"

"I was in the barn." He placed a hand on her shoulder. "Are you okay?"

"No thanks to him!" she snapped angrily.

"I'll have a talk with him," Ivan said, frowning and staring at the lane. "He starts work tomorrow."

"Tomorrow?" she repeated, stunned. "Why?"

"'Cause I need help, that's why," Ivan replied. "The mares will start foaling next week, and I'll be planting grain soon, not to mention the regular chores."

"But why Ryan Ferguson? Denver McLean fired him because—"

"I know why Denver claims he fired him, but Ryan swears he was innocent. No charges were ever filed, you know."

"Then why did Ryan leave town?"

"He says he quit, that he just needed some time away. Can't say as I blame him. Workin' for the McLeans must be hell."

"Oh, Dad, that's crazy. John McLean stood by Curtis Kramer when everyone else in town blamed him for the fire on the McLean Ranch. And some of those hands at the McLean place have been there for years. They love it."

Ivan clenched his teeth. "Don't mention John McLean to me!" he ordered, starting for the back porch at a furious pace.

"But he did."

"So now he's a saint, right? And I give another wrongly accused man a job and I'm not right in the head," he called over his shoulder.

"I didn't say—"

Her father reached the porch and whirled, his eyes bright. "John McLean is the single reason Vanessa left me and you grew up without a mother!" he reminded her, his words slicing open an old, painful wound. The back of Ivan's neck was flushed scarlet. "You know how I feel about the McLeans, so let's drop it!"

Cassie heard the rumble of an engine and glanced toward the drive. "I, uh, don't think that's possible."

"And just why the hell not?"

Cassie's heart felt like it had dropped to the ground. "Because it looks like Colton is on his way."

"What?" Ivan turned his gaze to the front drive. "Blast that man! What's he doin' here?"

"I guess we'll just have to wait and find out," she said, but she wished Colton's timing were better. Right now her father would like to tear anyone with the name of McLean limb from limb.

"He's not welcome here!" Ivan snapped.

"He knows that. So why don't you listen to what he has to say? It must be important," she said, trying to calm him

down before another confrontation between her father and
Colton exploded.

Ivan's eyes narrowed. "I've heard enough McLean lies to
last me a lifetime, and I would have thought the same goes
for you!"

"Colton never lied to me," she said, her back stiffening.

"No," Ivan allowed, "but what he did was worse! He
accused you of lying, using him, trying to trick him into a
marriage he didn't want." The flush on his neck spread upward, and his eyes flared. "Don't ever forget, Cassie, Colton McLean tried to destroy you!"

"I can handle myself!"

"Can you?" her father tossed back, the lines of strain
near his eyes becoming less harsh. "I hope so." With that,
he stormed into the house, Erasmus on his heels.

The screen door banged shut, and Cassie flinched. Her
father was right, of course. Colton had wounded her so
deeply, she thought she'd never be the same. And she
wasn't. Colton had single-handedly devastated the young
naive girl she'd once been. It wouldn't happen again. Now
she was older and, she hoped, much wiser. That young girl
could never be hurt again, and she would try her best to
make sure the woman she'd become wouldn't suffer at any
man's hands, including those of Colton McLean.

Watching as Colton parked his Jeep near her truck, she
waited by the steps. As he got out of the truck, his gaze met
hers, and one side of his mouth lifted in that same irreverent smile she'd always found so fascinating.

"I just couldn't stay away," he said, as if answering the
questions in her eyes.

"Seems you didn't have much trouble for eight years,"
she pointed out.

"Ouch." He shoved his hat back on his head and studied
her thoughtfully. "Am I back on the bad list?"

"You were never off," she said, trying to remain firm, but she couldn't keep the twinkle out of her eyes. "Face it, McLean, you're bad news."

"You've been talking to your father again."

"Maybe he's just been setting me straight."

Colton chuckled. "You know, Cass, you can be positively mean when you want to be."

"And you deserve it."

Without warning, he grabbed her arm and spun her around so quickly, she slammed into him.

"Hey—"

"Let's start over," he suggested, his gaze warm, the scent of him as fresh as a sun-drenched Montana morning. His breath touched her face in a gentle caress.

"Too late," she said, trying to keep her voice light, attempting not to notice that her breasts were crushed against his chest, her thighs pressed against the hard length of his, her body responding to the closeness of his.

Strong arms held her prisoner. "I thought we'd gotten past all that."

"Past the fact that you accused my father of horse thievery? Or past the feud? Or past the night you accused me of lying to you before you walked out the door?" she asked, the words tumbling out in a rush.

He tensed, every muscle suddenly rigid. "I think we'd better leave well enough alone."

"But nothing was ever 'well enough,' was it?"

"What do you want from me?"

"The chance to explain why I couldn't tell you that I wasn't pregnant eight years ago," she shot back, her insides quaking. Standing so close to him stirred up all her old insecurities, but this time she wasn't going to back down.

Something flashed in his eyes. Pain? Or pity? "Does it matter?"

She gasped. Of course it mattered! More than anything had ever mattered. "Eight years ago it was all that mattered."

"Eight years is a long time," he said, his eyes focused on her lips.

"It seems like yesterday."

Colton just stared at her. "Clichés, Cass?" he drawled, suppressing a laugh, his mouth curving into an amused smile.

Instantly infuriated, she sputtered, "You are, without question, the most insufferable, egotistical, bloody bastard that ever walked this earth!"

Colton laughed, a deep rumbling sound that erupted into the evening air.

"You think that's funny?" she said, jerking away, her black hair flying in front of her eyes, her fingers curling into fists of frustration.

"No, I think it's probably the truth," he admitted with an exasperating, devilish grin. Quick as a cat, he tugged on her arm, yanking her back against him. "What is it about you?" he wondered aloud. "One minute I think you're the most intriguing woman I've ever met, the next I realize you're a pain in the backside."

"Like you."

"Exactly," he said, his eyes growing dark as they focused on her lips.

Cassie's throat closed.

Slowly, with painstaking deliberation, he lowered his head and brushed his lips over hers.

Cassie had to bite back a moan.

His lips molded over hers, and her knees nearly buckled. Her conscience told her to stop this madness, and she tried. Though she attempted to push him away, he wouldn't relent, holding on to her with a fierceness bordering on desperation.

Her palms against a solid, denim-clad chest, she struggled a little as his tongue touched the inner recesses of her mouth.

A seeping warmth flooded her limbs, and though she thought perversely that she should bite him, she didn't. Instead, she closed her eyes and sighed. What was the point of fighting when she'd been waiting for eight years for him to take her into his arms?

When he dragged his lips away, she whispered, "You're positively annoying!"

"And you love it."

"Don't flatter yourself!"

"Come on, Cass," he whispered suggestively, "admit it. It keeps you interested."

She slid a glance at him from beneath the fringe of her dark lashes. "I'm *not* interested."

"Bull!" He touched his forehead to hers. "Let's not argue."

"Seems inevitable."

"Nothing's inevitable," he whispered, and her heart turned over. "Now, tell me, is Ivan the Terrible around?"

"*Dad* is in the house. And he's not in a great mood. I wouldn't be calling him any names."

"I won't," Colton said, releasing her and starting up the back steps. "As a matter of fact, I'm here to apologize."

Cassie's brows lifted. "You're just full of surprises, aren't you?"

"It keeps you on your toes."

"Don't bother."

He grinned despite her sarcasm. "I decided that the other night when I told you that I was wrong wasn't enough; that I should tell Ivan he's off the hook."

"I don't think he really cared one way or the other," Cassie said. She tried to sound calm, but her spirits were soaring. Colton was taking the first step; maybe Ivan could find it in his heart to forgive him. And perhaps she could forgive him as well.

"At least I'll have tried."

Cassie smothered a smile. "Enter, Daniel, into the lion's den."

Colton laughed as Cassie opened the back door. Erasmus bolted through, nearly knocking her over as he ran, pell-mell, down the stairs and streaked across the backyard, startling a flock of blackbirds in the leafless apple tree. "You know, you're not on his top-ten list of favorite people right now."

"I figured that."

Together they walked into the kitchen. Ivan was seated at the table, a mug of coffee in one hand. "McLean," he said without preamble.

Colton stopped just inside the door and swept his Stetson from his head. "Thought you'd want to know Black Magic's been found."

"I heard." Ivan's gaze bored into the younger man's eyes, but Colton didn't flinch. "Rumor has it he just wandered off and decided to come back on his own."

Colton's lips thinned. "I doubt it. But I've decided that I judged you too quickly."

"Probably just force of habit."

Colton's jaw worked. "Look, I just stopped by to say I'm sorry I came down on you so hard."

Ivan shifted his gaze away. "A little late for apologies, isn't it?"

"It's probably too late for a lot of things," Colton admitted with a grim smile, flicking a glance at Cassie. "But that doesn't mean we can't bury the hatchet."

"Just like that?"

Leaning a hip against the counter, Colton shook his head. "I suppose it'll take a little effort."

"And a lot of forgetting." Ivan scowled into his coffee cup, then took a long, last swallow. Dropping his feet onto the cracked linoleum, he shoved himself upright, straightening slowly. "There's been too much bad blood between our families to pretend it didn't exist," he said deliberately, rubbing his stubbled jaw. "I don't think we can even begin to bury it all."

"Dad..." Cassie protested.

"Look, McLean, you've said your piece and I've listened. In all honesty, I'm glad the horse is back. As for the rest—" his brows drew together and he lifted one shoulder "—I see no reason to change things. As far as I'm concerned, you're still not welcome here."

Cassie's spirits crashed. "Please, Dad, think about this—"

"Think about it?" Ivan retorted, his lips thinning. "I've thought too long about the McLeans. You might be falling for his line, but I'm not!" he growled.

"I just think it's time we settled some things."

"Tell that to your mother, why don't you?" His old eyes gleaming, he stood. The cords in his neck had stretched taut as he warned, "Be careful, Cassie. You're twenty-five now—old enough to make your own decisions—and I can't tell you what to do. But just be damned careful."

"Dad, wait—I think we should talk about this...." Cassie followed him out of the room, but Ivan shook his head sadly, ran a shaking hand over his forehead and climbed the stairs.

"Get rid of him. Then we'll talk."

Cassie felt pulled and pushed. On one hand she wanted to shove aside all the pain of the past, get on with her life. On the other, she knew her father was right. One apology didn't erase years of agony and mistrust.

Her stomach in knots, she walked back to the kitchen where Colton, twirling the brim of his hat in his fingers, stared out the window. "Charming fellow, your father," he muttered.

"He can be."

"You couldn't prove it to me."

"That works two ways."

Colton frowned, his brows drawing together in a single, stubborn line. "Let's get out of here."

"I just got home!"

"I know, but I'd rather go someplace where I'm welcome. And I'd like you to come with me."

Cassie hesitated. Tempted not to ask any questions and just take off and follow him, she had to force herself to slow down. "Why?"

"Because I want to spend some time with you," he said simply, his expression still perturbed.

Her pulse jumped. "Do you think that's smart?"

"I *know* it isn't, but what could it hurt?" He flashed her an uncertain grin, and Cassie's heart lurched. Seeing a vulnerable side to Colton, a part he tried so hard to keep hidden, touched her as nothing else could.

"I'd hate to think—"

"Then don't think. Just come with me."

She attempted to swallow all her doubts. "Okay." Wondering if she were making the second-worst mistake of her life, she breezed past him and walked outside. Afternoon shadows had lengthened, the sunlight was weak, the air cool. Shivering, she stuffed her hands into the pockets of her down jacket and crossed the yard.

Colton opened the door of the Jeep and helped her inside.

As he slid behind the steering wheel, Cassie glanced at the house. "I hope you know I feel like Benedict Arnold."

"Your father'll get over it."

"I don't know," she thought aloud as the Jeep lurched backward and cut a wide circle near the barn.

"You're twenty-five—Ivan himself pointed out that fact."

"Oh, so now I'm old enough, is that it?" she said, a sad smile toying with her lips.

"Old enough?"

"Don't you remember? That was your big argument against 'us' way back when. You thought I was just a kid."

"You were," he said, grinding the Jeep's gears and taking off down the twin ruts of the lane.

At the highway he didn't turn toward Three Falls, but guided the old rig in the opposite direction.

"Where're you taking me?" she asked.

He cast a seductive glance in her direction. "If I told you, I'd spoil the surprise."

"What surprise?" she demanded, a ripple of delight darting up her spine. Unpredictable, mysterious and secretive, Colton was never dull. "You know, this is starting to look like a kidnapping."

"I thought we'd already established the fact that you're not a kid anymore. Besides, you came willingly."

"I guess I can't argue with that," she thought aloud, her nerve endings tingling in anticipation as she leaned back in the seat and squinted through the windshield.

They were headed west, and cathedral-spired mountains, their craggy slopes snow-laden and sheer, pierced the dusky sky.

Cassie gnawed nervously on the inside of her lip. Where was Colton taking her? she wondered, and more important, *why*?

## Chapter Eight

Colton drove through a neighboring town and into the mountains. "We're going to Garner's Ridge?" she asked, surprised. "A ghost town?"

Colton laughed, and the rich sound filled the interior of the Jeep. The road twisted upward, turning to gravel as it wound through the pines and brush. The Jeep bounced and shimmied. Eventually the gravel turned to dirt. A sheer granite wall rose on one side of the deserted road, while forested cliffs fell away on the other.

When Colton shifted, his fingers nearly brushed her knee. As the Jeep rocked, their shoulders touched fleetingly.

The road narrowed around a final bend, and he slowed the Jeep to a stop at the end of what once had been the main street. A row of dilapidated buildings with sagging roofs and listing walls lined the narrow alley.

"Not much, is it?"

Together they walked through the old mining town where, nearly a hundred years before, gold had been discovered. In the beginning miners had flooded the area but later moved on because the mother lode had never been found. The few settlers who had arrived had left within twenty years.

Colton stepped onto the ramshackle boardwalk and shouldered open a door, which groaned as the rusted hinges gave way. Mice scurried across ancient floorboards, and a huge hole in the roof allowed a view of the darkening sky.

"Why did you bring me here?" Cassie asked, cautiously peeking through what little glass remained in the broken windows.

"I thought we needed a chance to be alone."

"You, me and the ghosts?"

Colton chuckled and grabbed her hand. "I thought we needed to put everything into perspective," he admitted. "Sometimes too many other people and things get in the way."

"Meaning Dad?"

"For one. Uncle John for another."

"Not to mention Black Magic."

"Right," he said quietly, walking back through the front door of the old general store and down the uneven steps. Outside, he propped one shoulder against the rough bark of a huge pine tree.

Mist rose eerily from the forest floor, forming pale clouds near the buildings and giving the shadowy old town an aura of mystery. "You could almost believe real ghosts live in this town," Colton murmured.

"And do you see any spirits?" Cassie stood next to him, her gaze following his. "Any ghosts from your past?"

"The only ghost I've had to deal with is you," he admitted.

"Me?"

"That's right." Touching her lightly under the chin, he tipped her face up to his, staring into near-perfect features that were already indelibly etched in his mind. Her cheeks were rosy, her hazel eyes wide as they searched his, her ebony hair curling softly around her face. "I've been trying to exorcise you for eight years."

"And were you successful?"

His mouth tightening at the corners, he said, "Doesn't look like it, does it?"

"It did for eight years."

His eyelids lowered to half-mast. "Not really."

Cassie's heart pounded. If only she could believe him. "And now?"

"Now is difficult, Cass," he admitted. "A real problem. Every time I shove you out of my mind, you find a way to push yourself right back in."

"Not true. I haven't bothered you once."

"Ah, Cassie," he said with a world-weary sigh, his defenses slipping. "You didn't have to try. You were always there—even when I thought I'd forgotten you, something would trigger a memory, and there you'd be."

"If you expect me to believe that you've been pining for the past eight years—"

"I don't pine."

"I didn't think so."

"But I was bothered."

"Not enough to call, or write, or stop by," she pointed out, trying to remember just how much pain he'd caused. But here in the half-light, alone with him, those agonizing memories seemed to slip away.

"I wasn't around."

"Your choice," she reminded him, aware of his fingers, hard and warm, against her chilled skin, and angry with herself for even listening to him.

"I didn't *want* to be bothered," he said tightly, slowly caressing the column of her throat, his gaze delving even deeper into hers.

Darkness settled between the decrepit facades of the time-worn buildings, and Cassie wished she had the willpower to draw away, to demand to be taken home, to tell him she never wanted to see him again as long as she lived. But she didn't. Mesmerized by his silvery eyes, she asked, "What made you change your mind?"

"You."

She laughed, and the sound echoed through the trees.

"I'm serious," he said softly. "As long as I was in another city, or state or country, I could keep away from you. But once I was back here—"

"You've been here for months," she cut in, forcing herself not to fall under his spell. "You didn't come see me until Black Magic disappeared."

A crooked smile twisted his lips. "Part of the time I was laid up," he replied, bending to push his face closer to hers.

"And the rest?"

"Willpower."

"So much for my powers of seduction," she mocked.

"Oh, you've got them," Colton whispered, his breath fanning her face, "and I'm not immune. But I had everything under control. Until I saw you again."

"What's this all about, Colton?" she asked, her voice sounding more ragged than she'd hoped. She wanted to appear in control when all of her senses were reeling; her nerve endings tingled from his touch, her nostrils were filled with his scent, her eyes were riveted to the sensual line of his lips.

"I just wanted to be alone with you," he admitted, his voice as rough as her own.

"In a ghost town?"

"Anywhere." Suddenly his mouth crashed down on hers, his fingers winding in her hair. The sounds of the night disappeared, and all Cassie heard was the wild cadence of her heart and the answering drum of Colton's. All she felt was the strength of his arms surrounding her and the force of desire raging between them, a desire so strong it destroyed all rational thought, a desire so potent it heated more quickly than it had eight years before.

"This—this is a big mistake," she murmured, dragging her mouth from his and searching for some shred of her sanity. *What am I doing?* she wondered, her breath short and shallow.

"Not our first." He kissed her again, thrusting his tongue wondrously between her teeth. With one set of fingers tangled in her hair, he pressed his other hand insistently against the small of her back.

Through her clothes she could feel the sheer force of his body, the strength of his muscles, the passion racing through his blood.

*Think, Cassie!* But she couldn't, and as the weight of his body dragged her down to a bed of pine needles and soft boughs, she sighed and wound her arms around his neck. *I love you,* she realized with a sinking heart. *I always have.*

His mouth covered hers, and she didn't fight the warmth invading her. A familiar heat rushed through her blood like quicksilver, pounding in her eardrums as she lay with him.

He slipped his fingers beneath her sweater, reaching up, touching the silky lace of her bra, causing her skin to tingle. Her nipple grew hard with anticipation, and when the tips of his fingers brushed lightly against her burgeoning breast, she shuddered.

"I've missed you, Cass," he admitted, kissing her lips gently as his hand surrounded her breast.

Her heart clamored crazily as he stroked. Her concentration scattered in the wind. "I—It was hard to tell."

"Because I didn't want to admit it," he conceded, his teeth tugging gently on her lower lip, his hands moving erotically beneath her sweater, kneading her warm, soft flesh, causing a maelstrom of emotions to roil within her.

With her own fingers she found the buttons of his shirt, slipped under the coarse fabric, and touched skin stretched taut over a washboard of corded muscles.

He sucked in a swift breath, his eyes fluttering closed. "You're a witch," he whispered.

"First I'm a ghost, now a witch," she murmured. "No wonder I'm crazy about you."

"Are you, Cass?" he asked, his eyes suddenly flying open.

"I must be—crazy, that is. Creeping around a ghost town, falling into the arms of a man who swore vengeance on my family. Honestly, Colton," she said, her good humor surfacing, "this is something out of a bad horror movie."

His grin was a slash of white in the darkness. "Don't worry, I'll protect you. Trust me."

The last words spilled over her like a bucket of ice water. "Trust *you*?" she said, all warmth instantly seeping from her body. "After everything that's happened between us?" Though Colton's grip on her tightened, she pushed him away. She needed to be free to think. "What about you, huh? Trust is a two-way street, Colton, and last time I looked, you didn't trust me or my dad!"

He reached for her, but she withered at his touch, straightening her sweater and drawing her jacket around her. Pine needles scratched against her back.

What was she doing here with him? What had she been thinking? "I think we'd better go!" she said, her teeth chattering as she scrambled to her feet.

Colton was on his feet in an instant, pinning her against the prickly bark of the pine tree. "What is it, Cassie?" he demanded, his square chin thrust forward, his gray eyes slits. "What's on your mind?"

"Trust isn't something given, it's earned," she said, her own chin inching upward mutinously. "And you can never expect me to trust a man who, without waiting for a word of explanation, walked out on me."

"There was nothing to explain!"

"There was plenty!" she nearly screamed, the words that had burned so bright in her mind leaping to her tongue. "I thought I was pregnant, Colton, and I was scared. Scared to death that you'd reject me.''

"Bah!"

''I had all the symptoms. I threw up at least once a day, my period was late and I'd been sleeping with you without a thought for birth control!''

Under the shifting moonlight she witnessed the blanching of his face.

''But it didn't matter, you see. You were right. I was too young to care, to understand what a burden a child would be. I could only see the good side, the thrill and joy of sharing everything with you, of bearing your son or daughter—''

''Cassie, don't,'' he warned, his skin stretching tight across his rugged features.

But she couldn't stop. As if a dam had suddenly given way, Cassie's words tumbled out in a rush. ''I trusted you once, Colton. And I loved you. Good Lord, how I loved you. But you took that love and trust and turned it against me, believing what you wanted to believe so that you could leave Montana and not look back! You told me over and over again that you didn't want a wife, that we were too young, that we had dreams we had to chase, and the first chance you got, you turned your back on me and took off! So don't talk to me about trust!''

Colton's jaw had become rigid, and the hands imprisoning her against the tree had curled into fists. Under the wrath of Cassie's fury, Colton didn't notice the splinters in his palms nor the pain. ''Are you finished?''

''There isn't any more to say.'' She tried to duck under his arm, but he captured her wrist, spinning her back.

''There's a helluva lot.''

''You have *reasons* for the way you behaved? *Excuses*?''

"Just the truth. You were pushing too hard, Cassie. You'd been hinting at marriage for a long time. The baby seemed convenient, especially when it never existed."

"Maybe I was just hoping."

"And maybe I didn't like being played for a fool!"

"Only one person can make a person look like a fool, Colton," she snapped. "And that's the person himself." Wrenching her arm free of his grasp, she started for the Jeep. But in three swift strides he was walking with her, matching her furious steps with those of his own. "Would it help if I said I'm sorry?"

"No!"

"Why not?"

"Because you don't *believe* me, Colt. And that's what this is all about!" She couldn't stop the hot tears that burned in her eyes. At the Jeep she spun to face him. "You were right, you know. We were too young. But I would've waited if only I'd felt you cared."

Leveling an oath at himself, Colt swore, his emotions battling deep inside. He brushed his finger over the slope of her cheek, sweeping aside a tear. "I cared," he said, his voice raw with emotion. "God, I cared. And it scared the hell out of me." He drew her into the circle of his arms and kissed her forehead. "I'm sorry," he whispered, sighing heavily. "I never meant to hurt you. If you don't believe anything else, please believe that I never intended to cause you any kind of pain. I should've told you all this a long time ago, but I couldn't. I didn't understand it myself for a long time, and when I finally did, my pride stood in my way."

She felt a shudder rip through him and heard the catch in his voice. After eight long years, she believed him. Deep, racking sobs tore through her soul. She cupped his face between her hands, feeling his warm skin beneath her fingers, knowing in her heart that he was finally baring his soul.

He turned his face in her hands, kissing her palms. "If there were a way to erase all our mistakes, I'd do it, Cass," he said. "And if I knew how to prove that I cared then and I care now, I'd do it." He kissed her forehead and held her close.

She buried her face against his leather jacket and took in long, calming breaths.

Time passed, the silence a balm to old wounds. Cassie felt suddenly freed, unburdened from a weight so old it had become a part of her.

"Come on," he cajoled. "I'll take you to dinner. Anywhere you want!"

"Paris?" she replied, blinking and smiling through unshed tears.

He chuckled, though his gaze, staring deep into her eyes, remained sober. "If that's what you want."

"I guess it doesn't really matter." She sniffed to keep from crying and made a valiant attempt to disguise the depth of her emotions.

"How about if we take a rain check on Paris and try something closer?"

"I'll hold you to it, you know. I won't forget."

"Oh, yeah. I know, Cass," he said, opening the passenger door of the Jeep and helping her inside. "I know."

The minute they stepped through the door of the Pinewood Café, Cassie knew they'd made an irreversible mistake. Every eye in the small restaurant seemed to have turned curiously in their direction.

Most of the booths, upholstered in a forest-green Naugahyde, were filled. Smoke curled lazily to the ceiling, where a wheezing air-conditioning unit was fighting a losing battle to clean the air. Voices buzzed in low tones, glasses clinked and waitresses bustled from one table to the next.

As Colton touched Cassie's elbow and guided her to a booth near the back, she recognized Matt Wilkerson and

Bill Simpson at one table, Nate and Paula Edwards at another, and Vince Monroe with his wife, Nadine, and daughter, Jessica, just being seated. Half the town seemed to have decided to have dinner at the Pinewood.

Cassie nodded to a few people who waved to her, smiling at those who didn't. She wondered if her lips still looked swollen, or if mascara darkened her cheeks. She'd swiped at her eyes in the Jeep and run her fingers through her loose, bedraggled curls, but she knew she must look like something the cat had dragged in, only to toss out again.

Most people in Three Falls knew her since she'd grown up in this small town and become one of two veterinarians who helped the neighboring ranchers with their stock and the townspeople with their pets. Managing a bright smile, she tried to act as if dining with Colton McLean were the most natural thing in the world.

"Popular spot," Colton observed, glancing around the room as he hung both their jackets on a post separating their booth from the next.

"Maybe everyone knew we were coming," she quipped, sliding into the bench across from him.

Colton laughed, and Cassie felt most of the interested gazes turn back to their meals, though she was sure that Jessica as well as her father cast more than one sidelong glance in their direction.

A slow smile spread across Colton's face, and he leaned back casually, his dark hair falling over his forehead, his face a mask of ease.

A tiny waitress with a brunette ponytail swinging behind her and a uniform that matched the upholstery hurried toward their table. "Hi, I'm Penny," she said a trifle breathlessly as she handed them each a plastic-covered menu. "The specials tonight are stuffed trout and prime rib. I'll give you a few minutes to look over the menu, then I'll be back for your order." With a quick smile she scurried to the next table. She seemed nervous and flustered, as if this were her first night on the job.

Cassie quickly scanned the menu, which she knew by heart. After Vanessa had left, her father had brought her to the Pinewood every Thursday night. Though the restaurant had changed hands and decor several times, the menu hadn't varied much.

"I'll have the game hen," she decided when Penny appeared again. Colton ordered a steak and fries. Penny scribbled furiously, biting on her lower lip as she concentrated.

"Dessert?"

"Not for me," Cassie replied.

"I'll wait until after my meal," Colton put in.

"It'll just be a few minutes." Penny walked quickly to the counter, filled their drink orders and returned to set a glass of iced tea in front of Cassie and a chilled glass and bottle of beer on Colton's side of the table.

"If you need anything else, just let me know," she said, eager to please. As she dashed through swinging doors leading to the kitchen, Cassie sipped her tea and Colton nursed his beer. The front door swung open again, and a rush of cool night air followed a young man into the pine-paneled room.

Cassie looked casually toward the door, and her fingers tightened over her glass. Ryan Ferguson, his helmet tucked under one arm, strode to a booth near the front window, where a pulsating green-and-yellow neon sign promoted a local brand of beer.

Colton saw her lips part in surprise. "See a ghost?"

"We're not in the ghost town anymore," she replied, turning back to him.

But Colton's eyes narrowed on the man Cassie had watched entering the room. Tall and fit, with unkempt dusty blond hair and small brown eyes, he carried himself with a cocky aloofness that was emphasized by his black leather jacket and pants. Colton guessed his age around twenty-five, give or take a couple of years.

With obvious disdain, the man tossed his motorcycle helmet onto the seat next to him, unzipped his jacket and searched in a pocket for a pack of cigarettes. He didn't glance around the room at all and seemed in a world of his own as he lit up and blew a stream of smoke toward the ceiling.

"You know him?" Colton asked, wondering if the man had been Cassie's lover, then immediately discarded the idea. Cassie may have had her share of half-baked love affairs in the past years, but instinctively Colton guessed this guy wasn't her type.

"Don't you?"

Colton shook his head. "Should I?"

"He grew up around here. Worked for Denver. And now I guess he's going to work for Dad. His name is Ryan Ferguson."

The name sent off warning bells clanging through the back of Colton's mind. "Isn't he the guy you thought might have been out to get Denver because Denver fired him a while back?"

"One and the same. He's back in town."

"As of when?" Colton's mind raced to new conclusions. Was Ryan Ferguson the key to the puzzle of Black Magic's disappearance? Colton's gaze shifted quickly around the room. Several people had noticed Ryan's entrance. Bill Simpson's gray brows rose, then he turned back to his wife. Vince Monroe's eyes narrowed on the younger man. Colton swung his gaze back to Cassie. He asked again, "When did Ferguson blow back into town?"

Lifting a shoulder, Cassie swirled her straw in her tea. A lemon wedge shifted between the ice cubes. "I don't really know—a little while."

"And he's been working for your dad?"

"No. Dad just hired him this afternoon."

Colton's thoughts turned a new corner. Was it possible that Ryan Ferguson and Ivan Aldridge had been in on the horse-napping together? He didn't want to think so. "He doesn't look like the type your father would want hanging around."

"Dad needs help." She offered a feeble smile. "Because of my job, I'm gone a lot—a lot more than either Dad or I imagined. And I'll be moving out soon."

Colton's head snapped up. This was news. Cassie was actually going to cut the strings that bound her to Ivan? "Where to? When?"

"Probably an apartment here in town, sometime this summer."

Colton's concerns about Ryan Ferguson were shoved to the back of his mind. "Why?"

"It's time, don't you think? I just moved back home until some of my college debt was paid off and to lend Dad a hand. But as I said, I'm not around enough to help much, and now that I'm out of school, he can afford to pay someone."

"So why did he choose Ferguson?"

*I wish I knew,* Cassie thought. "Ryan needed a job, I guess."

Colton settled back in his booth and watched Ferguson throughout the meal. The man, though dressed in basic *Road Warrior* attire, seemed harmless enough. But, as Colton had learned from years of dealing with some of the most deadly terrorists in the world, looks could be deceiving. Ryan Ferguson was worth checking out.

Vince Monroe scraped back his chair. Colton glanced his way and caught the older man staring at him—hard—and the warning hairs on the back of his neck rose. Though Vince's big face remained bland, his eyes gave him away. Colton recognized cold, hard hatred in Vince's stare.

Jessica turned her head in Colton's direction, offered a wobbly smile, which Colton returned with a friendly grin, then walked out on her father's arm without a word.

"I get the impression the Monroes aren't crazy about me," Colton thought aloud, wondering just how many of the local ranchers felt alienated from the McLeans.

"Vince has had some bad luck."

"That's my fault?"

"No," Cassie admitted, rolling her napkin nervously. "But there is Jessica."

"I told you, there was never anything between Jessica and me."

"Does she know that? You know, it's just possible you hurt her, Colton, and if you did, her father wouldn't count you on his list of ten favorites."

Colton rubbed his jaw pensively. The hate sizzling in Monroe's glance couldn't be explained by the fact that Colton had gone out with Jessica a couple of times, then left town. "I don't think this has anything to do with Jessica. There's got to be more. What happened between the Monroes and the McLeans while I was gone?"

"I don't know, except that Vince was forced to sell some of his stock to Denver last year."

"I'd think he'd be pleased that Denver would bail him out," Colton said, his gaze following the stiff set of Vince's shoulders as the big man shoved the door open.

"I doubt it," she said, her appetite disappearing. "The same thing happened to Dad a few years ago. He had to sell a horse to Tessa before she married your brother. It never set well with him."

"Anything remotely associated with the McLeans doesn't set well with Ivan."

"He has his reasons," she added. "You know, Dad can be a wonderful, caring man. He's done nothing but take care of me all of my life. You just have to give him a chance."

To her surprise, he reached across the table and placed his hand over hers. "I'm trying, Cass. Believe me, I'm trying." His work-roughened fingers smoothed the skin across the back of her hand, and a ripple of pleasure ran up her arm. "Come on, I'd better get you home," he said with a cynical grin. "I wouldn't want to get on the bad side of your father."

"Right," she retorted, but grinned as he helped her into her coat.

Outside, the night was cool and still. Together they walked to the Jeep beneath a night-black sky. Cassie's lips felt cold, her skin chilled, and yet being with Colton created an inner warmth that radiated to her fingers.

As he opened the door for her, he grabbed her hand, gently pulling her against him and kissing her with all the passion of eight lost years. "Thanks for coming with me tonight," he whispered.

"Thanks for asking."

They drove back to the Aldridge ranch in silence, but Colton remembered the people in the café and the hostility he'd sensed, the crackle of unspoken anger. Not from everyone, of course, but the Monroes and the Wilkersons had been far from friendly—and then there was Ferguson. Ivan's hiring Ryan bothered him a great deal without his really knowing why.

Cassie touched his shoulder. "You look like you're a million miles away," she said, tucking her arm through his.

One corner of his lip lifted. "Not that far."

"Where?"

"Back at the restaurant." He shifted down and turned into the lane. The windshield wipers slapped the raindrops aside. "Has your father known Ferguson long?"

"All his life. Ryan grew up around here, too," she said. "Why?"

He drove into the yard. "Just curious."

"Or suspicious," she challenged.

"I guess I'm a little of both."

"Oh, Colton, I thought this was over," she said with a sigh. "I thought that since Black Magic was back, you'd be satisfied."

"Relieved. Not satisfied."

"Good night, Colton," she whispered, refusing to get into another argument. She grabbed the door handle, but Colton reached out and trapped her next to him.

"Don't go," he whispered against her ear. "Not yet."

"You could come inside."

Colton chuckled. "Ivan wouldn't like that much."

"He'd get over it." She smiled almost shyly and traced the hard line of his jaw with one finger. "Despite what you may think, he's not an ogre. He's been very good to me."

"And you've been good to him."

Blushing a little, she said, "Except where you're concerned."

Colton's teeth gleamed in the dark interior. "I haven't completely corrupted you yet," he murmured, his lips moving gently over her hair, causing goose bumps to rise on her skin. "But just give me time."

"I can't wait," she teased back, then caught her breath as he lowered his mouth over hers. Her heart began to beat wildly.

"Oh, Cass," he murmured thickly as he lifted his lips from hers. His eyes were glazed; his hands trembled as he touched her cheek. "What am I going to do with you?"

"I was just wondering the same about you," she admitted, her voice so husky she barely recognized it as her own.

"I'll call," he promised.

"And I'll hold you to it." She kissed him on the cheek, then scrambled out of his rig, waving as he shoved the Jeep into gear and took off in a spray of gravel. She stood in the yard, oblivious to the quiet, moonless night, as his taillights disappeared in the distance.

Lighthearted, she gathered her skirt in her fists and ran quickly along the path to the back porch.

She was still smiling to herself when she let herself into the house and found her father in the living room, his reading glasses poised on the tip of his nose as he worked on another crossword puzzle. Only one lamp burned, and the television, turned down so low she could barely hear a sound, gave off a pale gray glow.

"Have a good time?" Ivan asked. His voice was flat. He didn't bother looking up.

"The best!" She wasn't going to let her father's disapproval destroy her good mood. Not tonight.

Frowning, he slipped his glasses from his nose, then polished the lenses with the tail of his shirt. "I wish I knew what it was about Colton McLean that mixes you up."

"I'm *not* mixed up," she said, plopping down on a tired-looking ottoman and noticing the lines of strain that had deepened near the corners of her father's eyes.

"So now Colton McLean is a god again?"

"Not a god."

"Then a hero."

"No—but not a villain, either. He's just a man."

He snorted, tossing his folded newspaper aside. "You've gone out with a lot of men," he said quietly, "and not one of them has even made you smile."

"Not true, Dad."

"You never gave them a chance."

Cassie frowned. "What're you getting at?"

"Four years of college—then veterinary school. All that time and you didn't let one man get close to you—not really. And now Colton McLean blows back into town, sticking around only long enough for the bullet wound to heal, and you're acting like a schoolgirl with a fresh case of puppy love." He sighed heavily. "It's beyond me why you'd give a man who's only caused you heartache a chance to hurt you again."

Cassie didn't want her father to deflate her soaring spirits, so she said, "Look, we've been over this." Bending down, she placed a kiss on his forehead. "I'm okay."

"I hope so," she heard him whisper over the rustle of newspapers as she dashed up the stairs to her bedroom. In a way, her father was right, she supposed as she stared at her room with new eyes. It was a young girl's room. Though the movie posters and ruffles had been replaced years ago and her canopied bed was long gone, the evidence of her childhood remained. Everywhere, from the neglected records stacked in the closet to blue ribbons she'd won at a local fair, there were reminders of her youth, a girlhood devoid of a mother and an adolescence dominated by one single obsession: Colton McLean.

She swallowed hard as her father's advice rang in her ears. She was falling in love with Colton again, and there wasn't much she could or would do about it. But this time she was older, a grown professional woman with an education, a fledgling veterinary practice and a purpose in life. Colton McLean could never change that, nor could he determine her happiness as he once had. Or could he?

With a frustrated scowl, she dropped onto the eiderdown quilt of her brass bed and stared at the ceiling. Unconsciously she hugged a pillow to her chest and shoved aside any lingering doubts about her own future. She was her own woman, and nothing, not even Colton, could change that.

## Chapter Nine

The next afternoon, while she was handing a recuperating Himalayan kitten to its owner, Colton burst through the waiting room door. His gaze collided with Cassie's. "I need you," he said the minute Mrs. Anderson walked outside.

The look on his face was desperate. His jaw sported a day's growth of beard, his eyes seemed sunken and his knuckles were white as he rammed his fingers through his hair.

Cassie swallowed hard. How many years had she waited to hear those three words. But uttered in the middle of the waiting room, they didn't ring with the desperation and love she'd hoped to hear. "What's wrong?"

"It's Black Magic."

*Of course.* Cassie clamped her jaw together. *Always Black Magic.* "What about him?"

"Oh, hell, I don't know. But he's not right. He's not eating—and he seems weak. His temperature is over 103 degrees."

Cassie felt a stab of instant remorse for her selfish thoughts. "Is he coughing?"

"No."

"Nasal discharge?"

Colton rubbed his jaw pensively. "Not that I noticed. But he was restless last night."

"What about his vaccinations?" Cassie asked, considering the symptoms. "Are they up to date?"

"I assume so—Tessa and her old man are pretty sticky about that. They don't fool around when it comes to the animals and their health."

Cassie lifted an eyebrow. So Curtis Kramer had managed to change Colton's opinion about him. Maybe there was hope for the Aldridge team. "Let me check our records." Quickly Cassie flipped through the files, pulled up the chart for the McLean Ranch and scanned Black Magic's immunization record. "It looks current," she murmured, mentally checking off the most common problems as she read Black Magic's history. "Any other symptoms?"

Colton, his lips compressed, shook his head. "All I know is that this came on like that!" He snapped his fingers for emphasis. "I showed him to you just the other day. He was fine."

Nodding, Cassie remembered the sleek black stallion, the health that fairly oozed from his mischievous eyes and glossy ebony coat.

No wonder Colton was worried. "I'll come out and have a look," she said, managing a practiced, professional smile, which belied the fact she was concerned. "Maybe he's just having a bad couple of days." But she didn't believe it for a minute. Black Magic was healthy and young; there was no reason for him to be listless or out of sorts. "Craig should be back any minute," she said, checking her watch and the appointment book. Fortunately she'd seen her last scheduled case of the day.

Shrugging out of her lab coat, she said to Sandy, "If we get an emergency call or someone comes in before Craig gets back, telephone me at the McLean Ranch. Someone will be near a phone." She glanced at Colton for confirmation.

He nodded. "Milly's back at the house, and we have extensions in the barns."

"Good." With a few last-minute instructions to Sandy, she grabbed her veterinary bag and followed Colton outside.

"I'll give you a ride," he suggested, but Cassie shook her head. As much as she'd have liked to have a few minutes alone with him, she didn't want to end up stuck at the McLean Ranch depending upon him to take her home to her father's house.

"I'd better take my own truck. I'll meet you there."

Colton gave her a quick nod and hopped into his rig. Less than a minute later he'd headed out of town.

Cassie followed at a safe distance behind, wondering what could be wrong with Denver's prize stallion. Worries plagued her. Fever. Fever from what? Infection? Virus? She gnawed on her lower lip as she drove. The McLean Ranch was known for the high-quality care given its stock. Petty jealousies aside, most of the ranchers in the area respected Tessa Kramer McLean's handling of the horses and cattle. And Denver, since he'd returned, had proved himself a capable, caring rancher.

But both Tessa and Denver were gone—and had been for several weeks. What kind of a rancher was Colton? Hadn't he sworn to hate everything to do with the ranch? Wasn't he here only to recuperate?

"Stop it!" she muttered angrily to herself as she flipped on the radio. Obviously Colton cared about the ranch or he wouldn't have raced to the clinic, looking haggard and worn. Nor would he have assumed the responsibility for the ranch and stock if he hadn't been prepared to give it his all.

He was already out of his Jeep and talking to Curtis by the time she drove into the yard, which separated the main house from the stables and barns. His arms crossed over his chest, his face drawn, he listened as Curtis talked.

"...Afraid so," Curtis was saying as he puffed on the cigarette dangling from his lips and squinted through the smoke. "Whatever it is must be contagious." Casting a skeptical glance at Cassie, he added, "I hope you know your stuff." He tossed his cigarette to the gravel and ground it out with the toe of his boot.

"Contagious?" Her heart sank. "Another horse has symptoms?"

"See for yourself." Without another word, the wiry ranch foreman led Cassie and Colton into the stallion barn.

The minute she saw Black Magic, Cassie knew Colton's fears were well-founded. Something was wrong—very wrong.

Gone was the handsome, vital stallion she'd seen only days before. Now Black Magic held his head stiffly; his eyes, once bright, were dull. "Poor baby," Cassie murmured as she examined him carefully, running her fingers over his body, checking nose, mouth, ears and eyes. His temperature had climbed to 104 degrees, his pulse had elevated significantly, and there was some nasal discharge.

"Well?" Colton asked, frowning as she carefully touched the stallion's jaw. Her fingers encountered hot swelling over his lymph nodes, and Black Magic tossed back his head, knocking Cassie's hand away from the abscess.

"It looks like strangles," she said.

"Strangles? What the hell is that?"

Curtis swore roundly and shook his head. "Distemper."

"Damn!" Colton pressed his lips together in mute frustration.

"He's got to be isolated immediately."

"Might already be too late," Curtis muttered.

"Too late for what?" Colton demanded.

"To protect the other animals. This stuff runs through a stable like wildfire," Cassie said. "Anything he's come in contact with could be contaminated. All his feeding and grooming utensils should be disinfected daily in an antiseptic solution. All the straw in his box will have to be burned." She flipped her bag open, located a hypodermic and bottle of penicillin. "His throat's sore, so I want him fed warm mashes. And don't feed him on the ground—use a sterile bucket. Keep him inside for the next couple of days, but make sure he gets plenty of fresh air." Quickly she injected Black Magic, then reached into her bag again and handed Colton a tube of medication. "Apply this liniment over his abscess so it will mature faster and can be drained."

Colton stared at the sick stallion. "Isn't there some vaccine against this sort of thing?"

Cassie nodded thoughtfully. "There is, but it's controversial. I don't even use it on our stock. Too many side effects. The best prevention is to avoid exposure." She glanced down the row of stalls in the stallion barn. "What's he been in contact with? Any other horses?"

"That's the million-dollar question, isn't it?" Colton tossed back at her, his eyes narrowing. "No one here knows."

"But—" she started to argue, then understood.

"Obviously he caught something while he was gone," he surmised sardonically. "Son of a—"

"You don't know when he contracted the disease," she cut in.

"It's a pretty damned good guess!"

Curtis stepped in before Cassie could answer. "Let's just calm down," he suggested, eyeing both Cassie and Colton. "Is this going around?"

Stung by Colton's hot retort, she said, "Not that I know of, but Craig was called over to the Monroe ranch this morning and he's been at Matt Wilkerson's this afternoon."

"What for?"

"I'm not sure," she said worriedly. "But some of their horses weren't feeling well."

Colton clamped his jaw tight. "Looks like there might be an epidemic, although this stallion—" he hooked a thumb at Black Magic "—hasn't been in contact with any horse other than those on this ranch and those he met while he was gone!" He glared at Cassie for a second before his face slackened as if he'd realized arguing wouldn't help. He swung his gaze to Curtis. "You said there was another horse with symptoms?"

"Tempest."

Colton sucked in a swift breath. Tempest wasn't one of the finest horses on the ranch. In fact he was pretty much mean-tempered and nondescript. For those very reasons he appealed to Colton. In the past few months Tempest had become Colton's favorite mount. "Great," he murmured sarcastically. "Let's check him out."

Cassie had to run to keep up with Colton's long strides. His boots sounded on the concrete, and inquisitive dark heads poked from the stalls as Cassie walked quickly to the far end of the stables.

Colton stopped at one box, and Cassie nearly ran into him. She looked into the stall and sighed inwardly. Tempest was sick all right. The sorrel stallion looked listless and weak. His water and feed hadn't been touched. Cassie guessed his temperature was high, his pulse elevated. She washed her hands, snapped on a new pair of gloves and examined him as she had Black Magic.

"Has he got it, too?" Colton asked.

"Yes." Wearily Cassie blew a strand of hair from her eyes. These two horses were just the first in the McLean stable to come down with the disease. She found a new needle and a dose of antibiotic, which she gave to Tempest before patting the stallion's shoulder.

She slipped out of the stall, stripped out of her gloves and reached again into her veterinary bag. Handing a large bottle of antibiotic tablets to Colton, she instructed, "I want Tempest and Black Magic quarantined."

"How serious is this?" Colton asked.

Cassie didn't mince words. "It's serious, but unless either horse develops complications, they should survive."

"What kind of complications?"

"Pneumonia for starters."

Colton exhaled heavily. "Pneumonia, huh? Great. Just goddamn great."

Wishing she could offer him some consolation, she said, "Pneumonia's just one of the complications, but let's not worry about that now. Both your stallions are young and strong. The antibiotics usually work. Tempest and Black Magic should make it, but the next few weeks are going to be rough."

"As long as they pull through."

"They should—really." Without thinking, she touched his arm, and the muscles beneath his sleeve flexed. Cassie turned to the foreman. "Are there any other horses with symptoms?"

"Not so far. Len checked the entire herd."

"Including Tessa's animals?" she asked, knowing how dear Tessa's horses were to Colton's sister-in-law.

Curtis nodded stiffly. "They looked fine."

"What about any neighboring mares the stallions may have serviced?"

"The first mares were due to arrive next week." His lips pursed together as if pulled on a drawstring. "I suppose that's out, right?"

"Absolutely. You have no choice but to cancel."

Curtis's old shoulders drooped.

"Now wait a minute," Colton cut in. "We can't—"

"You don't have a choice! You're lucky only two of your horses are infected!"

"She's right," Curtis said, frowning so deeply his face became a mass of lines.

"I'll have Len clean out their stalls and disinfect everything," Curtis said as he snapped a lead rope on Tempest. "We'll stable them in the old foaling shed. Come along." Curtis clucked his tongue and gently pulled on the lead. Tempest, his head extended rigidly, followed docilely behind.

Colton, leading an equally sluggish Black Magic, opened the door, trailing Curtis toward a weathered older building that was now used only for storage.

Slowly the unhappy caravan made its way across the yard and through two paddock gates to the small building. Inside, the shed was clean and light. While Cassie held the horses, Curtis and Colton swabbed the floor with antiseptic, then quickly spread straw and carried feed and water to the horses. Neither stallion took any notice.

Cassie's heart went out to the sick animals. Though, if lucky, they would both survive, the disease could disable and scar them. Once the stallions were settled, she said, "I think I'd better look over the rest of your herd." Mentally crossing her fingers, she silently prayed she'd find no other horse with symptoms.

"You think it's spread?" Colton's voice was grim, as if he was steeling himself for the worst.

"I hope not," she whispered, stuffing her hands into the pockets of her skirt. For the next three hours she examined every horse on the McLean Ranch, including the swollen-bellied mares ready to foal.

Colton never left her side, studying each animal as she did, waiting, his face gaunt, to hear that yet another horse was stricken.

"So far, so good," Cassie said as she examined the last of the horses, a chestnut with a crooked white blaze—Tessa's favorite stallion, Brigadier.

Impatient at being examined, Brigadier minced this way and that in his stall, shifting his sleek rump and hind-quarters away from Cassie's expert hands or jerking his head away when she attempted to look into his eyes and nostrils. "Feisty one, aren't you?" Cassie murmured, relieved she hadn't found any more cases of strangles than the first two.

Brigadier snorted haughtily, and Cassie gave him a play-ful slap on the rump. "This one's healthy!" Encouraged slightly, she squeezed through the stall gate and walked outside with Colton.

"For how long?" Colton asked.

"I wish I knew. It depends. Has he been in contact with the infected horses?"

Colton shook his head. "Tessa's always kept her horses separate, even after she and Denver married."

"And the rest of the herd?"

"You've seen it. The mares and foals are in one field, the yearlings in another, the stallions and geldings even more isolated. In fact, since Black Magic's been back, he hasn't been around any of the other horses—including Tempest."

"Then maybe you're safe," she said as she scanned the maze of pastures and paddocks comprising the ranch. The evening air was moist, but warm. The last streaks of sun-light blazed across the mountains, gilding the highest peaks and streaking the sky with swatches of lavender and ma-genta. Playful fillies and colts scampered through the lush grass, kicking and bucking, galloping in uneven strides through the fields.

"Aside from another animal, how does a horse get it?"

"Contaminated surroundings, water or food. Some-times from droppings or from contaminated utensils."

"What's the incubation period?"

"Two days to a couple of weeks."

He raked stiff fingers through his hair, shoving a way-ward clump that hung over his forehead back. "So any horse that's come in contact with Black Magic could be infected?"

"Yes." She could tell by Colton's grim expression that he understood the size of the epidemic he might have on his hands.

Guilt weighting his shoulders, Colton felt as if he hadn't slept in days. "I guess I'd better call Denver." Absently rubbing his wounded shoulder, he grimaced. He'd kept Black Magic's disappearance from Denver to save him any worry, and it had blown up in his face. Denver would be furious!

"Do you want me to talk to him?" Cassie asked.

"This is my problem," he snapped. Then, hearing the bite in his words, Colton forced a thin smile. "I mean, I'll handle it. But why don't you come with me—as my backup. Just in case Denver wants a more professional opinion."

"Fair enough."

Gritting his teeth, Colton strode into the house, marched into the den, picked up the phone and dialed.

As he waited for the connection, he sat on a corner of the desk and drummed his fingers on the scarred wood. Explaining this would be hell. The phone rang four times before a recording answered. "Great," Colton muttered. He wasn't about to tell a recording machine what was going on. Instead, he just asked Denver to call him as soon as possible.

"No luck?" Cassie asked.

Colton laughed bitterly. "I think I ran out of luck about six months ago."

"Things'll get better."

"Will they?" he asked, squinting through the window to the yard beyond. He watched as Len and Curtis, their backs bowed with feed sacks, trudged into the broodmare barn. "Is that your *professional* opinion?"

"No."

"I didn't think so." He rubbed the tight knot forming in the muscles between his shoulders. God, he was tired. He'd been awake most of the night, tossing and turning on that damned cot, his mind filled with images of Cassie and the ranch and a future that was far away. A future spent looking through the lens of a camera in some godforsaken land. Alone. Without Cassie.

She had dropped onto the arm of a worn couch and was staring at him with those wide, soul-searching eyes. The kindness and concern in her gaze bothered him. "Are you okay?" she asked.

"Do I look okay?"

Cassie smiled faintly. "The truth?"

"Don't hold back."

"You look like hell," she said.

"Thanks for the compliment." He forced one corner of his mouth up. "That's better than I feel."

"It's not your fault."

"Isn't it? I lost the horse, didn't I? It happened while I was in charge!"

"Wait a minute, Colt! Before you go on an extended guilt trip, let's look at the facts, okay?" She pushed herself to her feet, and her cheeks flushed. "We're not certain Black Magic caught this while he was 'lost.' And as far as you being responsible, I don't think you should be beating yourself up over it. The same thing happened last year and you weren't even here!"

"Last year Black Magic survived."

"And he just might this year," she said, crossing the room to stand only bare inches from him, "unless we all give up on him! Have some faith."

"Do you?"

"I told you, usually the disease isn't deadly."

She was so close that Colton could see the ribbons of green in her hazel eyes, smell the scent of her. Her black hair gleamed in soft, tangled curls that rested against her cheeks and fell past her shoulders. "And what else do you have faith in Cass?" he asked, reaching forward, curling his fingers around her arms.

Cassie didn't breathe. Her gaze flickered downward to where his long legs swung from the corner of the desk, brushing intimately against her skirt.

"That . . ." She swallowed hard. "That depends."

"On?" Colton's blood began to surge through his body. She was, without a doubt, the most bewitching woman he'd ever met.

"On you, Mr. McLean," she said, her lips parting, the pulse at the hollow of her throat leaping out of control. "I'd like to have faith in you."

His insides turned molten.

"Maybe you should."

She tilted her chin. "Should I? Why?" she asked, her warm breath fanning his face.

"Colton? You in there?" Milly Samms's voice drifted through the door. A loud rap echoed through the room.

Cassie froze in his arms for just a second. Blushing like a teenager, she quickly stepped back.

Colton, slightly amused, cleared his throat, but his voice was still raspy. "Come in."

"It's time for din—" Milly stopped in mid-sentence as she stepped into the room. "Oh, Cassie! I didn't realize you were still here."

Cassie stuffed her hands into the pockets of her skirt. "I thought I'd stay awhile, until we were sure none of the horses came down with the virus."

"Virus?" Milly asked.

Colton explained about Black Magic and Tempest, and told the housekeeper about the possibility of an epidemic. "I tried to get hold of Denver, but he was out. If he calls back, I want to talk to him. Immediately."

Milly's round face had turned ashen. "What about the foals?"

"So far, so good," Cassie said, "but I think I'd better stick around for a while."

"Then come on in to dinner," Milly insisted.

Cassie held up a hand. "No, I couldn't—"

"Nonsense. I always make enough to feed the entire third battalion, so you just come along." Before Cassie could protest any further, Milly swept out the door and hurried off toward the kitchen.

"I really can't," Cassie said to Colton once the house-keeper's footsteps had faded.

"Why not?"

"Because. I don't want to intrude—"

"You won't. Besides, I want you to stay." He touched her lightly under the chin, forcing her gaze to his, and for the first time that day Cassie saw tenderness tempering the passion in his eyes.

She swallowed nervously. Staying with Colton seemed natural and right, and she might be able to help if any of the rest of the stock came down with the virus.

"Don't tell me," Colton joked, "you've got a better offer."

"Millions of them."

"I thought so."

Cassie's lips turned up at the corners. "Actually I'm on my own tonight. Dad's playing cards with some friends."

"Then I insist."

"And I accept," she said, burying any lingering doubts. Tonight Colton needed her, and, unfortunately, she needed him.


Milly Samms proved an excellent cook. By the time the pork chops, potatoes, gravy, fresh asparagus and cherry pie had been served and devoured, Cassie was stuffed.

Curtis and Len had already left. Only she, Milly and Colton lingered over half-full cups of coffee at the Mc-

Leans' large dining room table. "I'll help with the dishes," she offered, but Milly wouldn't hear of it.

"You go tend to the horses, and I'll handle this."

"But—"

Colton reached over and squeezed her hand. "Don't argue," he said. "The kitchen is Milly's turf. She kicked me out just the other day."

"And a lucky thing, too," Milly said, picking up a few of the platters of leftover meat and potatoes. "This place was fallin' down around your ears and you didn't even know it."

"It was just a little messy."

"A little? A little, he says," she muttered under her breath, chuckling to herself.

Cassie reached for the butter dish. "At least let me clear—"

"No way. You're the guest, remember? Now put that down." Casting Cassie a look that dared her to defy her authority, Milly carried a stack of dishes through the swinging doors to the kitchen.

Cassie felt a bitter pang of disbelief. Milly had referred to her as a guest. In the McLean house. Never in all of her twenty-five years had she entered the house as a guest; not even when, years before, she'd thought she would marry Colton. She was an Aldridge—not a friend.

"I'm the veterinarian," she corrected, shoving her chair back. "And I'd better go check on Black Magic."

The phone rang, and Colton jumped. "Denver," he said just as Milly called, "Colt—Denver wants to talk to you."

"Here goes nothing," he mumbled under his breath, but said more loudly, "I'll get it in the den." Cassie shoved back her chair and started for the door, but Colton added, "Don't leave until I'm done talking with my brother."

She glanced over her shoulder. "I wasn't planning on it."

"Good." Colton walked into the den and snatched up the telephone receiver. "I'm glad you called," he said, stretching the truth a little. "We've got a problem." Blow by blow, he explained about Black Magic's disappearance, return and subsequent poor health.

Denver didn't say a word—not one comment as Colton continued. But the tension stretching over the telephone wires was nearly palpable.

"...So hopefully, none of the other horses are infected," Colton finished.

"Hopefully? *Hopefully*?"

"It's still too early to tell."

"Damn!" Denver swore long and loud. When he was through ranting and raving, he growled, "And you're sure Tessa's horses are okay?"

"I can't be sure of anything," Colton admitted, running a hand over his scratchy jaw. "But they're the least likely as they haven't been near Magic or Tempest."

"I guess I should be thankful for small favors."

"I suppose," Colton said, feeling defensive. Was this really his fault? Or should someone have clued him in that Magic was lost last year? He leaned a hip against the desk. There was no reason to start pointing fingers anyway. It wouldn't change a thing.

"Son of a bitch!" Denver was still showing off his rather limited vocabulary.

"Exactly."

"We can't leave tonight—but we can cut the trip short by a week."

"I don't see why. There's nothing more you can do."

"Except wring the neck of the bastard who stole Black Magic in the first place! Obviously Magic caught the virus while he was gone."

"Looks that way." Colton heard Denver's swift intake of breath.

"Do you think it was deliberate?"

"Deliberate?" Colton repeated, his gaze shifting around the room.

"Yeah. Isn't it possible that whoever's behind all this is more deadly than you think? Maybe stealing Black Magic was more than just an irritating prank."

Colton didn't like Denver's line of reasoning. "You honestly think someone would infect Black Magic on purpose?"

"Hell, I don't know!" Denver thundered. "But you have to admit it's a distinct possibility. In fact, it's downright plausible!"

"That's a little farfetched," Colton said, wondering if his brother were even more jaded than he.

"Is it? **No** more farfetched than someone stealing the horse just to cause a little trouble! Think about it, for God's sake! Strangles could cripple the ranch. Not only could we lose livestock and rack up a fortune in vet bills, but the stallions will be out of commission during the breeding season. No one in his right mind would send a mare to a ranch with that virus floating around. This was no accident!"

"No way—"

"It's happening, damn it!" Denver nearly shouted.

Colton suddenly felt tired. What if Denver was right? He closed his eyes and listened to his brother's rapid, angry breathing. "Look, I'll warn Curtis and tell him what you think. I'm not saying you're right, but I suppose there's the chance someone's that vindictive."

"Someone like Ivan Aldridge."

Colton didn't comment. Even he didn't think Ivan was capable of anything so treacherous. "It's not Aldridge."

"How do you know? Has anyone talked to him?"

"I have. He and Cassie swear he's not involved."

"He and *Cassie?* What's she got to do with it?"

"She's here now. She's the one who diagnosed Black Magic."

Denver's breath hissed between his teeth. "Why not Fulton?"

Colton's back stiffened. "He was busy," he snapped.

For a minute Denver didn't say anything, but Colton could feel the anger, the unspoken accusations crackling over the thin telephone wires. "Keep me posted," he finally ordered.

"Will do." Colton hung up feeling oddly protective of Cassie and her father. Though there was no love lost between Ivan and himself, Colton couldn't imagine the man intentionally hurting any animal—even an animal belonging to the McLeans. Nor did he think anyone around here would. Ranching stock was looked upon with a reverence that couldn't be compromised.

He walked through the kitchen and found Milly putting the last of the dishes in the dishwasher. "How did Denver take the news?" she asked as Colton reached for his hat and jacket near the door.

"About as well as I expected."

"That bad?" she quipped, but the joke fell flat.

"Worse," he muttered, glancing around the kitchen. Nearly everything was put away. "Why don't you take off?"

"In a few minutes." She polished the bottom of a gleaming copper pot and looked up to offer an encouraging smile.

Colton kicked open the door and strode quickly down the back steps. Outside, the sky was dark. A few pale clouds drifted across a half moon, and the breeze brushing his cheeks held the lingering chill of winter.

His boots crunched on the gravel as he strode across the yard. Was it possible? Would someone intentionally try to destroy the McLeans—and use the livestock to do it? The ugly thought soured his stomach as he yanked open the door to the old foaling shed.

There he found Cassie with Black Magic. She was talking quietly to the horse, her voice soothing, her hands gentle as they ran along his neck and shoulders. Glancing up at Colton, she forced a thin smile. "His fever hasn't gone up."

"Is that good?"

"I think so—but it's still too early to tell."

"And Tempest?"

"No change. Neither one has eaten anything." She slipped out of the stall and washed her hands while Colton observed both stallions. Listless and dull, Tempest barely flicked his ears when Colton walked to his stall. His head was still painfully extended, and his eyes held no spark.

"Hang in there," Colton whispered, wondering if the once-ornery stallion would take a turn for the worse.

"What did Denver have to say?"

"Nothing good," Colton evaded. There wasn't any reason to confide in Cassie—not yet. Denver's theory was just angry words. When he calmed down a little, he would probably change his mind. Or would he? Uncomfortable, Colton glanced from Cassie back to Black Magic, wondering who was responsible for this mess and coming up with only his own name.

"I want to check the other horses again before I leave," Cassie said. "Just in case."

"Right." Colton led the way through the various buildings. Fortunately all the horses, though disturbed slightly at the unusual intrusion, looked fine. Colton waited for Cassie at the door and snapped out the lights as she walked outside.

Aside from her truck and Colton's Jeep, the parking lot was empty. Milly and the hands had already left. With Colton at her side, Cassie started for her car, but he grabbed her hand, turning her to face him. He didn't want her to leave, not just yet. Having her here was comforting. She looked up at him expectantly, and his insides quivered. "If I didn't say it before, thanks for dropping everything and coming over."

"All part of my job," she replied.

He didn't let go of her hand. "But you stayed. That was above and beyond the call of duty."

"Not really." Somewhere in the distance a night bird called plaintively, and a mild breeze caught in her hair and murmured through the trees. Cassie's eyes were luminous in the pale moonlight. Withdrawing her hand, she wrapped her arms around herself, as if she were chilled to the bone.

"Cold?"

"I'll survive."

"Come here." Before he really knew what he was doing, he reached forward and drew her into the circle of his arms, pulled her close against him, her legs inside his.

Closing his eyes, he blocked out his worries about the ranch, his doubts about his occupation, and even the past. He only thought about the here and now. His heart slammed out of control as he lowered his head and brushed his lips over hers.

"Colton..." she whispered in protest. "Maybe we should think about this—"

"Too late," he murmured into her mouth, and any other arguments were stilled as he pressed his tongue insistently against her teeth. With a soft moan, she parted her lips.

Colton's pulse pounded in his brain. Desire became an obsession, fortifying his blood, numbing his mind to anything but this one, gorgeous woman. She didn't resist any longer. Her body was soft and pliant as he spread his hands across her back. Her mouth opened willingly, deliciously. He touched her tongue, and it danced with his.

She wound her arms around his chest, her fingers pressed against his back.

He couldn't stop himself. He groaned, kissing her harder, his lips demanding, hers yielding. His mind forgot everything but Cassie—sweet, beautiful Cassie.

Unbuttoning her blouse, he let the fabric fall open, exposing the swell of her breast, her creamy white skin mounding gently over the white lace of her bra. Beneath the sculpted lace, her nipple was dusky and taut, poking out enticingly.

The fire in Colton's loins burned hotter, and without a thought to time or space, he slid a silky strap from her shoulder with one hand, while pressing against the small of her back with the other. Her breast spilled over the lace, full and ripe, her tiny veins visible beneath the creamy skin.

Colton wound his legs around hers as he took her nipple in his mouth and pulled gently with tongue and teeth.

"Oh, Lord," she murmured as he suckled and nuzzled, her sweet, sure femininity enveloping him in a seductive cloud of passion and promise.

His hands shook as he lifted the gentle white swell and licked the dark button to hardness. Cassie's head lolled back, her throat arched, her hips fit snug against his.

Colton could barely stand as he turned his attention to the other lace-ensnared nipple, and he fanned his breath across the flimsy fabric. Her fingers twined in his hair, Cassie guided his mouth to the sweet, dark bud, and he took her breast, lace and all, into his mouth, leaving the other to be cooled by the chill spring breeze.

He could no longer stand on unsteady legs, and he dragged Cassie to the ground. Oblivious to the grass, he caressed her body, found her lips again and kissed her with an intensity that numbed his brain. "Stay with me," he whispered against her ear, feeling her tremble beneath him.

"I—I can't."

"Sure you can."

"Oh, Colton..." Knowing she was courting disaster, Cassie felt herself giving in. She'd simply have to find some way to explain her absence to her father... and she was old enough to make her own decisions.

Colton moved his hands seductively against her skin, and her mind spun in crazy, delicious circles. A liquid warmth deep in her center swept through her blood, carrying her away on a moon-kissed cloud of passion.

The cool night air touched her bare breast, then Colton's hot lips followed, dipping lower to her abdomen, his fingers finding the waistband of her skirt.

"Make love to me, Cassie," he rasped, his voice sounding far away. "Make love to me and never stop. Don't stop."

Where had she heard those words before? she wondered vaguely. Then, with searing clarity she remembered that it had been she who had pleaded with him to make love to her, to take away her virginity, to *love* her.

She froze, and the desire burning so bright only moments before cooled. "I—I think I'd better leave," she said, squirming under his insistent caress.

Colton lifted his head, and her heart constricted. His features, washed in the pale moon glow, seemed more clearly defined and angular than usual. His eyes, as silver as the moon-washed land, burned with passion. "Why?" he asked, his voice so low she could barely hear it.

"I'm not ready to make the same mistake twice."

"This is *not* a mistake."

"Then it'll wait," she said, swallowing back the urge to tell him she loved him. She sat up then to adjust her bra and, afterward, forced her hands to her sides when all she wanted was to place her palms against his cheeks and kiss him.

"What happened, Cass?"

"A severe case of déjà vu." Straightening her blouse, she was glad for the shadows in the night, thankful he couldn't see the blush burning her neck and staining her cheeks.

Colton pulled himself into a sitting position and jammed his fingers through his hair. "We're not kids anymore."

"Then maybe we'd better stop acting like them!"

His eyes blazed. "All right. Let's start again—more mature this time. I want you to stay with me, Cassie," he said, his gaze piercing hers with an intensity so powerful, she couldn't look away. "Stay here. In my bed. Spend the night with me."

*Oh, God.* The temptation was almost too much. *Alone with Colton—for an entire night!* "Sorry," she replied, hoping to sound sophisticated, though her voice was strangled. "I'm not into one-night stands . . . Ooh!"

As quickly as a cat, Colton shoved her back onto the ground, pinning her shoulders against the earth. "I wouldn't call eight years a one-night stand."

"Eight years?" she repeated. "Eight years? When were we together in the past eight years? And where were you? Who were you with?"

Some of the anger disappeared from his eyes. "There weren't many, Cass," he admitted with a sigh. "And none of them held a candle to you."

Her throat burned, and she wanted to believe him. Oh, God, how she wanted to believe him.

The fingers forcing her down became gentler. "What about you?" he asked quietly.

"You want to know about my lovers? All of them?" she asked, and was surprised at the pain in his eyes.

"No—that's your business, I suppose."

"Well, there were none. Not in college and not here," she admitted, suddenly wanting him to know, to understand just how important he'd been.

"None?" he hurled back at her, disbelieving.

"*Nada.*"

"Oh, Cass," he whispered, releasing her. "No wonder your father hates me."

"He doesn't—"

"Of course he does." Standing, he dusted off his hands, then offered one to her.

She took his hand, and he pulled her up but didn't let go of her fingers. "You know," he admitted. "I've always cared about you. Always."

The lump in her throat swelled, and she could barely get out her reply. "S-so you said."

He kissed her forehead so tenderly she nearly broke apart inside. "Please," he whispered, "stay."

"Not tonight." Pulling her hand away, she shook her head. "Not yet. Before I sleep with you, Colton, I want to think things through."

"That sounds a little cold and calculating."

"No. It sounds smart." Placing her hands on his shoulders, she lifted herself to her toes and kissed him on his forehead. "Last time I thought with my heart, this time I'll use my head."

Before she could draw away, his arms circled her waist. "Tell me," he asked, "just how much does your father hate me and Denver?"

"Denver I'm not sure about, but he detests you."

Colton was silent, his expression unreadable.

"That isn't a surprise, is it?"

"No." He lifted a shoulder as if he didn't care, but Cassie felt there was something he was holding back—something he wasn't telling her as he released her.

He walked her back to her pickup, but he didn't say another word. And as she drove away, she saw him standing in the moonlight, his shoulders rigid, his back ramrod straight, his fists planted on his hips.

## Chapter Ten

Confounded things!" Ivan yanked on his boots, grimacing until his foot slid inside. Seated near the wood stove, he glared up at Cassie. "You got in late last night."

Cassie nodded. "I was at the McLean place. Two of their horses have come down with strangles."

"Strangles?" His booted foot clattered to the floor. "Around here?"

"Looks that way to me."

"Which horses?"

"Black Magic and another stallion—a sorrel named Tempest."

Glancing at his watch, Ivan straightened and massaged a kink from his back. He crossed the kitchen and filled a blue enamel cup with the coffee warming on the stove. Was it her imagination, or had he paled slightly? "The rest of the herd okay?" He offered her the mug.

"As far as I can tell. But I was going to stop by on my way into town." She took a sip of the bitter coffee and made a face. "Why can't you learn to make a decent cup of coffee?"

"It's fine," he grumbled, "you're just picky. I sent you off to college, and what did you come home with?"

"A degree," she teased.

"That and some 'refined' tastes," he kidded back, but the familiar spark in his eyes didn't appear. "You gonna be late again?"

"I don't know," she said, thinking of Colton and Denver McLean's ailing horses.

Ivan dashed his coffee into the sink, then grabbed his jacket. "I'll see you later," he said. "I've got to feed the stock, then run into town to order some parts for the John Deere." Whistling to Erasmus, he sauntered outside.

Through the window, Cassie watched him cross the yard. He stopped to pet a few of the mares' muzzles and laughed out loud at a skittish colt's antics before he disappeared into the barn. He'd been good to her, she thought as she slung the strap of her purse over her shoulder and pushed open the screen door. She was greeted by the dewy scent of morning and the obtrusive whine of a motorcycle engine shattering the crisp air.

Ryan Ferguson was on his way to work. His employment shouldn't bother her, she told herself as she tossed her purse into the cab of her truck, but it did. She waited until he'd brought the cycle to a stop, switched off the engine, yanked off his helmet and swung off the bike. His hair stuck out in uneven blond tufts, and he smoothed it with the flat of his hand.

"You nearly ran me off the road the other day," she said as he lifted interested brown eyes to hers.

"Didn't mean to."

"You should look where you're going."

"I do." One side of his thin mouth lifted cynically. "You shouldn't hog the entire lane. There was room enough. Besides, Ivan gave me enough of a lecture." He glanced around the yard. "Is he here?"

"In the barn."

"Don't bother showing me in," he mocked. "I'll find my way." He left his helmet on the seat of his motorcycle and without a backward glance turned toward the barn. Erasmus, startled as he'd been lying under his favorite juniper bush, growled a little. "Ah, shut up," Ryan muttered, pushing hard on the barn's creaking door.

"Wonderful man," Cassie told herself, wishing her father hadn't hired him as she climbed into the cab. Ryan Ferguson had never done anything wrong—at least nothing that had been proven—and yet she didn't like him. Nor did she trust him.

She sent a scathing glance toward the gleaming black motorcycle before shoving the old truck into gear. She clenched her fingers over the wheel, and her thoughts turned to Colton and how close she'd come to staying with him.

As she'd driven home, she'd argued with herself and been glad that her father had already turned in for the night. She, too, had been bone-tired, and even though she'd thought about Colton McLean, even fantasized about him a bit, she'd fallen asleep quickly. So she hadn't had too much time to consider the subtle change in their relationship.

"Don't kid yourself," she said, shooting a glance at her reflection in the rearview mirror, "nothing about your relationship is subtle. Nothing about Colton is subtle. That's the problem."

Shifting down, she turned into the lane leading up to the small rise on which the McLean house stood so grandly. The two-storied farmhouse gleamed in the morning sunlight, though for years it had been allowed to run down until Denver had returned. Denver had brought with him the cash for a fresh coat of paint, new shingles and repairs.

Spying Colton's Jeep, she caught her lower lip between her teeth and tried not to notice that her pulse had quickened. *This is business*, she told herself as she parked near the garage, grabbed her veterinary bag and hurried to the front door, where she pounded on the thick, painted panels. Within seconds she heard a scurrying of feet.

The door swung open, and Milly, wiping her hands on her ever-present apron, forced a tired smile. "Thank goodness you're here. The men are up at the old foaling shed."

Cassie's heart sank. She knew instantly from the deep lines between Milly's eyebrows that one or both of the horses had taken a turn for the worse.

"It's Tempest. He was down this morning," Milly said.

"Why didn't Colton call me?" Cassie asked.

"He did. Just a little while ago. Your father said you were on your way."

Cassie didn't wait for any further explanation. She raced down the steps, rounded the house and ran through long grass to the smallest of the outbuildings.

She shoved against the door, and it creaked open. Inside, the scents of horses, leather and dust mingled together. Dust motes swirled in front of the windows as she breezed down the short corridor to the end stall.

Colton and Curtis, their shoulders drooped, were already inside the stall. "How is he?"

"Not good," Curtis bit out.

The foreman was right. Tempest seemed weak. His head hung at an alarming angle.

Cassie didn't waste any time. She slipped into the stall and examined him quickly. His temperature was soaring, and his pulse was much too rapid. "Come on, boy," she whispered, wishing there were something she could do and feeling absolutely helpless. What good were degrees and all her training when she couldn't save this horse? "Just hang in there." She patted his shoulder, then checked his food and water. "Has he eaten anything?"

"Isn't interested." Curtis shoved his hair beneath his hat. "We forced the antibiotics down him, but that's about it."

"Water?"

"A little."

"I don't want him to dehydrate," she snapped.

Curtis shoved his hat back on his head. "Neither do we."

Feeling helpless, she patted Tempest's soft muzzle, then walked back to Black Magic's stall. "This one looks better," she said, a little relieved. A cantankerous spark flared in Black Magic's gaze.

Colton's lips thinned. "But for how long?"

"I don't know," she admitted. "Has anyone checked on the other horses?"

"Yep." Curtis dug in his breast pocket, reaching for a crumpled pack of cigarettes. "Len and I looked 'em all over this morning. Everything looks okay."

"That's the good news," Colton said thoughtfully as they walked outside and he shut the door securely behind him. "What little of it there is."

Curtis lit up and blew a stream of smoke toward the blue Montana sky. "I'll see about cleaning all the tack—makin' sure that Black Magic's and Tempest's things are gone over. And we'll clean out the stalls and wash all the equipment again." He ambled toward the tack room, leaving Colton and Cassie alone.

Colton rammed his hands into the back pockets of his jeans. His expression pensive, he scoured the valley floor with his gaze, as if he could find some clue to an unsolved puzzle. "When I got through to Denver last night, I told him everything that had been going on in the past few weeks—including the fact that Black Magic was missing for a while."

Cassie's stomach knotted. She could tell just by looking at him that something important was to follow, and she guessed what it was. "He thinks the horse was stolen and that Dad did it," she said without any emotion.

"He's *convinced* the horse was stolen. What he's not sure about is if the horse contracted the disease by accident or if it was done on purpose."

"On purpose?" she repeated, her mouth dropping open. "What do you mean?" But the ugly realization was beginning to dawn on her. "Oh, Colton, no! He couldn't think someone would intentionally hurt one of your horses!" she said, horrified at the implications. "That's—that's tantamount to germ warfare!"

Colton nodded, shoving the brim of his hat away from his eyes. "I'm just telling you what his gut reaction was."

"Then his gut reaction was wrong!"

"He didn't seem to think so."

"And you? What about you?" She grabbed at the smooth leather sleeve of his jacket. "Tell me you think he's wrong," she demanded, her eyes boring into his, her fingers clenched anxiously. He couldn't think Ivan was involved in anything so sinister.

"I hope he's wrong."

"*Hope?*" she repeated, nearly shrieking. "Don't you know? Oh, Colton—"

"Look, Cass, I'm just telling you, that's all," he said sharply.

She dropped his arm as if it were a red-hot coal. "This time Denver's gone off the deep end," she said angrily. "But then he has a history of that, doesn't he?"

"So does your father."

The wound cut deep—like the slice of a razor. Whirling, she poked a single finger at his chest. "My father has his reasons for not trusting you and for hating your uncle. But I thought we were going to bury the hatchet and try to forget all that. I even thought we were going to try to 'start over,' isn't that what you said? Well, someone better clue Denver in!"

"I will. When he gets back."

"And when will that be?"

"As soon as he can."

"Great! I can't wait to give him a piece of my mind," she declared, turning on her heel and starting for her pickup. Of all the insane, horrid notions! If Denver McLean were here right now, Cassie would personally throttle him!

Righteous indignation staining her cheeks the color of the dawn, she threw open the door of the truck and climbed inside. But before she could slam it closed, Colton had wedged himself between the door and seat. "Now who's jumping off the deep end?" he demanded.

"Excuse me, but I think my reputation and my father's were just assassinated." She jammed the key into the ignition. The old engine caught. "I'd just like to know, Colton," she said, looking down at him from her perch in the truck's cab, "what happened between last night and this morning! Remember last night—out here in this very yard? Weren't you the guy trying to get me to stay with you? Sleep with you? Make love to you?"

His fingers flexed, the knuckles white.

"Well, I'm not interested," she said. "Not until you and I have some *mutual* trust!" With a toss of her head, she slammed the truck into gear.

By the time she reached the clinic, Cassie had cooled off. Her anger had given way to incredulity, disappointment and indignation.

"Any messages?" she asked, letting herself in through the back door and catching Sandy feeding the few patients housed in the cages of the back room.

"No—and your first appointment isn't until nine." She poured feed pellets into a small dish and placed them inside the hutch of an ailing white rabbit. "Coffee's on if you want some."

"Thanks. I could use a cup. I just hope it's *not* decaf."

"Ouch. Bad morning?" Sandy asked.

"You could say that." Cassie checked on the Edwards's poodle and the three puppies that had been brought into the world via Cesarean section. "How're you?" she whispered, petting the dog's soft gray head as the tiny puppies squirmed and squeaked, shifting into position against their mother's shaved belly. Cassie eyed the neat row of stitches and the ochre color of disinfectant staining the bitch's underside.

"Puppies are doing fine—Mom feels a little ragged," Sandy said.

"I don't blame her," Cassie murmured to the dog, and was rewarded with a sloppy tongue against her palm. "You are feeling better, aren't you?" she said, grinning as she stood and gratefully accepted a steaming cup of coffee from Sandy.

"Craig wanted me to remind you about the Edwards's party Friday."

Cassie made a face. She'd completely forgotten about the annual event. As this was her first full year working with Craig, and Nate Edwards brought a lot of business into the clinic, Craig was adamant she attend. "I don't suppose you know of a way to get out of it?"

"Why would you want to?"

"I hate those things!" Cassie replied.

"Oh, but it's great! No one can throw a party like Paula Edwards!"

"No one would want to." After examining the animals housed in the cages, she asked, "Has anyone called in about sick horses? Horses with an elevated temperature or pulse?"

"Only Colton McLean yesterday and Vince Monroe a few days ago. Craig went out to see the mare."

Vince Monroe! One of her father's best friends. Her palms began to sweat. "Do we have that file?"

"Unless Craig has it with him." Sandy walked through a connecting door to a small file room, ran one finger across the color-coded tabs and pulled out a thick folder for the

Monroe ranch. "Here it is," she said, handing the bound sheaf of papers to Cassie.

The most recent entries were in the top pages. Cassie saw where Craig examined a foal with a bowed leg and a mare with a slight fever. But there was no hint of strangles. She felt immediate relief.

"Craig hasn't mentioned anything more serious—like strangles, has he?"

Sandy frowned as the back door opened, letting in a breath of cool morning air. "Nope—at least not to me."

"Did I hear someone talking about me?" Craig asked as he stepped into the back room.

"That's right, and we've been saying hideous and vile things about you," Cassie teased, her black mood lifting at the sight of Craig's frizzy hair and flushed cheeks.

"I thought so." He hung his jacket on a hook near the door, then slid his arms through the sleeves of a starched green lab coat. "What's up?"

"There's an outbreak of strangles at the McLean Ranch."

"Strangles?" Craig let out a low whistle. "Which horse?"

"Black Magic and Tempest. Both stallions." While Craig walked into the tiny kitchen area and poured himself a cup of coffee, Cassie told him everything that had happened.

"And Colton thinks Black Magic picked it up while he was missing?" he asked thoughtfully, stirring sweetener into his cup.

"That's the way he figures it."

Craig's lower lip protruded thoughtfully. "Makes sense, I suppose. And the timing's right. There are some wild horses that live up in the mountains. McLean's stallion could've gotten mixed up with them."

Cassie shook her head. "I don't think so. The way Colton and Curtis Kramer tell it, Black Magic looked as good when he returned as when he left. He was groomed and cared for. I saw him soon after, and I'd say he hadn't spent any time in the wild."

Craig frowned. "So Colton still thinks he was stolen."

"Yes." *And more, much more.* Cassie placed her empty cup into the small sink. "If he's right, and some rancher 'borrowed' the stallion, we've got at least one more case of strangles. Probably more."

"More like an epidemic." Craig scowled into his coffee as he swirled a spoon in his cup. "I haven't heard of any other cases, but I'll call around to the other clinics in the county."

The front bell tinkled, signaling the arrival of the first appointment.

"Oh-oh, duty calls. That's probably Mrs. Silvan for her rabbit. She'll want to talk to you," Sandy said to Craig.

Craig took one gulp from his cup, then set it aside. "I'll bring Herman into room two."

"Great." Sandy hurried to her desk in the reception area, which was located on the other side of the file room and separated the waiting area from the examining rooms.

Craig motioned to the half-empty kennels and said to Cassie, "Look, if you want to take off early this afternoon and check on the McLean horses, feel free. Unless we get swamped with emergencies, I can handle things here. The same goes for tomorrow. I don't have any surgeries scheduled, so I'll hold down the fort."

"You're sure?"

"I think you're due for a day off," he said, then grimaced. "But dealing with strangles won't be any picnic."

"Don't I know," Cassie agreed as the front bell chimed again, and Craig lifted the fat white rabbit from its cage.

Inside the broodmare barn Colton studied the swollen-bodied bay with a jaundiced eye. Red Wing was anxious, her eyes rolling backward, her ears flattening as Curtis tried to examine her for signs indicating she was about to foal.

"Yep. She's ready," Curtis said, patting the mare fondly.

Colton wanted to swear. The last thing he needed was new, fragile horses being exposed to god-only-knew-what. "You're sure about this?"

"Sure as I can be. My money says she'll foal tonight—tomorrow night at the latest."

"Great." Colton grumbled.

"Too bad Tessa won't be here to see it," Curtis said wistfully as he slipped out of the mare's stall. "She's waited a long time for this."

Colton didn't answer. In a mood as dark as Black Magic's hide, he strode outside, barely noticing that the wind had turned, kicking up from the west.

Though it was barely four o'clock, Milly had already snapped on the kitchen lights. The windows glowed from within. Colton climbed up the back steps, kicked off his boots and hung his jacket and hat on pegs in the porch, then shouldered his way into the house.

It was filled with the scents of nutmeg, strong coffee and pot roast. Milly was sweeping what appeared to be a spotless kitchen floor. She glanced up when he appeared. "You got a call this afternoon. Some guy from a magazine. Grover, he said his name was."

Colton didn't really care. "What'd he want?"

"To talk to you." Milly leaned on her broom, looking miffed. "Wouldn't tell me any more than that. I left his number in the den."

Colton couldn't help but smile. He'd gotten used to Milly and her bossing, Curtis and his cantankerous ways, and Cassie—Lord, how she'd gotten under his skin. He knew what Steve Grover wanted, and for the first time in his life, he wasn't interested.

In the den, he glanced at the number, dialed and worked his way past a receptionist and a secretary before being connected with Steve.

"McLean!" Steve nearly shouted. "I'd about given up on you. Thought you might have dropped off the face of the earth."

"Not yet," Colton said, a slow smile spreading over his face as he pictured Steve Grover, a man of about five foot eight, whip-thin and charged with energy. He would give odds that even now Grover was pacing in his office, stretching the phone cord taut.

"Ready for a new assignment?"

"I could be," Colton evaded, propping one hip against the desk and staring out the window to the ranch beyond. Playful colts cavorted in one field while red-and-white Hereford cattle lumbered in the next. "Where?"

"South Korea."

"When?"

"Yesterday."

Colton laughed. "I guess you should've called sooner."

"You're right." Grover let out a long breath. "All kidding aside, the plane leaves Sunday night from Seattle."

"Seattle," Colton repeated, watching Cassie's white truck pull into the side yard.

"Right. Direct to Seoul. We're sending a team. Knox, Winston, Overgaard and you, if you'll go."

Colton watched as Cassie slid out of the cab, tugged on her jean jacket, then hurried up the front walk. His heart lurched, and he couldn't help but smile. "Sorry, I can't make it," he said without even thinking.

"What?"

"Can't do it," he said again. "I've got some problems here to tend to."

"But this might be the biggest story of the year. The students are rioting, the militia's been called in and there's talk of a North Korean offensive."

"Send someone else."

"But—"

"Talk to you later." Colton dropped the receiver, severing the connection. His blood pumping, he strode straight to the front door, opening it just as Cassie pushed the doorbell.

Folding his arms over his chest and leaning one shoulder against the doorjamb, he drawled, "I didn't expect to see you again so soon."

Cassie tossed her hair away from her face. "I'm on my way home; I thought I'd see if Tempest was any better."

"About the same."

"And Black Magic?"

"He's a little improved," Colton said, taking her chilled fingers in his large hands. "Come on, you can take a look for yourself." He pulled her through the door, kicked it closed and walked along the hall toward the back of the house.

"Cassie!" Milly chimed as Colton led her through the kitchen. "You're just in time for dinner!"

"Not tonight—really," she said when she read the disappointment in Milly's eyes. "Another time."

"I'll hold you to it."

"Other plans?" Colton asked, one dark brow rising.

She didn't respond.

"Seriously, why not stay?" Colton asked. He had let go of her hand long enough to open the back door to the porch and start yanking on his boots.

Cassie's eyes narrowed. "Unfinished business."

Looking at Milly, Colton cocked his head in Cassie's direction and explained, "I insulted Cassie this morning."

"Did you?" Milly smothered a smile as she glanced from Colton to Cassie and back again. "Then I guess you'd better apologize and ask her to dinner."

A lazy smile tacked to his face, he drawled, "I just might."

Cassie's blood began to boil. How ingratiating! How absolutely conceited!

Milly lifted the lid of a pot on the stove. Spicy-scented steam filled the room. "Did you get hold of that Grover fella?"

Colton grunted as he pulled on his other boot. "I did."

"And?"

"And I told him I was too busy to hop the next jet to South Korea."

Cassie glanced up at him sharply. Was he serious? His responsibilities here superseded his need to live life on the edge? *That* would be a first.

"Come on," he insisted, reaching for her hand again. He held open the door as she slipped through. "There's another reason I decided to stay."

"Oh? And what was that?"

"A beautiful woman."

He heard her swift intake of breath, saw a glimmer of hope spark in her gray-green eyes. "I saw you getting out of the truck and I..." He let his voice trail off. Colton had never been good at making promises he wasn't sure he could keep. Nor did he believe in painting a rosy picture that might someday dim.

Cassie angled her face up at him, her cheeks flushed from the cold, her expression serious. His hands felt so warm.

"Well, I guess you were right," he admitted. "There is some unfinished business between us. Lots of it."

"And you want to finish it?" she asked, doubting him, pulling away so she could think.

His eyelids lowered a fraction. "I don't think we can leave it as it is."

"Don't try to snow me, McLean," she said, remembering all too vividly the accusations that hung between them. Marching stiffly along the trail leading through the grass to the stable yard, she said, "I'm not as easily conned as I was when I was seventeen. Dad was right, you know. You McLeans are all cut from the same cloth!"

"I never conned you."

"Seemed that way." She reached the old foaling shed and grabbed for the door, but as she pulled on the latch, the flat of Colton's hand slammed the door back against its casing. Looking up so that her gaze collided with his, she thrust out her chin mutinously.

"Let's not get into all that, Cassie. What we're talking about is the here and now. The reasons these horses are sick. That's all."

"And that includes insinuating that my father would intentionally cause an animal suffering and pain!" Her face burned with a simmering anger.

Colton's frustration was plain in his expression. "If it's any consolation, I don't think Ivan would hurt the animals."

"Not even to get back at you?" she taunted, unable to resist baiting him.

"Not even then."

"Good. Now all you've got to do is convince Denver."

*And that won't be easy,* Colton thought as he slid the latch away from the door and held it open.

Cassie stepped inside and was greeted by a soft nicker. "Look at you," she whispered, walking up to Black Magic and patting his nose. Turning her head, she grinned at Colton. "He's already better." But when she touched the swelling under his jaw, the horse flinched, snorting impatiently and tossing back his head. "Steady, boy, I didn't mean to hurt you."

The shed was warm and dry. Fresh, sweet-smelling straw had been scattered over the floor, and Magic's box was filled with oats.

Tempest, however, hadn't improved. In fact, he looked worse. Whereas Black Magic's temperature was slowly falling, Tempest's continued to rise, and his nasal discharge was constant and opaque. "Has he eaten anything yet?" Cassie asked, already guessing the answer.

Colton shook his head. "Curtis has tried to get him to eat. So has Len. But it's a major battle just to force the antibiotics down his throat."

"Come on, boy," Cassie whispered, frowning a little. "You can do it."

The big sorrel didn't move, didn't so much as flick an ear in her direction. Patting his strong shoulder, she sent up a silent prayer for this horse and the rest of the McLean stock.

Together, she and Colton made the rounds again. One of the yearlings had started to cough, and Cassie ordered him isolated immediately. "It might be nothing more than a cold," she said, crossing her fingers as Curtis led the horse to a stall far from the others, "but we can't take any chances."

Curtis, Len and Daniel started the task of cleaning out the yearling's old stall, and Colton, more charming than usual, convinced Cassie to stay for dinner.

Later, he and Cassie walked to the broodmare barn and found Red Wing shifting anxiously, pawing at the straw.

"She's ready," Cassie said, keeping a watchful eye on Tessa's little mare. She leaned her elbows on the top rail of the stall and bent forward to get a closer look.

Colton stood behind her, so close she could feel the body heat radiating from him. "Maybe you should stick around," he suggested, his breath on her nape. "She might need you." He slipped his arms familiarly around Cassie's waist, linking them at her abdomen, pressing gently so that her hips rested against the firm saddle of his thighs.

*Think, Cassie,* she told herself, wishing she had the willpower to squirm away from him. But she didn't, and the tips of his thumbs gently pressing against the underside of her breasts caused a stirring deep inside her.

"I—I should go home."

"You told me your father never expects you."

"I do work odd hours, but—"

"But nothing. Stay here. The horses need you. And so do I."

She closed her eyes and swallowed against the huge, burning lump that suddenly filled her throat. "Colton, don't—"

"You said we had unfinished business."

"I didn't mean *this*!"

"But I did." How could she concentrate when his lips were hovering over her crown, his fingers splaying possessively across her abdomen, his warmth seeping through her clothes to caress her skin?

Gathering all her strength, she turned to face him. "So now you want me. Is that it?"

"Yes."

Her stomach fluttered and her heart pumped faster as she noticed the sexy slant of his mouth, the cocksure lift of his brows. *Cassie, use your head!* She forced her chin up, challenging him with her piercing gaze. "After all these years, all the heartache, all the misunderstandings and even this— this accusation of Denver's that my father was part of some insidious plot to destroy your livestock and your ranch—you want me?"

"Don't confuse me with my brother," he warned.

"And don't blame me *or my father* for something we didn't do!"

The corners of his mouth moved slightly, and she couldn't help but drop her gaze to the thin, sensual line of his lips that hid all-too-perfect teeth. Her heartbeat went wild; her breath fairly burst in her lungs as he tightened his arms around her, crushed her breasts against his chest and kissed her long and hard and lazily, as if they had all the time in the world.

Cassie closed her eyes, holding on to this one breathless instant and telling herself what had gone before didn't matter. His tongue slid between her teeth, and she welcomed its touch. All thoughts of denying him vanished.

Colton groaned, a deep primal sound that caused an answering moan from her. His hands moved up slowly, lifting, surrounding her breasts with a sweet, tortured reverence
that nearly moved Cassie to tears. His thumbs stroked gently
across her blouse. Her nipples hardened, the skin stretching tight, an ache forming deep in her center. "Stay, Cass,"
he whispered. "At least for a little while."

She wanted to say no. Deep in her heart she knew she was
making an irreversible mistake. "For a while," she agreed,
and his lips moved hungrily over hers.

He lifted her from her feet and carried her to the far end
of the barn. Still holding her, he switched off the lights and
kicked open the gate to an empty stall. Fresh, sweet-smelling
straw covered the floor.

Colton grabbed a clean blanket with one hand, dropped
it over the straw and gently laid Cassie on the makeshift bed.
"What if someone comes here?" she said, though her mind
was fuzzy.

"No one will."

"But—"

"Shh. Milly's busy, and Curtis and the rest of the hands
are in the fields. It's just you and me." Covering her mouth
with his, he lay with her, his legs entwined with hers, his
arms holding her tight against him.

Outside, the wind whispered through the trees. Cattle
lowed, and a night bird called softly. The inside of the barn
was warm; horses shifted and sighed, and Colton carefully
lifted her sweater over her head.

In the half-light, Cassie stared up at him. No longer a
naive girl of seventeen, she curled her hand around his neck
and bent his head so that their lips could mesh. She sighed
when he pushed the strap of her camisole off her shoulder.

His lips nibbled at the sculpted lace, and his tongue traced
a sensual pattern against her skin. She shivered, but not
from the cold. Anticipation caused tiny bumps to rise on her
flesh. He warmed them with the caress of his tongue.

"Colton," she whispered, arching closer.

"I'm right here, love." He lifted his head and stared at her, and for an instant Cassie forgot about the pain of the past, forgot how he'd abandoned her, forgot that he'd sworn never to trust her again. "God, you're beautiful," he murmured, tucking his palms under her breasts and tenderly lifting them upward until both nipples peeked over the lace.

With a moan he took one little bud in his mouth and laved it with his tongue, lashing and flicking, causing Cassie's mind to spin, her breath to come in short gasps.

She wound her fingers in his hair, holding him close as he moved from one breast to the other, letting the night air cool the wet trail against her skin while he stoked a fire already raging through her blood.

Her hands moved of their own accord, tugging on his jacket and shoving it impatiently over his shoulders. Colton struggled out of it and flung it into a corner of the stall. It was quickly followed by his shirt, and she ran her fingers intimately over the hard, corded muscles of his chest and back. He kissed her again, his mouth molding over hers.

Strong and lean and sinewy, his hard body fit against her softer flesh. The mat of dark hair on his chest brushed and tickled her breasts. His dark, stubbled jaw prickled her cheeks.

His hands moved swiftly and without hesitation. Easily he unbuttoned her skirt and slid it, along with her pantyhose and panties down her legs, stripping her bare. Then, once she was lying naked in the straw, her breasts rising and falling as rapidly as her breath, he knelt above her, unbuckled his belt, slid the leather strap through the loops and let it drop.

Her throat was suddenly desert-dry, and their gazes touched, locked, ignited. With one deft movement he slid his jeans over his own hips and thighs.

Cassie had trouble swallowing. For years she'd dreamed of just this moment. Unashamed, she stared at him, his raw

nakedness, the downy hair on his legs, the shadowy apex of
his legs.

Teeth sinking into her lip, she watched as he lazily lay over
her, his weight settling comfortably against her, his skin
fusing with hers.

"This is the time to say no," he said, swallowing, his voice
deep and husky, one hand slowly running from her rib cage
to her ankle and back again. "Stop me before it's too late."

"I . . . I don't want to," she admitted.

His gaze shifted to her face, then to the darkened corners
of the huge room. "Oh, Cass," he murmured, his hands
twining in her cloud of dark curls, his face twisted into a
tortured expression. "Why couldn't I ever forget you?"

"Probably for the same reason I couldn't forget you."

His lips crashed down on hers, and there was no turning
back. Their tongues met and danced while they explored,
caressed and teased with their hands. She traced the scars on
his shoulder; he trailed his fingers along the curve of her
spine, and a dewy sheen of sweat melded his body to hers.

The ache within her stretched wide as his manhood
brushed against her abdomen and thighs, teasing, titillat-
ing, driving any last-minute doubts from her mind.

Balanced on his elbows, he held her face between his
hands and stared down at her flushed, sweat-dampened
face. "I love you, Cass," he admitted, his eyes burning
bright with passion. "I always have."

Tears sprang to her eyes. His buttocks flexed, and he entered her, thrusting long and hard into the aching empti-
ness only he could ever fill.

Cassie's breath escaped in a rush. As he moved, she
moved, too, her body responding to his rhythm, her mind
void of all but this one, virile man.

"Cassie, oh, love," he whispered over and over as his
tempo quickened, his thrusts driving deeper.

Blood thundered through her head, and brilliant sparks of gold and red flashed in her eyes. She convulsed, her nails biting into his back.

"I can't—hold back..." And he didn't. In a powerful explosion that was answered only by her own, he fell on her, his muscles straining, his voice crying out her name lustily.

Collapsing on her, his heart thudding as wildly as her own, Colton held her close. The edge of his hairline was damp, his breathing hard and fast.

Cassie wound her arms and legs around him, wishing she never had to let him go—and knowing that she would. Colton McLean wasn't a man to be tied down, and she wasn't fool enough to think she would change him. She fought a losing battle with tears and kissed him over and over again—afraid she'd never get another chance.

## Chapter Eleven

Cassie had nearly fallen asleep when she felt Colton's muscles tense. Instinctively she clung to him. "Mmm. What's wrong?" she murmured, then stretched languidly.

"Nothing," he whispered, kissing her crown and levering up on one elbow. The barn was dark, but even so, she knew he was squinting, listening.

She heard it, too. A horse's low painful moan. *Tessa's mare! Red Wing!* Instantly awake, she scrambled into her clothes, shook the straw from her hair and fumbled for the light switch. Colton found it first, snapping it on. Harsh illumination flooded the huge room, accompanied by the nickers, snorts and whinnies of the other horses.

Tucking her sweater into the band of her skirt, Cassie hurried to Red Wing's stall. Inside, the mare was laboring, her breathing rapid, her eyes wide. Cassie reached for the latch of the stall gate.

Red Wing's water broke in a gush, filling the air with the scent of birthing.

*Here we go,* Cassie thought, her hands on the gate. If Red Wing could deliver alone, Cassie wouldn't offer any help. "Calm down, girl."

But Red Wing, her ears flicking nervously, eyes bulging and sweat darkening her coat, moved nervously. Veins stood out beneath her glossy hide. She shuddered with the next contraction.

"Come on, Red Wing, easy now," Cassie coaxed. Still, Red Wing paced restlessly. Cassie felt Colton beside her. "I'll need clean towels, water and iodine," she said softly as Red Wing moaned again. Cassie opened the gate and slipped into the stall. Gently, careful of Red Wing's shifting hindquarters, Cassie examined her. "Steady, girl." Part of the amniotic sac was visible, and gently, Cassie probed at the big white balloon. She found the foal's nose and one foot. Only one. Not good.

"Here you go," Colton said softly, hauling the towels and water bucket into the stall.

"I'll need your help."

"Problems?"

"One foot is twisted back on itself," she said, trying to keep the worry from her voice. "This way it won't fit through the birth canal. We'll have to push the foal back in, straighten the leg and then help it out."

Colton rolled up his sleeves. "Just tell me what to do."

Gently, so as not to break the umbilical cord or the sac, Cassie nudged the foal backward, then eased the bent foot forward. The entire procedure took only a few minutes, but it felt like a lifetime. Fortunately Red Wing didn't lash out with teeth or hooves.

"Okay, now…" She guided Colton's hand. "Now, when the mare contracts again, pull down, gently of course, to help the foal out."

He glanced her way. "Got it."

The next contraction ripped through the mare a second later, and both Cassie and Colton tugged on the tiny legs until the feet and head were free. An instant later Red Wing moaned painfully, and another contraction pushed the foal's shoulders through. Once the shoulders were out, the rest of the foal slid to the floor in a rush of birthing fluid.

The umbilical cord broke. Cassie quickly ripped open the sac and cleaned out the colt's nose. "Come on, breathe," she whispered, trying to infuse life into the tiny horse.

As Red Wing hadn't yet claimed her foal by licking it, Colton grabbed a towel and began rubbing its wet sides. The little horse's eyelids and lips were blue. "Come on, come on," Cassie begged, waiting for the colt to breathe as she slipped her hand beneath its nose and felt the first warm rush of breath from its lungs. The foal's small ribs expanded, its huge eyes blinked open curiously, and Cassie wanted to shout with joy. "Isn't he beautiful?" she cried, reaching for the iodine and dousing the colt's umbilical stump.

Red Wing snorted, eyeing the dark, straw-flecked, spindly legged bundle.

"Watch out," Cassie warned. Colton jumped before Red Wing's teeth found his back. "I think Mama wants to take over."

He flashed her a quick grin. "Good. Let her. I don't think I'm much of a midwife." He moved out of the mare's range.

"Oh, I don't know, McLean," she teased, unable to stop smiling over the lump swelling in her throat. "For a man who swears he hates anything to do with ranching, you did a fair job."

"I'll take that as a compliment."

"It was meant as one." She glimpsed at him from the corner of her eye. His shirt still open, Colton fastened his gaze on mare and foal. Virile and tough, yet tender and caring—no wonder she'd never stopped loving him. Quickly Cassie worked on the mare, making sure that eventually all the afterbirth would fall from the mare naturally.

Ignoring Cassie, Red Wing washed her new charge with her tongue, stimulating the colt's circulation and cleaning him. She nudged him with her huge head, nickering softly, urging him up on spindly legs that refused to hold him.

He would struggle upright only to fall in a cross-legged heap or to land on his head.

"He could use a few ballet lessons," Colton said.

"Maybe you should name him Misha."

They stepped out of the stall and washed as best they could. Colton chuckled. "I'll tell Tessa when she gets back."

"Do." She didn't pull away when Colton's arm surrounded her, and yet she felt suddenly awkward. There were still tremendous hurdles between them. Denver's accusations for starters. Did Colton really think her father could be a part of such a heinous crime as deliberately infecting Black Magic with a virus? Once that was cleared up, which she was sure would happen soon, then there was still Colton's need for danger and thirst for faraway places, while she belonged here. And the past—there was always that black cloud threatening to spill over them. Had Colton really put it to rest?

The little colt nuzzled his mother's flank and finally found his first meal. A huge smile spread across Colton's square jaw, and he hugged Cassie even tighter. "Finally!" he muttered.

"Tessa will be proud."

"She should be." He glanced down at her, and the kindness shining in his flinty eyes received an answering grin. "You, Ms. Aldridge, are a first-class mess."

"I am?"

To prove his point, he plucked a piece of straw from her hair. Cassie stared down at her clothes, ruined with blood and amniotic fluid. "I guess you're right."

"How about a shower?" he suggested, his eyelashes lowering seductively.

"Not a chance." But she laughed, imagining a rush of water tumbling over Colton's bare skin and thick, dark hair.

"Why not?"

"Oh, I can think of about a dozen reasons. Let's start with Curtis, Len, Daniel, Milly—"

"I already told you the hands are busy, and we could have Milly run an errand to town."

"No way." But she giggled.

"It could be fun."

His gaze delved into hers, and she suddenly felt as if a tight leather strap had been placed around her chest, making it impossible to breathe. Her stomach trembled. "You're positively wicked, Colton McLean."

"One of my most endearing qualities."

As the foal suckled and a few of the other horses nickered softly, Cassie was caught in the magnetism of Colton's eyes. "I, uh, think we'd better find Curtis," she said. "He'll want to see Red Wing's new foal. And then I think I'd better go home."

Colton leaned a shoulder against the rough boards of the wall. His jaw slid to the side. "Afraid?" he asked.

"Of what?"

"Of me?"

"No!"

"Of us?"

"There is no 'us.' There never was. Remember?" Her heart pounded crazily, and the atmosphere in the barn became even more intimate.

"No us—then what was that a little while ago?"

"Passion."

"So you're afraid of passion."

"No!"

"Then why not stay?"

She gulped, her mind spinning. All these years she'd wanted to be with him, and now her emotions were stretched taut. Their relationship had gathered the steam of a freight train running out of control. "You're the one who so graciously pointed out what a mess I am," she said, not ready to tackle the more serious issues.

"You could change here. Wear something of Tessa's. Or—" his voice lowered "—something of mine." He slid a sizzling glance her way.

"I'd look pretty silly in a Stetson, leather jacket and Levi's." Shaking her head, she said, "Thanks for the offer, but I don't think so. I've—I've got to get home."

"Why? Ivan's not expecting you."

Ramming his hands into the back pockets of his jeans, he focused an intense gaze on her and crossed the small space separating them. "Things have changed between us, Cass."

"Have they?" She thought about making wonderful love to him in the straw, and blushed like a schoolgirl. "Yes, I suppose they have." She began to twist her fingers in the folds of her skirt, and she mentally shook herself, kept her hands steady and tilted her face to his. "So where do we go from here?"

"I wish I knew." As if unable to help himself, he cupped her determined chin. Her skin quivered, and she knew that if she didn't leave now, she wouldn't be able to.

"So do I," she admitted, stepping away, needing time and space to think. Years ago she'd rushed things, chased him with all the foolishness of a teenage girl in the throes of puppy love, and she wasn't about to play the fool again—not even for Colton.

"Are you going to the Edwards's party?" he asked as she reached the door.

"I have to. Command performance."

He smiled at her irreverence. "Would you go with me?"

"I'd like it very much," she admitted.

"Then I'll pick you up at seven."

Nodding, she pushed open the door and called over her shoulder, "I'll see you later."

"You can count on it."

She climbed into her pickup and glanced at her reflection in the rearview mirror. Twinkling hazel eyes returned her stare, and her heart pounded crazily in her chest. Time and distance wouldn't matter much, she realized, because, like it or not, she was in love.

She didn't see Colton for two days. Though she dropped by the ranch several times to check on Black Magic and Tempest, she never caught a glimpse of Denver McLean's younger brother. Milly explained that he had "business in town," Curtis was evasive but polite, and Cassie couldn't help thinking that Colton might be trying to give her a hint. Had the love they'd shared been a mistake—just like before?

Though wounded, she hid her feelings and went about her job. Black Magic was recovering well. His temperature had dropped to normal and his abscess had matured. Cassie drained the abscess, then cleaned the cavity with a mild antiseptic solution. Black Magic didn't like her ministrations much and tried to nip her.

Tempest seemed to have turned the corner, but his recovery was much slower than Black Magic's, and the yearling was following the path of Tempest. Cassie was worried about those two horses because of the threat of complications such as pneumonia or, more rarely, abscesses in the internal organs. She crossed her fingers as she left the old foaling shed and started for her pickup. Unwittingly she scanned the near-empty yard for Colton's Jeep.

Was he avoiding her? He hadn't called, nor stopped by. Maybe he regretted making love to her. And perhaps his change of heart was for the best.

Frowning, she drove home and parked near the garage, wedging her truck into the small space left between Vince Monroe's pickup and Ryan Ferguson's motorcycle.

She wasn't in the mood to face either of the two men, but she had no choice, she supposed, as she climbed out of the cab. Erasmus streaked out of the kitchen, yipping at the sight of her and bounding across the yard. He jumped up, placed huge muddy paws against her skirt and barked.

"It's good to see you, too," Cassie said, eyeing the dirty streaks on her skirt. "Come on, let's see what's going on."

With Erasmus bounding at her heels, Cassie climbed the back steps and shoved open the door. Inside, the men had gathered around the kitchen table. Newspapers, coffee cups and ashtrays covered the scarred surface. Smoke drifted to the ceiling, and all conversation stopped abruptly. Three sets of eyes turned toward her, and she felt as if she, in the very house where she'd grown up, was an intruder.

"Am I interrupting?" she asked, and her father waved her question aside.

"'Course not."

Vince Monroe cast her a cursory glance. "Evening, Cassie," he drawled, scraping back his chair and standing.

*Always the gentleman,* Cassie thought uneasily, noticing that Ryan hadn't bothered getting to his feet. Not that she cared. His eyes followed her, and he inclined his head, though he didn't move the one booted foot propped against her favorite chair. A cigarette dangled from the corner of his mouth, and smoke curled lazily over his head. His helmet sat on the floor next to him, and an insolent smile curved his lips.

A tense undercurrent charged the room. Cassie forced a playful grin in an effort to lighten the mood. "What is this?" she asked. "An old hens' meeting?"

Ivan laughed, Vince guffawed, and Ryan's dark eyes glinted.

"Yeah, that's what it is." Ryan finally lifted his foot and kicked the chair toward her. "Except that it's an old roosters' meeting. We could use a hen or two. Join us," he invited.

Ivan's smile fell from his face, and he sent Ferguson a warning glare.

"I can't," she said, glancing toward her father. "I've got to get ready. You, too."

"For?"

"Nate and Paula's party."

"Oh, that." Ivan shook his head and glowered at the thought of the Edwards's annual event. "I'm not going."

"Why not? Nate's one of your friends."

"I know, I know. But I got things to do," her father said gruffly. "I think Sylvia's going to foal tonight." Sylvia was her father's favorite mare—the best on the ranch. "But you go along. McLean called. Said he'd take you."

Cassie's heart somersaulted joyously. So he hadn't been avoiding her! But still, that didn't explain her father's change of heart. Or did it?

Vince drained his coffee cup. "It's time I was rollin' along," he remarked, stretching his big arms. "Otherwise the wife'll be callin'." He snatched his huge, gray Stetson and stuffed it onto his head, walked to the door, then paused, as if he'd had a sudden thought. His eyes found Cassie's, and the pale blue orbs glittered a bit. "So how're things at the McLean Ranch—those horses of his getting any better?"

"Much," Cassie replied, experiencing a sudden chill. Vince Monroe had always made her uncomfortable, but this evening the feeling was even stronger. "Black Magic should be good as new in a few weeks, and the others—well, they're coming along."

"Good," Monroe said gruffly. "Helluva thing that strangles. McLean's lucky no more than a few horses got it."

"I don't think he's feeling very lucky about it," Cassie said, eyeing the older man warily.

"All a part of ranching. The bad part. Good night, Aldridge." He squared his hat, exchanged glances with the other men and strode outside.

Ryan took a final drag on his cigarette and snatched up his helmet. "I've got to be shovin' off, too." His sultry gaze touched Cassie's before he stubbed out the butt and glanced at Ivan. "I'll see you in the morning."

Ivan nodded. "If I'm not here, I'll probably be with the mares. My guess is that Sylvia won't wait too long."

"I thought she wasn't due for a couple of weeks," Cassie said.

"She isn't, but you try and tell her that," her father joked, though his eyes didn't sparkle as they usually did.

"Later," Ryan called over his shoulder as the door banged shut behind him.

"Do you want me to stay?" she asked.

"Nope. Go along. I'll handle things here." Glancing down at his hands, he scratched one finger nervously across his thumb.

"I thought you were going to Nate's party."

Ivan scowled, his forehead creasing. "You know how I feel about gettin' all dressed up."

"It can be fun," she said, remembering Sandy's words and feeling like a hypocrite. Before Colton's invitation, Cassie hadn't been looking forward to the party, either.

"It's a pain in the butt."

"Since when?" she asked, knowing how her father loved a few drinks, a dance or two and a chance to see all his friends gathered together.

"Since that mule-headed mare decided to deliver."

"Or since I decided to go with Colton," she prodded, feeling there was more to it than he was admitting.

Ivan made a face. "As you're so fond of tellin' me, it's your life. It goes without sayin' how I feel about you going anywhere with Colton McLean. It was all I could do not to hang up on the bastard today—but I didn't. Because of you."

"Thanks."

He bit the corner of his mouth. "I don't suppose I can change your mind?"

"Not a chance."

He sighed and turned his gaze to the table. He clamped his jaw hard, and a muscle worked furiously at the side of his neck. "I can't give you any more advice, Cassie. Even if I did, you're too stubborn to listen. But just—" at a sudden loss for words, he shook his head "—don't rush into anything you can't get out of."

"I won't," she promised, wondering if being careful where Colton was concerned was possible and knowing in her heart that it didn't matter.

Glaring at his reflection in the hallway mirror, wondering if he'd had one sane thought since making love to Cassie, Colton tugged at the impossible knot of his tie.

He hadn't talked to her in two days, and it hadn't been his choice. He'd known she wanted breathing room and, because he'd felt the same way years before, he'd given it to her.

He twisted his head, loosening the knot. His fingers were sweaty as he thought about the evening stretching out before him. Tonight Colton planned to enjoy every second of Cassie's company. He'd even managed to talk to her father on the phone and keep his temper in check. Hurdle number one. There was just one more: Denver.

Colton heard the old truck rattle up the drive, and he braced himself. Denver had called last night with the news that he and Tessa would be arriving today. Curtis had left several hours earlier to pick them up at the airport. And now they were back.

Colton wasn't looking forward to confronting Denver, but he didn't have much choice. With a last scowl at the tie, he ripped it from around his neck and hurried downstairs and through the back door.

Before Curtis could crank on the emergency brake, Denver sprang from the cab and helped Tessa, her pregnancy in full bloom, from the truck.

They made a striking couple, Colton decided. Denver, tall and broad-shouldered with raven-black hair and piercing blue eyes, and Tessa, her hair a vibrant red-gold, billowing behind her, her skin tanned, the bridge of her nose dusted with a smattering of freckles. Together, fingers linked, they dashed up the path.

Colton tensed. His relationship with his older brother had always been volatile. Though they respected each other, and probably would defend each other to the death, there was always a keen sense of competition between them—a love-hate relationship that had mellowed only slightly over the years. Their pride and hot tempers often got in the way of their common sense.

Tessa dashed up to her brother-in-law and gave him a fierce hug. "Dad said Red Wing foaled the other night!" she cried, her hazel eyes bright. "A colt! Brigadier's first! I can't wait to see him!" She turned her eager face up to her husband's. "Come on."

Denver looked about to argue, but the delight so evident on her face must have changed his mind. "Can't it wait?"

"No! Denver, come on! You know how important this is!"

"Yeah, I know," Denver said with a half smile. "Let's check him out."

Tessa was already heading toward the broodmare barn, striding ahead of her father and the two McLean brothers. Inside, in a large, straw-covered stall, Red Wing guarded the gangly bay colt. His eyes were round and wide, his nostrils flared, his ears twitching nervously.

Red Wing, usually calm and friendly, placed her body squarely between the intruders and her foal. Her ears flattened to her head, and she eyed everyone, including Tessa, suspiciously.

"Look at him," Tessa cried, fairly glowing. "He's gorgeous."

Curtis laughed. "You wouldn't have thought so if you'd been here when he was born."

Colton's guts twisted at the memory, and his vivid recollection of the hour before, lying in the straw, filled with the scent and feel of Cassie . . .

"Good thing Cassie was here," Curtis rambled on, and Denver shot his brother a killing glance. "This little guy was all twisted up, one foot caught back. Cassie had to help Red Wing out."

"I should've been here," Tessa said, staring guiltily at the inquisitive colt. Peeking from behind his mother's rump, he stretched his long neck and blinked. "He's perfect!"

Her father hugged her shoulders. "That he is, gal."

"It worked out," Colton replied. He glanced to the far wall and the box stall where he'd spent nearly an hour in the delicious rapture of Cassie Aldridge. His insides melted. Just at the thought of their lovemaking, he felt his passion surge.

Jamming a fist into his pocket, he shifted, ignoring the lofty lift of one of Denver's dark brows.

Denver pinned Curtis with a cool glance. "So now you're a fan of Cassie Aldridge?"

"The girl knows her stuff," Curtis said.

"And her father?"

He snorted. "Him I could live without."

"Enough," Tessa insisted. "Let's not spoil all this." She slipped into the box.

"I don't know if this is such a good idea," Denver said, turning his attention on his wife, but, as usual, when it came to horses, she ignored him and stroked Red Wing's soft muzzle.

"It's okay," Tessa said, either to Denver or to the horse. Colton couldn't tell which.

Denver's gaze slid to his brother, and he eyed Colton's suit. "Going somewhere?"

"To Nate and Paula Edwards's party. You're invited, too."

Tessa gasped. "I'd forgotten all about it!"

Denver frowned at his pregnant wife. "It's been a long day—"

"Don't you try to weasel out of it," she warned, eyeing him over her shoulder. "I promised Paula months ago!"

Denver's scowl deepened. "I thought pregnant women were supposed to slow down."

She laughed gaily. "Well, I guess you thought wrong. Paula's pregnant, too, you know."

Colton couldn't swallow the smile that pulled on the corners of his mouth. He loved watching Tessa bully Denver. No one else had ever been able to tell his mule-headed brother anything, but Tessa, half his size and as clever as a fox, had managed to wrap Denver McLean around her little finger.

Denver, disconcerted, sighed. "Maybe we should look at the other animals. "How's Black Magic?"

"Better. But Tempest's just not snapping out of it as quickly," Curtis muttered, running a leathery hand around his neck and squinting thoughtfully. "Why don't you two get changed, have a cup of Milly's coffee, then we'll take a look?"

"Let's just do it now," Denver said impatiently.

Tessa could barely tear herself away from Red Wing and the new foal, but Denver convinced her.

Inside the old foaling shed, Denver studied Black Magic, Tempest and the buckskin yearling, who was improving, though slowly.

Tessa's face fell, her expression becoming dark. "Denver thinks this happened when Black Magic was stolen," she said, her fingers gripping the top rail of the stall so tightly her knuckles blanched white.

Colton whispered, "So do I."

She glanced up at him, then to Denver, who was talking with Curtis at the far end of the shed, near Tempest's stall. "But he thinks someone did it on purpose."

"You don't?"

"I can't imagine it. Hurting innocent animals to get back at us?" She shook her head, and her hair shone pure gold under the artificial lights. "No way. No one around here is that mean."

"I hope you're right," Colton said, glancing to where Denver stood staring in frustration at Tempest. Grim lines creased Denver's forehead, and his fists had curled angrily. "I hope to God you're right."

## Chapter Twelve

By the time Colton knocked on the front door, Cassie had already been waiting fifteen minutes. She flew down the stairs, the skirt of her silk dress billowing behind her like a trailing scarlet cloud.

At the door she paused, took in a long, steadying breath, then turned the knob.

Colton stood under the porch light. His dark hair gleamed, and he looked totally uncomfortable in a dark gray suit, starched white shirt and crimson tie. If not for the jaded glint in his eyes and the cynical twist of his lips, she might not have believed this dashing man to be the irreverent rogue of her dreams.

"Are you ready for this?" he asked, crossing his arms over his chest as he surveyed her from head to toe.

"As ready as I'll ever be," she quipped, though a nervous knot tightened in her stomach as she reached in the closet for her long black coat. She felt self-conscious with her hair twined away from her face in delicate French braids, her silk dress much more sophisticated than any she'd ever owned, her impractical high-heeled shoes.

Outside, the spring night was warm. A warm wind stole through the shadows, rushing around the corners of the buildings and soughing through the trees. Stars winked brightly, and beams from a half-moon washed the earth in blue-gray incandescence.

"Don't you have to say goodbye to your father?" Colton asked.

She shook her head. "Already did."

"He's not going? I thought every rancher in a four-county area was invited."

Cassie settled one shoulder against the passenger door. "He's staying with Sylvia, who's due to drop her foal anytime."

Colton didn't respond as he drove onto the main highway and turned west. They rode in silence until the Edwards's ranch came into view. One of the largest spreads in the state, Nate Edwards's ranch sprawled as far as the eye could see. The house, a plantation-style home that looked as if it belonged in Virginia, stood in stark relief against the black night. With white siding, brick facing, bow windows and blue shutters, the Edwards's home rose three full stories and was ablaze with lights. Cars, pickups and four-wheel drive rigs lined the circular drive.

"I guess I'd better warn you," Colton said as he parked, "Denver and Tessa got home today. They'll be here."

Though she felt a nervous jolt at the thought of meeting Colton's judgmental older brother, she tossed her head. "Why the warning?"

"Denver can be—"

"I know how Denver can be," she shot back. "A lot like you." With a sweet smile, she opened her side of his Jeep and stepped outside. She heard Colton's chuckle and pretended that her nerves weren't stretched tight.

Colton caught up with her on the brick steps just as she rang the bell. Laughter and conversation sifted through the closed windows.

Colton tucked his arm around her waist. "You know," she said, hearing footsteps approaching, "I thought you were avoiding me."

"Never." He squeezed her, and she couldn't help but grin.

"You haven't been around the ranch lately."

"Because of Denver. I had to talk to his attorney in Helena and get a few things ready…besides," he glanced down at her, and the hand against the small of her back felt suddenly warm, "I thought you wanted a little time to think things through."

"I did—"

The door flew open, and Paula Edwards, her red hair piled high on her head, abdomen protruding roundly, waved them inside. "Colton and Cassie! Come in, come in. Here, Nate, take Cassie's coat."

A burly, muscular man whose dark hair was shot with gray, Nate Edwards was fifteen years older than his young wife. He sported a gold-capped tooth and a recently added mustache. Wearing a western-cut suit and string tie, he reached for Cassie's coat and hung it in the closet. "How're things going?" he asked Colton.

"Better. Denver got back today."

"So now you can take off again, eh?" Nate asked, clapping Colton on the back. "You never were one to sit around much."

Colton slid a heart-stopping glance to Cassie. "Maybe I've changed."

"Sure you have," Nate agreed with a throaty chuckle. "I'll believe that when palm trees sprout in the Rockies. Come on in and let me buy you a drink." He led them into a huge living room where other guests mingled and sipped from tulip-shaped glasses. Quiet conversation was muted by the sound of music drifting from an adjoining room.

"Champagne or scotch?"

Colton glanced sideways at his host.

"Scotch," Nate decided, taking his place as bartender at a mirrored bar and pouring Cassie a glass of champagne. He handed them their respective drinks, then tugged at the strings surrounding his throat. "Damned things. I don't know why Paula insists we dress up."

"It's just her way of keeping you in line," Cassie teased, sipping from her glass.

"I s'pose. Sure is a bother, though." Nate poured himself a stiff shot and took a swallow. "Sorry to hear about all your trouble with Black Magic. A damned shame, that's what it is. Lost twice in two years and now strangles. Sometimes ranchin' can be a real bitch." He shook his head and smoothed his hair.

Cassie stiffened, expecting Colton to argue about the horse being stolen, instead he just nodded affably, though his jaw was clamped tight.

The doorbell pealed, and Nate, catching Paula's eye, finished his drink quickly. "Duty calls," he muttered, sauntering toward the foyer and leaving Colton and Cassie in a room crowded with neighboring ranchers and townspeople.

Cassie knew almost everyone. She smiled and waved, made small talk and mingled. Colton didn't leave her for a minute. More than a few people glanced their way, and some of the ranchers' smiles seemed forced. She felt hateful undercurrents in the air.

Matt Wilkerson's lips had flattened at the sight of Colton, and Vince Monroe's smile had fallen from his face.

Then Cassie saw Jessica Monroe sliding Colton secretive glances.

Jessica's blond hair spilled over her shoulders in luxurious waves, and her white satin-and-lace dress seemed almost bridal. She sipped champagne, giggled and kept her arm looped through Ryan Ferguson's, though her gaze wandered over the crowd and lingered on Colton. Colton didn't seem to notice.

"Cassie!" Beth Simpson waved from the far side of the room. She'd already kicked off her shoes and was seated in an apricot-colored velvet chair. Her dress, a billowing amber-and-yellow print, spilled over her distended belly.

Glad to see a friendly face, Cassie waved back and wound her way through the knots of people to her friend. "I thought you were supposed to be in the hospital," she said, remembering the gossip she'd heard in town. "What're you doing here?"

"Waiting for my water to break," Beth grumbled. "I did go into County General, but it was false labor. I felt like a fool, too, since this—" she tapped her abdomen "—isn't my first."

"Well, you fit right in," Cassie observed just as Denver and Tessa walked into the room. Tessa looked absolutely radiant. Her face was glowing; her strawberry-blond hair shimmered under the dimmed lights. "It looks like we've got an epidemic of pregnant ladies," she joked.

Beth laughed, but Cassie's eyes were drawn to Colton's older brother. Denver was as handsome as ever. Even though he'd suffered several plastic surgeries after the fire, he was as ruggedly good-looking as Colton. He never left Tessa's side as they wended through the crowd.

A few faces turned his way, and a few people exchanged meaningful glances. Ryan Ferguson noticed him and stopped dancing with Jessica. Hatred seemed to radiate from his body, and he took a step forward, but Jessica's hand restrained him.

Denver didn't seem to notice.

Tessa spied Colton and Cassie and, dragging her recalcitrant husband behind her, made a beeline across the room. Colton shifted closer to Cassie, keeping one arm around her waist as Tessa joined them. "I can't thank you enough," she said breathlessly, her hazel eyes shining on Cassie. "Dad says you single-handedly delivered Red Wing's colt."

"Not so single-handedly. Red Wing did all the work, and Colton helped."

"Did you?" Tessa arched one fine brow at her brother-in-law.

"I just took orders," Colton clarified.

"That I'd like to see!" Tessa said, giggling as Denver, standing behind her, wrapped possessive arms around her thick waist.

"I guess I owe you, too," Denver conceded, though he didn't smile and his blue eyes were dead serious. "You managed to save Black Magic and a couple of others."

"We all did." Cassie started to relax, but she felt Colton's muscles stiffen. "Hopefully you won't have any other cases."

Denver's eyes narrowed. "What about the other ranchers in the valley. Has anyone else had a problem?"

Cassie bristled, taking the hint. "None that I know of." When Denver didn't seem convinced, she added, "Craig and I talked about it—since strangles is so contagious. He's afraid that Black Magic linked up with some wild horses who have the disease."

"Just let me know if you hear of any other cases," Denver said before Tessa sent him a killing look.

"You, husband dear, have a one-track mind. Cassie didn't come here to discuss her work and, except to thank her for helping out at our ranch, neither did I. Let's dance."

"Good idea," Colton added as Tessa linked her fingers with her husband's. She led Denver toward an adjoining room that had been cleared of furniture. The oak floor had been polished to a golden shine, and a few couples were gliding over the gleaming parquet.

"No dancing for me," Beth said as Colton cupped Cassie's elbow.

Cassie chuckled despite Denver's pointed remarks. "Maybe it's just what you need to convince that baby to come into the world."

"The baby's not the problem," Beth replied as her husband, balancing two platters of food joined them, "my feet are!"

"Come on," Colton whispered into Cassie's ear. He tugged on her arm and guided her through a wide arch. Folding her expertly into his arms, he held her close, moving to the soft strains of a slow tune. Other couples swirled around them, but Colton didn't seem to notice. "If I haven't said it before, you look sensational."

"Thanks." She colored under his compliment and felt the warm whisper of his breath against her bare nape. "I feel ridiculous."

"Why?"

"This—" she looked down at her dress "—is out of character for me."

"You can't run around in jeans and lab coats all the time."

"Oh, and you're comfortable?" She arched her black brows, daring him to lie.

"As long as you're in my arms," he shot back, his steely eyes glinting wickedly.

"Where'd you read that?"

"I didn't. I saw it in some movie."

"Figures." She laughed, and they danced together, oblivious of the crowd or anything but each other. Colton swirled her and held her, and she forgot the hostility she'd felt when they'd first joined the party.

Laughing, she danced with him, held him, felt his lips press kisses against her hair until she thought she would drop. "I think we could use a break," he murmured against her ear.

"Amen."

"Would you like something to drink?"

She nodded and started to follow him to the bar, when she spied Craig talking with a tall, slender man she didn't recognize. Craig had one hand tucked in the pockets of his slacks, the other wrapped around a half-filled old fashioned glass. He caught her eye and waved her over.

Without waiting for Colton, she skirted the dancing couples and joined the two men. "Wonderful party," she said, smiling. "I'm glad you talked me into coming."

Craig chuckled. "Maybe next time I won't have to put a gun to your head."

Rolling her eyes, Cassie conceded, "Okay, okay. I was wrong."

"Now that that's settled, I'd like you to meet a friend of mine." He indicated the tall, slender man next to him. "This is Frank Belmont—Dr. Frank Belmont. We went to school together. Frank's got a clinic downstate. Cassie works with me—I think she plans to buy me out in the next couple of years."

Cassie smiled. "Maybe around two thousand and thirty— when you're ready to retire."

"I'll keep you to it." He swirled his drink and sobered. "Frank saw another case of strangles a few weeks ago," he said.

Cassie's eyes flew to the other man. "Where?"

The two men exchanged glances. "Around here," Craig explained. "One of Vince Monroe's mares. She was quarantined."

"But why didn't he call us..." she asked, already knowing the answer. Then they would have known that Vince had been involved in Black Magic's disappearance. An odd mixture of relief and fear coursed through her. Relief that Vince Monroe was most likely the culprit and fear that her father was involved. He and Vince had become thick as thieves lately. Her stomach turned over.

"I asked Vince about it earlier," Craig said, frowning into his drink.

"And?"

"He said he'd called, couldn't get through and stopped by but we were closed. He knew Frank and called him."

"We have an emergency number," Cassie pointed out.

"I know."

Cassie searched the room, but the towering form of Vince Monroe wasn't in sight. "Where is he?"

Craig lifted a shoulder. "Maybe he already left. It is getting late."

"Speaking of which, I'd better get going," Frank said. "It's a long drive home."

Cassie spied Colton leaning against the bar, his tie loose, his eyes filled with amusement as he stared at her. He hooked a finger in her direction and held up a tall glass of champagne.

Her heart turned over as she moved through the groups of people, and she wanted nothing more than to tell him about Vince Monroe, but she couldn't, not until she had more substantial proof. She wasn't going to accuse anyone before her facts were straight. If Colton had taught her anything eight years ago, it was to listen to all sides before hurling accusations.

"Talking shop?" he asked once she was close enough to hear.

"Umm." She accepted the glass from his hand and didn't protest when he wrapped one arm around her.

"Well, enough of that," he whispered in her ear, sending delicious tingling sensations down her spine. "We have more important things to do."

"Such as?"

"You'll see," he said mysteriously, and Cassie silently agreed. She had lots to do. As Colton took her hand and pulled her toward the dance floor, she spied Jessica Monroe leaving with Ryan Ferguson, and she wondered if Jessica or Ryan or both were involved with Vince. Or—worse yet—her father.

Hours later, when the guests began to leave, Cassie found Paula and thanked her, while Colton located her coat and slipped it over her shoulders. The tips of his fingers grazed her bare arms, and she shivered a little.

Outside, the night was surprisingly warm. Only a few clouds dared creep across the moon. A mild breeze caught in Cassie's hair and snatched at her skirt as she hurried to the Jeep.

She'd barely settled into the passenger seat when Colton started the rig. "It's too early to take you home," he announced.

"It's nearly midnight."

"Like I said—too early." Flashing a devilish grin, he cranked the wheel and the Jeep roared toward the main highway.

"Don't tell me, you're kidnapping me again."

"Nope."

"Then where are we going?"

"Somewhere we should've gone a long time ago," he replied. His voice had grown deep, his gaze thoughtful.

"And where's that?"

"The lake."

Her heart nearly stopped beating. Vivid memories haunted her—memories of making love with Colton, of cold water and a brilliant summer day, of the scent of pine mingled with the musky odor of sweat and of their sweet, precious day being ruined by Denver McLean astride a rangy bay gelding. "There's no road to the lake."

"Then we'll ride."

"Ride? You mean ride *horses*—like this?" she cried, glancing down at her dress, but couldn't help giggling at his wonderful sense of the ridiculous. She considered telling him about Vince Monroe's horse, but didn't—there was time later. For a while she didn't want anything to come between them. And until she had her facts straight, there wasn't much she could do.

"Why not?" he asked.

"If you don't know, I couldn't begin to tell you."

Colton laughed and yanked off his tie as the Jeep tore down the highway toward the McLean Ranch.

"You're out of your mind!"

"So you've told me." He guided the car up the lane leading to the house, parked in the yard and grabbed Cassie's hand, pulling her to the stables where the geldings were housed.

Inside, while Cassie blinked against the bright lights and her nostrils filled with the scent of horses, leather and musty hay, Colton saddled two geldings, a short gray creature named Lamont and a lanky buckskin called Joshua.

"I don't suppose you have a sidesaddle," she said as he tightened the cinch around Lamont's belly.

Colton shook his head and glanced at her from the corner of his eye. "You'll just have to hike up your skirts."

The joke had gone on long enough. "Colton, you're not serious..." she said when he slapped Lamont's reins into her hand and opened the stable door. The gray pricked his ears and lifted his head.

"Where's your sense of adventure?"

"I think I left it in the drawer with my common sense," she said, taking off her coat and tossing it over one of the stall gates before following him and Joshua through the door. "This is madness—sheer, unadulterated madness!"

Colton swung into the saddle, and Cassie, caught in the excitement of it all, followed suit. Her skirt bunched around her thighs as she prodded Lamont with her knees. The eager little horse took off, swinging into a gentle gallop and keeping up with the buckskin's longer strides.

The wind rushed at Cassie's face, yanking the pins from her hair, stealing the breath from her lungs and snapping her skirt like a long, scarlet banner. She leaned forward over the horse's shoulders, adrenaline pumping through her system, her spirits soaring as the gelding's hooves thundered against the thick spring grass.

Ahead, washed in the moon's silvery light, the pine forest loomed before them, and through the trees the reflection of the clear water appeared jewellike against the black tree trunks.

She felt her mount take the bit in his mouth and leap forward, his ears flattening back against his head as he challenged the bay. Colton's horse responded, and soon the animals were charging across the field, hoofbeats thundering, nostrils wide, eyes sparking with defiant fire.

Cassie leaned lower, urging the little horse on, whispering words of encouragement. Racing across the moonwashed fields beneath a spray of glittering stars, Cassie rode hard, tears smarting in her eyes.

Colton's laughter rang through the night, and her heart skipped a beat. How long had it been since she'd felt so carefree, so young?

At Colton's whoop, the bay leaped forward. Though Lamont labored, he couldn't catch the longer-legged horse.

Near the edge of the forest Colton reined his horse to a slow walk. Lamont, dancing and snorting, caught up with him and tried to take a nip out of Joshua's backside.

"Sore loser," Colton teased, guiding his horse along the overgrown path through the pines. Cassie followed a few steps behind. The sounds and smell of the forest closed in on her: the deep-throated hoot of an owl, the crackle of twigs and rustle of leaves and the fresh fragrance of pine and soil.

The trees gave way to the banks of the lake. Pale rocks rimmed the darker water. A ribbon of moonlight rippled across the glassy surface. Cassie felt as if she and Colton were the only man and woman on earth.

"You going to stay up there all night?" Colton asked.

Lost in the beauty of the night, she hadn't noticed he'd dismounted. Colton reached up, his hands slipping around her waist as he helped Cassie down from her mount. She

ouched ground, and his palms slid upward against her ribs.
He tightened his grip then and drew her close.

"I've thought about this from the minute you walked
down the stairs at your house," he whispered, running his
hands through her hair and yanking loose the few remain-
ng pins.

"We could've ditched the party."

"Oh, no." When her hair fell free, he framed her face
with his hands. "Then I couldn't have shown you off."

"Is that what you were doing?"

"Mmm. You were far and away the most gorgeous
woman there."

She laughed, the sound ringing through the surrounding
hills, and she shoved her thoughts of Vince Monroe aside.
'And did you see that in a movie, too?"

"No—that's my own."

"You're irrepressible." Loving him, she tilted her face up
to his.

He sighed. "You know," he whispered, taking a pin from
her hair and letting the long loose curl drop to her shoulder,
'I thought I'd leave you alone for a week, maybe two. Give
you time to realize just how miserable your life is without
me, but I couldn't make it."

She struggled against a giggle and failed. "Twenty-five
years of misery. It's a wonder I survived."

"A miracle," he said, taking another pin from her hair,
then lowering his mouth to hers. His lips were chilled and
tasted of Scotch. They fit across her mouth perfectly. With
strong arms he pulled her so close she could scarcely
breathe. He tugged at the zipper of her dress, and she felt
the breath of wind touch her bare back as the silk parted.

She wound her arms around his neck, and he lifted her
deftly from her feet. One shoe dropped on the bank, but she
didn't notice. He carried her to the base of the very tree
where so long ago they had made love.

Tenderly he laid her on the ground, her dress falling off one shoulder, her skin shimmering like pearls in the night. "I love you, Cassie," he whispered roughly. "I think I always have."

Her heart thrummed wildly, but she attempted to hang on to some tiny shred of her common sense. Placing a finger across his lips, she whispered, "Shh. You don't have to say anything."

"Wrong, Cass. I should've said what I've felt for a long time." He kissed the finger touching his lips and shuddered when she traced the outline of his mouth. "I didn't want to love you eight years ago. God knows I fought it. But I lost."

"No—"

"Yes." He tangled his hands in the wild strands of her windblown hair. "Why do you think I've been running away, Cass? Why haven't I married? Settled down? Had a family?"

She held her breath.

"Because of you," he admitted, his lips brushing over hers as her pulse quickened crazily. "Only you. Oh, I denied it," he conceded, "wouldn't even admit it to myself, but deep down I knew." With his tongue he tasted her lips, then forayed between her teeth, delving deep, tasting and exploring.

Cassie gave into the swelling in her chest, the ache burning hot and deep inside, the quiver of her skin as he brushed his hand across her breast.

"Marry me, Cass," he pleaded, nuzzling the hollow of her throat, moving his hands slowly across the red silk still draping her breast. "Say yes."

A thousand questions raced through her mind, a thousand questions without answers. "Shh," she whispered, searching beneath his shirt for the muscled wall of his chest. "Don't talk."

And he didn't, not until they were lying side by side, sated and sighing, arms and legs wound together as they watched a hawk circling in the moonlight. "I'm serious, you know," he said, levering himself up on one elbow and twirling one long strand of her hair around his finger. "I want you to marry me."

Cassie laughed. "And where would we live," she teased, "Beirut or Seoul?"

"Somewhere around here."

Shaking the pine needles from her hair, she eyed him thoughtfully. "And you'd be happy ranching?" She didn't believe him for a second.

"No. But I might be happy doing freelance work in the area."

"I hate to be the one to break the news to you, Colton," she teased, "but there hasn't been a major war around here in years."

"Maybe it's time I slowed down a little—"

"Ha!"

"—worked on stories stateside."

"You'd be bored," she said, wishing it weren't so. Unconsciously she traced the tiny purple scars on his shoulder.

"You wouldn't let me get bored," he insisted, throwing one leg across her and pinning her to the earth. "I know it won't be easy, because I won't be working an eight-to-five job, but I'll travel as little as I can."

"Why?"

"Believe it or not, I'm tired of covering my... butt."

"Are you?"

He seemed so sincere. His eyes were dark and serious. "I mean it, Cassie. Say you'll marry me."

His expression was a mixture of determination and love. For the first time since she'd seen him in the middle of her father's kitchen, she didn't doubt that he cared. "You're not kidding, are you?" she whispered, her voice filled with awe.

"No, Cassie, I'm not. I want you to be my wife."

"And everything else?" she whispered, thinking of the feud, her father, Black Magic's disappearance and their long, lost affair.

"Doesn't matter." He pushed his face so close to hers that she hardly dared breathe. "Marry me, Cassie."

Her heart took flight. He wanted her! He loved her! "Oh, Colton, yes! Yes! Yes! Yes!" Wrapping her arms around his neck, she sighed happily. Finally they'd crossed all the barriers between them and she was where she belonged, wrapped in the safety of Colton's arms.

Reaching into his pocket, he withdrew a ring—a diamond ring with a single winking stone. "Wear this," he said, his voice catching as he slid the ring over her finger. "It was my mother's."

*Katherine's?* "Oh, Colton." Her heart filled her throat, and tears pooled in her eyes when she thought of Colton's feisty mother and how she'd lost her life trying to save the horses. "You don't have to—"

"I've waited eight years for this," he said.

"Hardly—"

"Well, maybe I didn't know it, but I knew someday, if I did ever marry, I'd want my wife to wear this ring."

Cassie blinked rapidly. "Thank you," she whispered, her heart so full of love it threatened to burst.

"Don't thank me," he growled against her ear, "show me how much you love me."

"I will—oh, I will," she whispered, finding his lips and kissing him as if she'd never stop. She didn't think of the pain eight years before, nor the feud between the families, nor Black Magic. There was no room. Her heart, mind and body were filled with only Colton McLean.

## Chapter Thirteen

Cassie snuggled close to Colton, not caring that her dress was probably ruined, her hair a mess. Sighing contentedly, she closed her eyes as he drove from the McLean Ranch back to her father's house.

"Something's up," Colton said as he turned into the Aldridge lane. Ahead, though it was nearly three in the morning, the house lights were blazing. Across the broad expanse of yard, the broodmare barn, too, was illuminated. Yellow patches of light spilled through the windows.

"It's probably Sylvia," Cassie said as he braked the Jeep near the barn. She hurried from the Jeep and into the barn, where, as she expected, her father was settled on the top of an old barrel, staring over the slats of Sylvia's stall.

At her entrance, he glanced up, and his mouth tightened at the sight of Colton following her inside.

"Sylvia?" she asked.

Her father nodded.

Cassie grinned at the sight of a tiny black tail waggling as the filly nursed hungrily. Long-legged and spindly, the foal was coal-black against his mother's roan coat. Sylvia shifted, protecting her new one.

"She's a beauty," Cassie said, wondering at the lack of pride in her father's eyes.

"That she is."

"And so black."

"Same as Devil Dancer," he replied quickly, mentioning the foal's sire as he placed his hands on his knees and pushed himself to a standing position. He flicked a cold glance at Colton, then took in Cassie's soiled dress. "The party get a little out of hand?" he asked.

"A little," Cassie said, her eyes sparkling. Colton was standing behind her, with one arm slipped possessively around her waist. Her stomach had tightened into knots even though she'd never been happier in her life. "Dad..." she started, as her father slapped his hat against his thigh.

He glanced up, his skin losing some of its pallor, as if he expected what was to come. "What is it?"

"Colton and I are getting married."

Ivan's old shoulders slumped. His jaw slackened, and a heavy sigh fell from his lips. "I was afraid of that," he admitted, bracing one arm against the wall as if he'd been kicked hard in the gut.

The seconds ticked by, measured only by the drumming of her own heart and the soft sounds of the foal suckling nearby.

"I love him," she said simply. "I always have."

Ivan's throat worked. "And what's it got you, huh?" he demanded of Cassie before impaling Colton with his furious eyes. His face turned beet red, and one fist coiled angrily at his side. "Only heartache. And what did it get your mother when she fancied herself in love with a McLean? Nothing!" Big veins throbbed in his throat. "I always wanted what was best for you, Cassie. Always. I would have done anything to make you happy, but...ah, hell!'' He kicked a water pail and sent it rattling down the concrete corridor, then reached for the door.

Colton stopped him with a hand on Ivan's arm. ''Wait, Aldridge,'' he warned.

''For what?''

''To hear my side.''

''I'm not interested!'' Ivan roared, then glanced at Cassie and closed his eyes, obviously struggling with his temper. He shook off Colton's hand and glared at the younger man. ''Okay—so talk.''

''I'll take care of your daughter.''

Ivan didn't say a word.

''I love her.''

Cassie thought her heart might break right then and there.

''What do you know of love?''

''I know that I was a fool eight years ago. That I should have trusted her. That I made a mistake.''

Ivan cast his eyes to a far stall. ''So?''

''And I'll spend the rest of my life making it up to her if I have to.''

Blinking rapidly, Ivan studied the floor. His voice had dulled from a roar to a whisper. ''This is really what you want?'' he asked Cassie.

''Yes!''

Ivan's Adam's apple moved up and down his throat. He struggled with words that wouldn't come. ''I—uh—I won't stand in your way.'' Lifting his eyes to meet Colton's gaze, he added through tight lips, ''You'll be welcome in my house anytime.'' Then, without another word, he yanked open the door and marched stiffly outside.

''This isn't going to be easy,'' Colton said, staring after the older man.

''Did you think it would be?''

''Sure—a piece of cake.'' He chuckled and drew her to him, taking her lips in his. He kissed her for an endless moment, then chuckled. "And if you think this was bad, wait until we talk to Denver."

"Ooooh," Cassie groaned. "Let's not think about it." Happiness swelled deep in her heart. Resting her head against Colton's chest, she looked through the slats of Sylvia's stall just as the newborn turned his face to hers. For a minute she didn't say a word—just stared at the perfect little horse with the crooked white blaze. Her blood seemed to freeze in her veins as the curious colt lifted his head and tossed his ebony head. He was so like Black Magic.

Colton's eyes followed her gaze, and the blood drained from his face. His fingers curled tight.

Cassie's eyes pleaded with his. *Don't say it,* she seemed to whisper, though not a sound passed between them, *don't spoil this beautiful night.*

He didn't. His eyes narrowed on the little horse, but he didn't say a word. A cold stone settled in her stomach.

The stables seemed suddenly cold as if a wind from the north had silently blown through.

"I think I'd better go," Colton finally said, his voice suddenly distant, his eyes filled with an anger so hot it burned through her heart.

"You don't have to…"

He took a step toward her, then hesitated. "I think we both have a lot to think about." Turning, his broad shoulders stiff beneath his jacket, he left without another word. Cassie slumped against the wall, her fingers sliding down the rough wood. It couldn't be possible. Or could it?

Her feet felt like lead as she made her way to the open door and watched Colton get into his Jeep and drive away. Searching her heart, she tried to push her suspicions aside. Ivan wouldn't have stolen Black Magic; he *couldn't* have. The colt was sired by Devil Dancer and that was that.

But her throat was clogged with nagging doubts, and her mind wouldn't quit spinning with misgivings. The coldness that had started in her stomach chilled her heart as well. *Oh, please,* she cried inwardly, *let me be wrong!*

She took several bracing breaths, knowing what she had to do. Dread mounting with each step, she ran to her truck, found her veterinary bag, then headed back to the barn. She didn't like the idea of taking a vial of blood from a newborn colt, but she had to know the truth. And she had to know it soon.

*And then what? What if you find out your father's been lying to you?* Her legs threatened to give out on her, and she had to force herself onward.

At the door of the barn she paused, glancing down at her left hand. The diamond ring twinkled in the night, and she wondered if she'd made a gigantic mistake in not telling Colton.

"Too late now," she whispered pragmatically, and shoved the door to the barn open again.

Colton didn't drive back to the ranch. He was too keyed up. That foal—that new little Aldridge horse—had to have been sired by Black Magic. Cassie had seen the resemblance, too. Only a blind man wouldn't have recognized Black Magic's genes in the little ebony colt.

"Damn it all to hell!" he ground out, instinctively driving toward the hills. He couldn't ignore this—act like he didn't know. Obviously Ivan Aldridge had stolen Black Magic a year ago and bred his mare, Sylvia, to him. He must have stolen him again this year, and this time the horse could've died.

The Jeep hurtled off the main highway and up the twisting road leading to Garner's Ridge and the old ghost town. Once there, he climbed out of his rig and walked the desolate main street. But he didn't see the decrepit buildings, sagging porches or broken windows. No, each time he looked down that street, he envisioned Cassie. Cassie pointing the barrel of a gun at his chest, Cassie mussed and soiled as she pulled Red Wing's foal into the world, Cassie laughing, moonlight caressing her face as she rode the feisty little Lamont, Cassie as a girl, seductive and innocent, the lake lapping around her legs, and Cassie now, a woman, her throat clogged as she accepted his mother's ring, her eyes glittering with tears of happiness.

He kicked at a stone, sending it richocheting along the remains of a boardwalk, and wished he could just leave Montana and forget her. But the thought of chasing stories in war-torn countries held no allure for him. In fact, a life spent searching for the next front-page story seemed like exile. "Oh, Cassie, Cassie," he murmured, wondering how he'd ever become so maudlin, "what am I going to do with you? Just what the hell am I going to do with you?" He dropped his head into his hands.

By the time he finally left Garner's Ridge, the night was beginning to disappear as the eastern sky grew light. He turned into the lane of the McLean Ranch and caught a glimpse of cattle, white-faced Herefords, moving slowly through one field. This wasn't such a bad place, he realized with a jolt that rocked him to his very soul. He could find happiness here—and peace—as long as he could leave when he felt the urge. As long as Cassie was by his side.

He parked near the garage and had barely stepped out of his Jeep when Denver, nostrils flared, blue eyes angry, strode up to him. Still wearing suit pants and white shirt from the party, Denver didn't mince words. "Where the hell have you been?"

"Out."

"All hell's broken loose. Tempest died two hours ago."

Sickening bile filled Colton's stomach. He thought of the ornery stallion, and his throat constricted. "No—"

"It happened."

"Damn, how?"

"Pneumonia."

"But just yesterday he was better—much better." He couldn't believe it, wouldn't.

"That was yesterday. Last night he took a turn for the worse. By the time Curtis found him, he was too far gone."

"But the antibiotics—"

"Failed!" Denver's dark skin was white, the lines near his mouth deep grooves.

Colton's anger turned inward. He was the one who lost Black Magic, and he'd suspected all along who'd taken the beast. Ivan Aldridge. His soon-to-be father-in-law. "Sweet Lord," he whispered.

"That's not all."

Colton's head snapped up.

"By the time Curtis got hold of Craig Fulton, it was too late for Tempest."

"Fulton examined him?"

"That's right." Denver's eyes were dark with rage, though there was a tenderness akin to pity as he stared at his younger brother. "And he made a strange remark—one I think you should hear. He said he'd talked to another veterinarian at the Edwards's party, and that guy knew someone up here with a horse infected with strangles."

Every muscle in Colton's body went rigid. "Go on."

"Seems Vince Monroe had a horse come down right before Black Magic got the disease."

"Monroe?" God, was it possible? Was he wrong about Aldridge?

"The funny thing is, Craig already told Cassie Aldridge about it."

Colton didn't move. "When?"

"Last night—at the party." The skin on Denver's face had drawn tight. "She say anything to you?"

"No."

"Strange, isn't it?"

Colton's lungs constricted. *Oh, Cassie—oh, love!* Why hadn't she told him?

As if reading Colton's thoughts, Denver sighed. Some of the anger left his face. "If it's any consolation, I think she's protecting someone—maybe Monroe, maybe her father. They're pretty tight these days. Let's go see what she has to say."

"And Monroe?"

"I've already called the sheriff's office. A deputy's on his way to the Monroe place right now. And there's a quarantine on his horses."

"I think I'd better handle this myself."

"I'm coming with you."

"Not this time!"

"But—"

"Denver!" Tessa's voice cried out through the early dawn. Colton turned to see her grab hold of a post supporting the porch while her other arm wrapped around her stomach, and she bent over, wincing.

"What—?" Denver spun on his heel, his face draining of color.

"The baby," she cried, forcing a brave smile, though her face was twisted in pain.

"But it's not time!" He was racing across the yard and up the steps in long strides. When he reached the porch, he surrounded her with his arms. "I knew we shouldn't have gone to that party," he grumbled. "Are you all right?"

She forced a brave smile, but another contraction hit her full force, and she clung to her husband, eyes squeezing shut, her mouth pressed into his chest to muffle her cry.

Colton saw fear on Denver's face and felt a pang of his own. Tessa's baby wasn't due for another six weeks. "I'll drive you to the hospital," he said, but Denver was already shepherding Tessa toward his car.

"I'll handle this! Come on, Tessa . . ." His jaw was rigid as he helped her into the car, then climbed behind the wheel and took off.

Colton stood in the middle of the yard for a second, then climbed back into his Jeep. Bone-tired, he let out the clutch. Why hadn't Cassie told him about the strangles at the Monroe ranch? Why had she wanted so desperately to deny that Sylvia's raven black colt was sired by Black Magic? To protect her father? Somehow Ivan was involved, and Cassie cared so little about Colton that she couldn't confide in him. His boot pressed hard against the throttle.

Cassie didn't sleep a wink, but watched as dawn turned the sky gray and she heard her father in the kitchen below. She listened as Erasmus barked to be let out and watched through the window as her father, his shoulders stooped, made his way to the broodmare barn.

With a heavy heart she climbed out of the bed, showered, stepped into faded jeans and brushed her hair into a sleek ponytail. "It's now or never," she told her reflection, and she steeled herself for what was to come.

In the kitchen she poured herself a cup of coffee and waited at the table. She heard her father's heavy step on the back porch, and her heart turned over.

Her cup of coffee, untouched, was cradled between her hands, as if to give her warmth as he walked in. From the stoop of his shoulders and the lines near his eyes, she guessed he'd slept no better than she.

"'Mornin', Cassie," he muttered, not bothering to remove his hat or boots. "There's something I think we should talk about."

The lump in her throat swelled. "Does it have to do with the new foal?"

"What d'ya mean?"

Her fingers shook as she opened her veterinary bag and withdrew two purple vials of blood. "These," she replied, her voice the barest of whispers. "One of them is from the new colt, the other from Devil Dancer."

Her father sucked in his breath. "I see."

"Later, I thought I'd go to the McLean ranch and take a sample from Black Magic. Even though I cannot prove who the foal's sire is, I can prove which horse isn't the father."

Dropping his head into one hand, Ivan whispered, "You already know."

So it was true. Her stomach quaked. "Oh, Dad, why?" she cried, tears filling her eyes. She heard the rumble of a truck in the drive, and she knew instinctively that Colton had returned. What could she say to him? How would she explain? Setting her cup on the table, she noticed Katherine's ring on her finger. Her lungs and eyes burned.

"I did it for you," Ivan said.

"Me?" she cried. "No..."

He studied his thumb. "It was wrong, I know, but the way I saw it, the McLeans had it coming. All they'd ever caused us—you—was heartache."

Colton stepped through the door, his jaw set, his eyes blazing.

Ivan didn't look up. "I wanted the best for you, don't you see? And I couldn't afford it. I'd borrowed everything I could to help you through school, to get you away from here and all those memories."

"Oh, Dad—"

"Vince came to me with a plan—and it wouldn't really hurt anyone. We'd just borrow the horse, use him to service our mares and then put him back. Improve our herd and give old John McLean fits. It worked, too."

A muscle jumped in Colton's jaw, but he didn't cross the room. He lifted one foot to the seat of a chair and leaned forward, his gaze set on Ivan.

"Then, this year, Vince says we should do it again. I wasn't too crazy about the idea—John was dead."

"But I was around," Colton surmised.

Sighing, Ivan nodded, his neck bowed miserably. "It was a mistake from the beginning. All it did was get you riled up and stomping over here." He cast the younger man a weary glance. "I wanted to keep you and Cassie apart, but the whole thing backfired."

"What about the disease?"

Ivan's old head snapped up. "That was an accident."

"Was it?"

"Vince brought in a mare he'd bought down south somewhere. She developed a fever right after she'd been bred to Black Magic. That's when I brought him back." He glanced at Cassie. "None of our mares had even gotten near him. Thank God."

"Damn it all to hell, Aldridge, do you hate me that much?" Colton demanded, kicking at the chair and sending it across the room.

"I did."

"And where did you hide the horses?"

"That was the beauty of Vince's plan," Ivan explained. "They never left your land, except for the ride. They were up on the ridge—up in a shack in the old silver mines."

"You old bastard!" Colton roared.

Cassie couldn't take her eyes off him. His expression changed from love to hate, to pity, to disbelief. When he turned his gaze her way, she recognized his anger . . . and his pain. "You could've told me," he accused. "Last night, Cass. At the party. You knew most of this."

"I wanted to talk to Dad first."

"That's the problem, isn't it?" Colton muttered. "You never have been able to face me with the truth. You put things off—delude yourself into thinking you'll confide in me, but you wait until the timing's right. Well, when would it have been right this time? Today? Tomorrow? Or after the wedding? Tell me, Cassie, were you planning to dupe me again—trap me into marriage?"

"No!" She shook her head vehemently. "No! No! No! You can't think—"

"I don't know what to think," he snarled, his fists curling, his eyes black with fury.

"Leave her be!" Ivan shouted. "She had nothing to do with this! I already called the sheriff's office. They're sending a man over."

"*What?*" Cassie shrieked, bolting from her chair. "What do you mean?" she demanded.

"It's over, Cassie," he said, touching her hair fondly.

"No! Dad, you can't be serious." Her eyes flew to Colton's. "Tell him! Tell him you're not going to file charges!"

"Tempest died, Cass," Colton pointed out.

"Leave it alone, Cassie," Ivan said, ramming his hat on his head and whistling to his old dog. "I can deal with anything comin' to me."

"No! I won't let you! Dad—you're it. The only family I've got. Don't leave me, too."

But the door slammed behind him, and he crossed the yard.

She whirled on Colton. "Don't do this."

He hesitated.

"Please, it won't happen again. Look at him, for God's sake." She pointed a shaking finger to the window and beyond, to where her father leaned down to scratch Erasmus's shaggy ears. "He won't hurt you—he can't. And...and as for the damage, I'll pay you for Tempest and Monroe's damned stud fees and any other expenses." She advanced on him, her own eyes burning bright, her fingers struggling with the ring surrounding her finger. "I'll even pay for the cut fence and the antibiotics, any amount of money you lost, but you can't, *can't* send my father to jail!" The ring slid off, and she slapped it back in his hand. "My father is my family. He sacrificed everything for me, and no matter what he's done, I'm standing by him."

"And against me."

"It doesn't have to be so black and white," she said, struggling to keep her voice from shaking. He was leaving her—again. Again he was refusing to listen to reason or any of her explanations. She knew Ivan had been wrong, realized his hatred went much too far, but he'd already suffered. She could see it in his old eyes, and to send him to prison for a crime he'd committed because of her... It would kill him.

"What about trust?" she asked, her voice shaking as she advanced on Colton.

"You couldn't trust me last night."

"I had to have my facts straight."

"Bah!"

"What about love?"

He blinked. "I always loved you."

"And now?"

His gaze held hers, and though he didn't say the words, she could feel the intensity, the love lurking deep in those stormy gray depths. She reached up and curled her fingers into the smooth folds of his leather jacket. "I didn't lie to you eight years ago, Colton, and I didn't lie last night. But I do need time and space to work things out in my own mind. I would never manipulate you into marrying me," she said, blinking back the hot tears. "In fact, if you don't want me, believe me, I don't want you." She pressed his mother's ring against his palm and closed his fingers over the gold band. "If your love isn't as strong as this stone, as never-ending as this circle of gold, as complete as the ring itself, then I don't want you!"

Colton's breath was a desperate rasp. His eyes locked with hers.

"I won't have a man who doesn't love me."

"Cass—" He tried to fold her into his arms, but she stepped backward.

"I mean it, Colton. All or nothing!"

"I do love you, Cassie," he said, his voice thick, his words a whisper. "And I can't imagine living without you."

She waited.

He swallowed, looking down at the ring in his big palm. "There's been enough hate already," he said quietly. "Enough pain. Enough loneliness."

Her knees went weak as he took her hand and placed the ring on her finger. "I love you, Cass," he said again, caressing her cheek. "No matter what happens, I want you to be my wife."

A sharp, painful cry escaped from her lips, and she flung her arms around him.

"Marry me."

"I will," she vowed, her arms circling his neck, her tears flowing against his chest until he tilted her face to his and kissed her with all the emotions roiling deep in his chest.

"This is forever," he pointed out.

"It better be!"

A month later Ivan Aldridge gave his daughter to Colton McLean. The charges against him had been dropped, and despite a nagging feeling that he was losing something dear, Ivan realized stoically that Colton loved Cassie. He'd treat her right.

As a bride, Cassie was radiant. Kneeling in a hundred-year-old church, her ivory-colored gown spilling over ancient boards, she vowed her love for Colton.

Ivan's old eyes misted.

"You may kiss the bride," the preacher declared, and standing, Colton took her into his arms, lifted her veil and slanted eager lips over hers. Cassie melted against him. Finally they were together, and nothing, nothing could tear them apart.

Organ music began to throb through the little church, and one small voice, that of Katy McLean, Denver's four-week-old daughter, rang through the chapel as wedding bells chimed loudly, pealing across the valley and sounding beneath the wide Montana sky.

Mr. and Mrs. Colton McLean walked together along the flower-strewn runner, and as the door opened, they started a life together as bright as the morning sun.

"You've done it this time," Colton said.

"Oh?"

"Now you'll never get away from me."

She giggled, holding her skirt up off the dusty porch. "Is that a promise or a threat?"

"Both," he murmured, taking her into his arms again. Colton felt her heart begin to pound as loudly as his own. Finally, he knew, he'd come home.

\* \* \* \* \*

# Silhouette Special Edition

## COMING NEXT MONTH

**#571 RELUCTANT MISTRESS—Brooke Hastings**
The prophecy clearly stated that a tall blond *haole* would enter Leilani's Hawaiian paradise, bringing both love and anguish. Was irresistible Paul Lindstrom that man, and was their mutual destiny one of passion or pain?

**#572 POWDER RIVER REUNION—Myrna Temte**
Their feuding fathers had snuffed out JoAnna and Linc's teenage romance, but a Powder River High reunion relit the fuse. Could their own stubborn wills stem an explosion this time?

**#573 MISS LIZ'S PASSION—Sherryl Woods**
Locking horns with angry parents was elementary for passionate schoolteacher Elizabeth Gentry—until she confronted single father Todd Lewis, who offered *her* some *very* adult education....

**#574 STARGAZER—Jennifer Mikels**
With a family scandal to live down, high-principled attorney David Logan knew he should avoid kooky occultist Jillian Mulvane. But her love potion proved extremely potent....

**#575 THE LOVE EXPERT—Maggi Charles**
Stacy Mackenzie suddenly found herself in uncomfortably close quarters with sex psychologist James Ashley-Sinclair. Could she possibly hold her own with this notorious love expert?

**#576 'TIL THERE WAS YOU—Kathleen Eagle**
Forest ranger Seth Cantrell had chosen quiet solitude. Skier Mariah Crawford was always in the limelight. One night of passion changed their two lives forever... by making them reckon with a third.

## AVAILABLE THIS MONTH:

**#565 MISS ROBINSON CRUSOE**
Tracy Sinclair

**#566 RENEGADE**
Christine Flynn

**#567 UNFINISHED BUSINESS**
Carole Halston

**#568 COME GENTLE THE DAWN**
Eileen Nauman

**#569 TENDER TRAP**
Lisa Jackson

**#570 DENIM AND DIAMONDS**
Debbie Macomber

*Silhouette Intimate Moments*®

# It's time... for Nora Roberts

There's no time like the present to have an experience that's out of this world. When Caleb Hornblower "drops in" on Liberty Stone there's nothing casual about the results!

This month, look for Silhouette Intimate Moments #313

## TIME WAS

And there's something in the future for you, too! Coming next month, Jacob Hornblower is determined to stop his brother from making the mistake of his life—but his timing's off, and he encounters Sunny Stone instead. Can this mismatched couple learn to share their tomorrows? You won't want to miss Silhouette Intimate Moments #317

## TIMES CHANGE

Hurry and get your copy... while there's still time!

You'll flip . . . your pages won't!
Read paperbacks *hands-free* with

# Book Mate · I

**The perfect "mate" for all your romance paperbacks**

**Traveling • Vacationing • At Work • In Bed • Studying • Cooking • Eating**

Perfect size for all standard paperbacks, this wonderful invention makes reading a pure pleasure! Ingenious design holds paperback books OPEN and FLAT so even wind can't ruffle pages — leaves your hands free to do other things. Reinforced, wipe-clean vinyl-covered holder flexes to let you turn pages without undoing the strap . . . supports paperbacks so well, they have the strength of hardcovers!

Pages turn WITHOUT opening the strap.

**SEE-THROUGH STRAP**

Reinforced back stays flat.

Built in bookmark

BOOK MARK

BACK COVER HOLDING STRIP

10" x 7¼", opened.
Snaps closed for easy carrying, too.

# INDULGE A LITTLE SWEEPSTAKES

# OFFICIAL RULES

### SWEEPSTAKES RULES AND REGULATIONS. NO PURCHASE NECESSARY.

**1. NO PURCHASE NECESSARY.** To enter complete the official entry form and return with the invoice in the envelope provided. Or you may enter by printing your name, complete address and your daytime phone number on a 3 x 5 piece of paper. Include with your entry the hand printed words "Indulge A Little Sweepstakes." Mail your entry to: Indulge A Little Sweepstakes, P.O. Box 1397, Buffalo, NY 14269-1397. No mechanically reproduced entries accepted. Not responsible for late, lost, misdirected mail, or printing errors.

**2.** Three winners, one per month (Sept. 30, 1989, October 31, 1989 and November 30, 1989), will be selected in random drawings. All entries received prior to the drawing date will be eligible for that month's prize. This sweepstakes is under the supervision of MARDEN-KANE, INC. an independent judging organization whose decisions are final and binding. Winners will be notified by telephone and may be required to execute an affidavit of eligibility and release which must be returned within 14 days, or an alternate winner will be selected.

**3.** Prizes: 1st Grand Prize (1) a trip for two to Disneyworld in Orlando, Florida. Trip includes round trip air transportation, hotel accommodations for seven days and six nights, plus up to $700 expense money (ARV $3,500). 2nd Grand Prize (1) a seven-night Chandris Caribbean Cruise for two includes transportation from nearest major airport, accommodations, meals plus up to $1,000 in expense money (ARV $4,300). 3rd Grand Prize (1) a ten-day Hawaiian holiday for two includes round trip air transportation for two, hotel accommodations, sightseeing, plus up to $1,200 in spending money (ARV $7,700). All trips subject to availability and must be taken as outlined on the entry form.

**4.** Sweepstakes open to residents of the U.S. and Canada 18 years or older except employees and the families of Torstar Corp., its affiliates, subsidiaries and Marden-Kane, Inc. and all other agencies and persons connected with conducting this sweepstakes. All Federal, State and local laws and regulations apply. Void wherever prohibited or restricted by law. Taxes, if any are the sole responsibility of the prize winners. Canadian winners will be required to answer a skill testing question. Winners consent to the use of their name, photograph and/or likeness for publicity purposes without additional compensation.

**5.** For a list of prize winners, send a stamped, self-addressed envelope to Indulge A Little Sweepstakes Winners, P.O. Box 701, Sayreville, NJ 08871.

© 1989 HARLEQUIN ENTERPRISES LTD.

DL-SWPS

---

# INDULGE A LITTLE SWEEPSTAKES

# OFFICIAL RULES

### SWEEPSTAKES RULES AND REGULATIONS. NO PURCHASE NECESSARY.

**1. NO PURCHASE NECESSARY.** To enter complete the official entry form and return with the invoice in the envelope provided. Or you may enter by printing your name, complete address and your daytime phone number on a 3 x 5 piece of paper. Include with your entry the hand printed words "Indulge A Little Sweepstakes." Mail your entry to: Indulge A Little Sweepstakes, P.O. Box 1397, Buffalo, NY 14269-1397. No mechanically reproduced entries accepted. Not responsible for late, lost, misdirected mail, or printing errors.

**2.** Three winners, one per month (Sept. 30, 1989, October 31, 1989 and November 30, 1989), will be selected in random drawings. All entries received prior to the drawing date will be eligible for that month's prize. This sweepstakes is under the supervision of MARDEN-KANE, INC. an independent judging organization whose decisions are final and binding. Winners will be notified by telephone and may be required to execute an affidavit of eligibility and release which must be returned within 14 days, or an alternate winner will be selected.

**3.** Prizes: 1st Grand Prize (1) a trip for two to Disneyworld in Orlando, Florida. Trip includes round trip air transportation, hotel accommodations for seven days and six nights, plus up to $700 expense money (ARV $3,500). 2nd Grand Prize (1) a seven-night Chandris Caribbean Cruise for two includes transportation from nearest major airport, accommodations, meals plus up to $1,000 in expense money (ARV $4,300). 3rd Grand Prize (1) a ten-day Hawaiian holiday for two includes round trip air transportation for two, hotel accommodations, sightseeing, plus up to $1,200 in spending money (ARV $7,700). All trips subject to availability and must be taken as outlined on the entry form.

**4.** Sweepstakes open to residents of the U.S. and Canada 18 years or older except employees and the families of Torstar Corp., its affiliates, subsidiaries and Marden-Kane, Inc. and all other agencies and persons connected with conducting this sweepstakes. All Federal, State and local laws and regulations apply. Void wherever prohibited or restricted by law. Taxes, if any are the sole responsibility of the prize winners. Canadian winners will be required to answer a skill testing question. Winners consent to the use of their name, photograph and/or likeness for publicity purposes without additional compensation.

**5.** For a list of prize winners, send a stamped, self-addressed envelope to Indulge A Little Sweepstakes Winners, P.O. Box 701, Sayreville, NJ 08871.

© 1989 HARLEQUIN ENTERPRISES LTD.

DL-SWPS

## INDULGE A LITTLE—WIN A LOT!

## Summer of '89 Subscribers-Only Sweepstakes

# OFFICIAL ENTRY FORM

This entry must be received by: Nov. 30, 1989
This month's winner will be notified by: Dec. 7, 1989
Trip must be taken between: Jan. 7, 1990–Jan. 7, 1991

YES, I want to win the 3-Island Hawaiian vacation for two! I understand the prize includes round-trip airfare, first-class hotels, and a daily allowance as revealed on the "Wallet" scratch-off card.

Name_____

Address_____

City_____ State/Prov._____ Zip/Postal Code_____

Daytime phone number _____
                              Area code

Return entries with invoice in envelope provided. Each book in this shipment has two entry coupons—and the more coupons you enter, the better your chances of winning!

© 1989 HARLEQUIN ENTERPRISES LTD.

DINDL-3

---

## INDULGE A LITTLE—WIN A LOT!

## Summer of '89 Subscribers-Only Sweepstakes

# OFFICIAL ENTRY FORM

This entry must be received by: Nov. 30, 1989
This month's winner will be notified by: Dec. 7, 1989
Trip must be taken between: Jan. 7, 1990–Jan. 7, 1991

YES, I want to win the 3-Island Hawaiian vacation for two! I understand the prize includes round-trip airfare, first-class hotels, and a daily allowance as revealed on the "Wallet" scratch-off card.

Name_____

Address_____

City_____ State/Prov._____ Zip/Postal Code_____

Daytime phone number _____
                              Area code

Return entries with invoice in envelope provided. Each book in this shipment has two entry coupons—and the more coupons you enter, the better your chances of winning!

© 1989 HARLEQUIN ENTERPRISES LTD.

DINDL-3